[SUMMER OF CHAMPIONS

SUMMER of CHAMPIONS

DEWEY JOHNSON

To Joseph,
Best wishes,
Dewey

[TEXAS TECH UNIVERSITY PRESS

This book is typeset in Aldus Roman with Helvetica Neue display. The paper used in this book meets the minimum requirements of ANSI/NISO Z39.48-1992 (R1997). ∞

Designed by Lindsay Starr

Library of Congress Cataloging-in-Publication Data
Johnson, Dewey, 1946-
    Summer of champions / Dewey Johnson.
        p. cm.
    Summary: "In 1956 New Mexico, the Roswell Hondo All Stars are on their way to the Little League World Series, and fifth grader Joe Don and his widowed mother struggle to remain independent. When the teacher who inspires him to championship is arrested, Joe Don finds his own character tested"—Provided by publisher.
    ISBN-10: 0-89672-567-7 ISBN-13: 978-0-89672-567-6 (cloth : alk. paper) 1. Boys—Fiction. 2. Widows—Fiction. 3. New Mexico—Fiction. 4. Single mothers—Fiction. 5. Baseball players—Fiction. 6. Little League baseball—Fiction. 7. Teacher-student relationships—Fiction. I. Title.
    PS3610.O337S86 2005
    813'.6—dc22
                                                                          2005009163

Printed in the United States of America
05 06 07 08 09 10 11 12 13/ 9 8 7 6 5 4 3 2 1
SB

Texas Tech University Press
Box 41037
Lubbock, Texas 79409-1037 USA
800.832.4042
ttup@ttu.edu
www.ttup.ttu.edu

To small towns, where we learn life's big lessons

[ACKNOWLEDGMENTS

I want to thank Sandra Scofield, whom I met at the University of Iowa Summer Writing Festival, for her guidance and encouragement in the writing of *Summer of Champions*. She is not only a gifted author, but an inventive writing teacher.

Thanks to the 1956 Roswell Lions Hondo Little League All-Stars for providing a world championship context for this story. Team members: Harold Hobson, Jimmy Valdez, Randy Willis, Teddy Garrett, David Sherrod, Guy Bevell, Dick Story, Albert Palomino, Mike Sandry, Bill Turley, Ferrell Dunham, Blaine Stribling, Tommy Jordan, and David Smith. Coaches: Richard St. John and Pete Ellis.

Thanks to the members of Sandia Presbyterian Church, whose appreciation of story and humor have provided me a place to be myself.

And thanks to a supportive family: Cheri, Tag, Curran, and Reah.

DJ

BOOK I

a GOOD LIFE

the KITCHEN TABLE

IT WAS FRIDAY THE THIRTEENTH, January 1956, report card day. Cards had to be signed by a parent and returned the next Monday. Miss Sherelle, our no-nonsense principal, was strict. Failure to return a signed report card would subject you to the dreaded electric paddling machine kept behind the locked closet door in her office.

I presented my report card to Mom at the supper table. Friday night was special. It was "hamburger night." After work Mom would stop by Smiley's Restaurant and get two burgers and fries to go. She was a clerk at Allensworth's Five & Dime and happy on Fridays because she had only half a day of work left. Her workweek was over Saturday noon. She'd say, "Friday night is for putting my feet up. Saturday night's for letting my hair down," although she never did let her hair down. We were Southern Baptists.

Several times I had tried to talk Mom into going inside Smiley's and sitting at a booth. I was willing to pay a nickel tip, but she never would. Smiley's was crowded with families. I guessed that without a husband she would feel out of place.

We ate off the paper that the hamburgers came in. After the blessing I reached down into my right pants leg cuff and brought up my report card. I laid it on the table and pushed it over by Mom's fries.

She looked me in the eye penetrating-like and said, "I suppose you were unlucky today, found out you flunked everything."

"Yes, ma'am. It was my unlucky day."

"Let's have a look." She pulled the card out of its manila holder and took her time going over each side, both grades and deportment. "All A-pluses. You didn't have art this six weeks, did you? And all Satisfactories for deportment . . . Joe Don, this is the report card of a champion! Did Mr. Connell congratulate you?"

"Yes, ma'am, he did."

I was in the fifth grade and almost eleven and a half years old. My homeroom teacher, Mr. Connell, was teaching us how to be champions. He was a student of the ancient Greeks, the people who gave us the Olympics and heroes. He said that the Greeks sought excellence in all things, strove to be physically and mentally fit. I was doing the same. My report card was proof of my mental fitness.

Mom came around the table and hugged my neck. "I don't have much, Joe Don, but I have you! And you make me happy!"

She didn't have much. That was a fact. But once she did. Mom would say that she had it all, until she got a telegram telling her that Dad had been killed in the Korean War. Uncle Charlie said Dad had been murdered by "that arrogant MacArthur" because he had underestimated the Chinese. That was in 1950. MacArthur had been a dirty word around our family ever since.

I was just a kid at the time, but I had some memories. We lived in a nice house on the north side of town. I had a big room with a closet, and a front and back yard with grass. When we left I held Mom's hand. She cried as we walked out the front door and got into the car. Uncle Charlie had loaded his pickup with what was left of our furniture after we sold off much of it. He helped us move across town to the tiny house where we now lived. I no longer had a closet or chest of drawers or a lawn.

Mom had to go to work at Allenworth's, and for a year I stayed at a baby-sitter's house during the day. By New Mexico law, I could have gone to school that year, but my Uncle Caleb was a high school sports fan and had always argued that the kids in our family should start school late, to have an edge playing sports. So I didn't start school until I turned seven and was one of the older, larger kids in my class. It didn't hurt me. I had fun with my friends, and schoolwork came easy. I loved Missouri Avenue Elementary School.

My best friend, Jay Bob Jones, didn't like schoolwork. He liked working with his hands and, just for the fun of it, planning robberies. He wasn't a criminal, although he once stole a candy bar at the school store when he was in the third grade. It was just a phase he was going through. Jay Bob got a nickel for every B and a dime for every A he brought home on his report card. All I got was a hug for A-pluses, but that was all right. Another boy in our class, Raymond Spencer, got backhanded for his bad grades, and for a lot of other things, too.

"Mom, do you think there's any way we could afford a TV?" She had returned to her seat across the table.

"Not on what little I make. You know that."

"Then how about a baseball glove? I need a new one for next season."

"That we might do. You know how your Granddaddy and Grandmama Miller give you birthday money? Your birthday isn't until August, but I could talk to them about giving it to you early."

"But a glove costs more than a dollar. That's what they always give me."

"How about I ask your Grandma and Grandpa Snider? They could chip in too."

"A baseball glove costs more than two dollars."

"Uncle Charlie and Aunt Elvis?"

I couldn't remember what they had given me last year, but it probably cost seventy-nine cents. "Still not there."

"How much does a glove cost?"

"More than two dollars and seventy-nine cents. I need a Rawl-ings."

"Would you want me to chip in rather than buy you a present myself?"

"But then I wouldn't get any presents on my birthday, except maybe from Jay Bob and Curty." Curty McDonald was my second-best friend.

"But only because you got a big present earlier when you needed it."

Mom liked to make me count my blessings, but I couldn't see how a birthday without a present from her would be much of a blessing. I was afraid I'd be sad like some little kid. But I needed the new glove if I was going to be a champion on the baseball diamond. "Okay," I said. "I'll walk over to Del Beene's tomorrow and see how much one costs."

"And what if after all this there's still not enough? Are you willing to chip in what you earn at Whitman's Auto?"

"MOM! I only make twenty-five cents a week!"

"ONLY! Half the kids in this town would love the deal Mr. Rodman gives you! If you saved what you made, you might pay for the glove yourself."

"But it's my spending money, and we have a field trip coming up. It's gonna cost a dime, and I'll have to pay Raymond's way too else he can't go. His stupid dad never gives him anything."

"Don't talk that way about his dad," she corrected me. "You don't have to pay for Raymond, and you don't have to have a candy bar or a coke every day. As you get older you're going to have to learn how to save up for more important things."

"Cokes and candy are pretty important, Mom. 'Man does not live by bread alone.' And if Raymond doesn't go with us, he'll have to sit all day in the library while we're out having fun. He'd hate that."

"Still, it's a pretty big present you're asking for. How much do you want it? Enough to make a sacrifice?"

Oh man, anything but the sacrifice lecture. "Mom, if I sacrificed any more, it'd stunt my growth! I already tithe my Whitman's Auto quarter to the church, remember? You know how much candy I could buy with three more cents a week, or two if you'd let me round down?" I paused. "But here's an idea. Are you ever going to get married again?"

Mom made a little gasping sound. I had caught her off guard. We never talked about her remarrying. A little smile came to her lips as she pointed a French fry at me and said, "And what if I did? What would you think about it?"

"I think I'd have to take you out and shoot you, Mom, like a dog with rabies. Sad but necessary."

"What kind of answer is that! You know what me getting remarried would do for us. It would buy you a baseball mitt and both of us a better life."

"But he wouldn't be my dad."

"Nor my dreamboat," she said, dipping the fry into her ketchup. "You only get one dreamboat in this life, and mine was your dad. Why would you have to shoot me?"

I shouldn't have brought it up. Mom could talk your leg off. Give her an opening and she'd yak both of 'em off at the knees. "I'm afraid it would change things. You'd never be the same again if you got married."

I feared change. Dad's getting killed at that reservoir in Korea was enough change to last me a lifetime. Mom getting remarried would be in the same league. It would be worse than when I had to switch from a Big Chief tablet to notebook paper in the fourth grade. I hated it then, and I hated it still. *Classroom Teachers . . . Do Not Care . . . Big Chief Tablet . . . Oughta Scalp Their Hair . . . Burma Shave*

Another of my fears was that Mom would die. If it happened to Dad, it could happen to her. Mom said that she wouldn't, but if something did happen, like a car wreck, I'd go live with my Uncle Clifford and Aunt Dixie on their farm. But my hoodlum cousin Greg said different.

Greg was sixteen, a junior in high school. He was Uncle Charlie and Aunt Elvis's only child, a juvenile delinquent. They lived in a nice house in the north part of town. When Mom and I would go for supper, Greg used to get me off by myself and say things to scare me. He'd say, "I hope your Mom's heart problem gets better. If she has a heart attack and dies, you'll have to go live in the orphanage in Albuquerque."

"Unh uh! Women don't have heart attacks! But even if something did happen, like getting run over by a train, I'd go live with my uncle near Muleshoe."

"She just says that so you won't worry. She knows New Mexico is a poor state. It will never let you leave. The judge will make you live in an orphanage and work in a license plate factory. The adults are mean and give you whippings all the time. You'll never get to go to school or play ball or have enough to eat."

Greg had made me cry until third grade when Mom explained to me that he had been adopted from an orphanage in Albuquerque. I was to pay him no attention, but I found that hard to do. He could come up with scary things to think about! So scary that I imagined his real parents were Bonnie and Clyde, the bank robbers. When they were shot to death at the roadblock in Louisiana, their hoodlum baby Greg was in the backseat in a bulletproof crib. He was put up for adoption in New Mexico where no one knew what a public menace he would grow up to be.

One of my fears I got from Mom. She was afraid that we couldn't make a living in Roswell on what a store clerk earned. If we went broke, we'd have to go live with Grandpa and Grandma

Snider on their farm near Muleshoe. That would be a change we'd both hate. She didn't like farm life, and never wanted to live on one again. And I'd miss my friends if we had to move.

Mom was thirty-five, pretty, with blue eyes and light brown hair, but thin and not very strong. Grandma said Mom was so skinny that she looked in poor health. So I did what I could to help Mom keep up her strength and not miss any work. I'd sweep the floor and set the table and help out around the house. I toted things for her when I could, like laundry to the car when she went to do the washing.

Mom broke the silence. "We must be related, Joe Don. Ever since we lost your dad, I don't cotton much to change either. Guess that's why I never let my hair down. Don't want the attention. " She thought for a moment. "So here's a vocabulary word to look up, 'trepidation.' We have a trepidation about change."

We had a dictionary that we kept on the bottom shelf of the coffee table in the living room. I'd get it out after supper.

"And here's a joke for you, Mom." I told Mom jokes to make her happy. "Did you hear about the little moron from Oklahoma?"

"No, tell me about him."

"He flunked out of school."

"Why?"

"He was too poor to pay attention!"

She laughed. "Poor Okies. I feel sorry for them, but here's another. Do you know the difference between a Murphy bed and an Okie?

"No, what?"

"A Murphy bed puts the mattress on the wall. An Okie puts it on top of his car."

I laughed. When adults saw a car with a mattress on top, they'd say, "There goes an Okie down on his luck."

2

PART-TIME JOB

SATURDAY MORNING I RODE TO WORK WITH MOM. Although Whitman's Auto faced north on First Street, its backside was catty-cornered across a dirt parking lot from the rear of Allensworth's Five & Dime, which faced east on Main. Almost as many people went in both stores through the back door as they did the front. Mom parked our '49 Ford at the back of the parking lot. We would both work until noon and then be free for the rest of the day.

Mom's boss, Mr. Franks, seemed to hate her. I was lucky. Kyle Rodman, manager of Whitman's Auto, liked me. He had grown up with Dad in Abernathy, Texas. After Dad was killed he started helping us out. He provided parts and labor to keep Mom's car going. And ever since September he had let me work Saturday mornings helping throw away trash. He paid me out of his own pocket because I wasn't old enough to be on the payroll.

The shipping/receiving room was on the first floor by the loading dock and the freight elevator. Merchandise was brought down from the storeroom on the third floor to be uncrated and assembled there. Whitman's sold furniture, appliances, bicycles, and automotive goods. By the end of the week the room was filled with corrugated cardboard boxes, baling wire, and wood crating. Some of the corrugated boxes were bigger than I could carry. Before I hauled them to the trash bin, I had to cut them in pieces with a box cutter.

Using a box cutter had been hard at first because my hands weren't that strong. But they were getting stronger. A box cutter was a weapon used by junior high and high school kids in knife fights, and using one made me feel older. Jay Bob's brother, Gerald, who was fifteen, had seen a kid slashed by a box cutter in a fight at high school. His T-shirt was soaked with blood, and he had to have stitches in his stomach. There were several box cutters just lying around the shipping/receiving room. I was tempted to "liberate" one, as my hoodlum cousin Greg would say about stealing, but so far had not broken the eighth commandment.

I was cutting up a bicycle carton when Earl, the deliveryman, walked in. "Hey Miller," he grinned. "You're doin it right, just like I taught ya. Cut down the seams. It's easier."

I was happy to be caught doing something right. At school I could do no wrong other than in art class. I wanted to be a champion worker at Whitman's, but I made lots of mistakes. Work was complicated. "Hey Earl, there's an A-frame behind my house. My friend Jay Bob said so. You can have it if you want."

A couple of weeks earlier I had heard Earl telling a salesman that he was looking for an A-frame so he could pull out car motors and make some extra money. I had thought that was what the swing-set-looking thing was, but I had to ask Jay Bob to be sure. He was a genius about tools and equipment.

"Really? You got an A-frame?"

"Yeah, left by someone who used to live in my house."

"How much ya want for it?"

"Nothing, you can have it." I liked Earl. He was the only black man I had ever known, Roswell having so few Negroes. He was also one of the strongest men I knew. The salesmen agreed. No one messed with Earl even though he was a lay preacher at his church. He had been a boxer in the navy.

"It wouldn't be right to just give it to me. Have you asked your mom about this?"

"No, but it's all right by her."

"Ask her what she wants for it. I ain't gonna to take it for free. It's worth something to both of us. If I can borrow a pickup, I'll come by Sunday afternoon after church and get it. And thanks, Joe Don, for looking out for ole Earl!"

He started to walk off, but then stopped, turned around and smiled. "And how are those New Year's resolutions comin?"

"I haven't had time to do much yet." Earl had never known anyone who made New Year's resolutions. All he did was eat black-eyed peas on New Year's Day. He figured that if he started out the year with black-eyed peas, the rest of the year would have to get better. He was interested when I told him about my resolutions at break time New Year's Eve morning.

I told him that I had four, although I hadn't written them down at the time. You needed to write your resolutions down so you could look at them all year long. That helped them come true.

My first resolution was to become a champion. The second was to make the All-Star Little League baseball team that summer. Three was to help Mom so we wouldn't go broke and have to move from Roswell. And four was to win the school spelling bee, maybe even the city bee.

Then I made Earl swear that he wouldn't tell anyone. Only two people knew about my resolutions, Earl and Mr. Connell. I had told Mr. Connell after we came back from Christmas break. No one else in his class was as interested in becoming a champion as I was, and he thought my resolutions were good. He said that if I won the school spelling bee and made the All-Star Little League baseball team, that next December we should get together and determine what my 1957 resolutions would be. A champion was always open to new adventures. I looked forward to what he had in mind for me.

Earl left to go make a delivery, and I carried my first load to the trash bin. The trash bin was on the southeast corner of Whitman's and was also used by businesses that faced Main Street. It was a four-foot-high cinder block rectangle, with a wide, locked, wooden gate that swung open across the front so the trash men could empty it. The back and the two sides were enclosed by a five-foot chain-link fence, about three feet away, that caught overflow or blowing trash and kept the alley clean.

I was throwing in corrugated boxes when a magazine on the bottom of the bin caught my eye. There was something unusual about it. I jumped up, swung over the side, and dropped in to see what kind it was. It was a *Playboy* magazine! I looked around to make sure no one was watching. No one was. I ducked down so I could look at the pictures.

I had heard about *Playboy* from Jay Bob and Curty. What a find—naked ladies! It was like I was under a witch's spell as I leafed through the pages. I knew I shouldn't be looking, but I couldn't escape. The magazine had me in its power. And what a problem it presented! I couldn't just leave it there. It was the most valuable thing I'd ever found. I had to sneak it home, but how? I had two more hours of work and then a ride in the car with Mom.

I decided to put the *Playboy* in the trash bin corner nearest Whitman's back door. I placed a small cardboard box over it so no one else could see it. The trash bin was big. I'd toss trash everywhere else inside, going light on the one corner, so I could jump in after closing time and get it. Trip after trip I kept the corner clear as I tossed in trash. And as I worked, my mind figured out how to get the *Playboy* home.

I would stick it inside the front of my shirt, partially down inside my blue jeans. I'd tighten my belt to hold it in place. I'd have my jacket on over my shirt, and I'd keep it zipped up all the way home so Mom couldn't tell. I couldn't sneak it under my mattress,

which was where Curty said teenage boys kept *Playboys,* because it was Saturday. Mom would change and wash sheets that afternoon. She'd find it. I'd have to hide it in my special hiding place, a water-tight World War II ammo box, stored in the secret compartment under the floor of my fort beneath the elm tree behind the house.

It was break time, ten thirty. Earl was still out on his delivery, so I got a Dr. Pepper from the machine and sat by myself in the corner of the shipping/receiving room. Mom would snatch me bald headed if she caught me drinking a coke that early in the morning, but there wasn't anything else for me to drink. I didn't care for coffee. If Earl had been there, we would have sat together.

I got to thinking about the Saturday before. Curty's dad hired Jay Bob, Curty, and me to hand out handbills in the downtown area. We put them beneath windshield wipers, and we handed them to people on the sidewalk. Curty and Jay Bob had started midmorning after the stores opened. I worked with them after I finished at Whitman's. The handbills told about specials on the menu the next week at Jake's Grill.

Mr. McDonald owned Jake's Grill, which was next door to Allensworth's Five & Dime. He was open only for breakfasts and lunches, but he did well. The people who worked downtown ate there, and so did people who shopped downtown. The only person I knew who didn't eat there was Mom. She always took her lunch to work. Since Jake's wasn't filled with families like Smiley's, I figured she was trying to save money.

The politicians at city hall drank coffee at Jake's every day. They talked to Mr. McDonald as though he was their pal, which was how Curty got his interest in the news. He worked there part-time and sometimes knew the news before the *Roswell Daily Record* did. Reporters and editors would drop by Jake's to find out who had said what. If Jake was busy, Curty was happy to tell them what he knew.

He also told me which men talked about Mom. Some had asked her
to go on dates, which she never mentioned to me, but she had
turned them down. According to Curty, men thought Mom was
one of the most beautiful women in Roswell. They sometimes
bought things in Allensworth's just to talk to her.

In fourth grade the kids in our class used to say that there were
three ways to communicate—telegram, telephone, and tell-Alea,
referring to Alea Ritchy, a ready source of news. But Alea changed
between fourth and fifth grade. She was less on the phone nowadays and more into books. Her role was being taken over by Curty.
Curty was like the gospel song we sang in church. He "loved to tell
the story," any story, time after time, to anyone who would listen.

The previous fall he had told us details about the car wreck in
front of our school. Some robbers in a panel truck were being
chased by the police and ran the stop sign on Washington Street at
Deming. They were going south at eighty miles per hour when
they rammed into a family in a station wagon, killing both parents
and both kids. Those were the facts reported by the *Roswell Daily
Record.*

What wasn't in the newspaper was what Curty heard from
policemen eating at Jake's. The impact had knocked one of the dad's
shoes a city block away to the opposite side of the park, as well as
someone's tooth and a ring. The cops weren't sure whose tooth it
was—the ring belonged to one of the kids—but they were amazed
at the distance. So were we. The three of us went to the park after
school looking for jewelry and shoes and clothing. We didn't find
anything, but Jay Bob pointed out something we had never imagined about jockey straps.

Suppose, he said, high school football players weren't exagger-
ating when they said, "he got his jock knocked off." If a speeding
panel truck could hit a guy in a station wagon and knock his shoe

across the park, maybe a football player could get tackled so hard that he'd have to go pick up his jockey strap after the play. Since all three of us intended to play football, it was something to worry about. It would be embarrassing!

Mr. McDonald was a good cook. Mom said that was why Curty was roly-poly. I had eaten several times at the McDonald house. Each time they had what was left over that day from Jake's Grill. It was great food—club sandwiches, meatloaf, spaghetti—and Saturday afternoon, after we kids handed out handbills, the McDonalds invited Jay Bob and me over for a pancake supper. Curty immediately declared a contest and issued a challenge. He'd eat us under the table!

Jay Bob was the smallest and skinniest, but he had a hollow leg. Everyone who saw how much he ate couldn't believe their eyes. Mr. Connell said he must have a tapeworm. I was the tallest, not skinny and not fat and I ate a lot, but not as much as Jay Bob or Curty. Mr. Connell had helped me understand this. He said it was because there were more people at their tables, which meant more food on their tables. Day after day they ate more, their stomachs stretched more, and so their stomachs could hold more.

I didn't know who would win, Curty or Jay Bob. Even though I was most always up to a challenge, I wasn't going to enter the contest. Not only did I hate stomachaches, but why compete when I didn't have a chance?

Mr. McDonald was happy. Jake's Grill had great sales that day. He poured batter on the pancake grill while Curty's mom set the dining room table and poured milk. He also cooked bacon and gave us a pitcher of the best maple syrup I'd ever tasted. Curty said you couldn't buy it at the grocery store.

The pancakes were all the same size so the contest would be fair. We started with a stack of three. Jay Bob and Curty didn't eat any bacon or drink much more than enough milk to wash down their food so they could hold more pancakes. I ate bacon and drank lots of milk. They were working on their second stack while I was only halfway through my first.

Mrs. McDonald kept telling them to not eat too much. "Eat until you're pleasantly full and stop." She was mad at Curty's dad for going along with the contest, not wanting to be up all night with a sick kid. I ate three pancakes and three pieces of bacon and stopped. Curty ate seven pancakes, while Jay Bob, the champion, ate eight. Both were so stuffed they were miserable. After supper we went into Curty's room and talked.

"What I'd like for dessert is a hot fudge sundae," I said, "with lots of pecans, whipped cream, and a cherry on top. Is your mom going to serve us dessert?"

"Shut up, Joe Don!" Curty said. He was lying on his left side on the bed.

"Or you know those pastries you get at Mexican food restaurants in Old Town Albuquerque? Sofa pillows? Those hollow rolls that you fill with honey? Those are so good! Man, I'd like a whole basketful, with a six-pack of grape Nehi to wash 'em down."

"Get out of here!" Jay Bob said. "You're making me sick."

After I mentioned all the food I could think of, I suggested that we go play basketball at the hoop on Jay Bob's garage. "We gotta practice so we can grow up and beat the Hobbs Eagles. Practice jumping up and down, up and down, up and down. Hustle, hustle, hustle, move it, move it, move it!"

The thought of jumping up and down made the two of them even sicker. Jay Bob and I left when Curty had to go to the bathroom to vomit. As soon as we got outside, Jay Bob threw up in the flowerbed. I felt really good though. I had been paid a dime for distributing handbills and got a free supper to boot! A free supper saved Mom money, not only because she didn't have to feed me, but because she ate soup when she was by herself. A can of soup didn't cost that much.

· · · · · · ·

Earl had come back from his delivery. After break he needed me to help him pull stock on the third floor. I was there until closing time. Earl always made sure I didn't pick up anything too heavy. A kid could get hurt. We rearranged a bunch of boxes getting what Earl needed. I was good at climbing up in the racks and shoving boxes over to the edge so Earl could reach them. At closing time I picked up my quarter at Mr. Rodman's office and then raced out of the store to get my *Playboy* magazine.

No one was around the trash bin, but what on earth had happened? The bin was filled to overflowing with Christmas paper and cardboard and small trash of every kind! Allensworth's and the other Main Street stores must not have tossed their trash since Christmas, and had done so while I was on the third floor. Trash was everywhere! It overflowed the bin and filled much of the space between the bin and the chain-link fence. It looked like a trash mountain!

I climbed in and dug toward my buried treasure as fast as I could, but no sooner did I move trash out of the way than more trash filled in. It was as bad as trying to save a person caught in an avalanche. I was making like a Saint Bernard when I heard a voice say, "Joe Don, what in the world are you doing!"

It was Mom. "Uh . . . nothing."

"Then come out of there, you're getting filthy! No telling what all is in there."

I climbed out and she brushed me off. "Have you been to Del Beene's to price your baseball glove?"

"Not yet."

"I'll go with you. I want to see that new refrigerator everyone's talking about." Mom was a fan of appliances. She knew more about washers and dryers than baseball fans knew about Duke Snider.

"You go on ahead," I said. "It's been a busy day. I'll see if Mr. Rodman needs me for anything else. I'll meet you there."

"Silly, he doesn't need you for anything else. The back door is already locked. You couldn't get in if you wanted to. Let's go! I'd think you'd be busting a gut wanting to price baseball gloves."

I would have thought so too, but naked ladies change your plans.

3

BEST FRIENDS

THAT NIGHT I HAD A SLEEPOVER AT JAY BOB'S. Jay Bob's dad, Mr. Edgar
Jones, was the librarian at the Carnegie library and the smartest man
I knew. He had explained to Uncle Charlie how MacArthur's stu-
pidity led to Dad being killed on the Yalu. In my opinion, had Eisenhower been in charge, it wouldn't have happened. Ike would never
have sent thousands of brave men to a needless death, but he was in
Europe. I guessed he couldn't get to Korea in time to prevent it.

Jay Bob's mom was a kind lady, older and heavier than Mom.
She liked to fix things and did the repair work around the Joneses'.
She also looked out for me.

Late summer, when we were getting ready to go back to school,
Mom couldn't find a cigar box, and I had to have one. We used them
to store our school supplies. The tobacco shops were out. The
Roswell Daily Record referred to it as "The Great Cigar Box
Shortage." A reporter had determined that there were far more kids
in elementary school than there were men smoking cigars. Mr.
Connell joked that it was a communist conspiracy.

Housewives were in a panic, but Mrs. Jones found me one. It
was a Dutch Masters, just like the one she had found for Jay Bob a
few weeks earlier. She wouldn't say where she got it, but I figured
she bought it. She bought a whole box of cigars, emptied them out

for Mr. Jones to smoke later, and gave the box to me. But however she got it, Mom and I were thankful. On the first day of school, I took my cigar box, filled with scissors, glue, an eraser, crayons, pencils, and a six-inch ruler, and put it inside my Peabody desk.

I ate with Jay Bob's family at the dinner table. Jay Bob's brother, Gerald, was a sophomore in high school. He was tall, skinny, and not very strong, but was good enough to play first string on the junior varsity basketball team. A nice guy, he never picked on me. He told lots of jokes and liked imitating Charlie Chan. He called Jay Bob "Number Two Son" and himself "Number One Son."

We ate Jay Bob's favorite meal of chicken and rice. Mrs. Jones had made a chocolate pie with meringue, or what my West Texas cousins called calf slobbers, for dessert. I had a piece and then waited politely for her to ask if I wanted seconds, which I did. After supper Jay Bob and I went to his room and shut the door.

I loved his room. I daydreamed about having one like it. Jay Bob had two single beds, which allowed for sleepovers. A single bed filled up my entire room. He also had a closet and a desk and a chest of drawers. My room was so small I had to keep my clothes under the bed, stored in two drawers from a thrown-away chest of drawers, and I did my homework at the kitchen table. Jay Bob also had a card table, which stayed up most of the time. He used it for making model airplanes, ships, and, more recently, hot rods with flame decals.

I didn't have the money to spend on models like Jay Bob did, but that was all right. I wasn't very good at it. The few I had made came out more glue than plastic. I got glue all over the kitchen table and glue all over the model airplane. It looked like it had been painted with snot. By the time I finished, my fingers were stuck together, and I was lucky if I could stand up without the chair sticking to my blue jeans.

But Jay Bob was a craftsman. You could never detect a trace of glue on his models. They were perfect, and most of the time he didn't need the instruction sheet to put them together. He could figure the parts out as he went along. Not me. I could have learned Latin in the time I spent puzzling over instruction sheets. I rarely could find the part I needed, although whenever I finished, I always had a pile of parts left. And I wasn't much better with decals. One time I lost a star-and-stripes decal between the water glass and a Corsair's wing. Mom was the one who found it. When I went to take a bath that night, she pulled it from the hair on the back of my head.

Jay Bob was so good with his hands that he was making a soap box derby racer in the storage room attached to the Joneses' garage. He wouldn't let anyone see it, not even Curty or me. All he would tell us was that its name was *Hardesty,* in honor of the winner of the Sixth All-American Soap Box Derby in 1939. Cliff Hardesty had been Jay Bob's hero ever since Mr. Jones had given him a magazine article in an effort to get Jay Bob to read more. It was funny how Mr. Jones read all the time and Jay Bob hardly read at all.

The article said that the officials at Akron suspected that an adult had built Hardesty's racer. It was a weird design and had a suspension system superior to that of any other soap box derby racer. But when the inspection committee asked the eleven-year-old to show them how he built the suspension, he convinced them in only half an hour. They were astounded that a kid could work with tools the way he did. They let him race, and he beat out over a hundred racers to win the championship.

Jay Bob wanted to be as good as Cliff Hardesty, and so he didn't allow anyone else around his racer. No one else could make a suggestion or do the least bit of work. For a kid who liked to plan robberies, he ethically and meticulously observed the rules. There was a lock on the door to the storage room, and only Jay Bob had the key. When he brought out his racer in July for the race down North Hill, we all could swear that no one helped him. And if the officials didn't believe us, Jay Bob could show them how he built every bit of it.

Jay Bob was sitting on one bed, and I was sitting on the other facing him. We were digesting our supper. "Do you know why the little moron took a prune to the prom?" Jay Bob asked.

"No, why?"

"Because he couldn't get a date! Get it?"

"Yeah, I get it, but it's not that funny. Who told you, Gerald?"

"Yeah. Someone on the B-team told it to him."

"Figures, teenagers laugh at anything. I think hormones make them goofy. Do you think the varsity is going to win state this year?"

"Nope, not even district. The Coyotes are only good at football."

The Roswell Coyotes were great at football. They had won two of the first three official New Mexico State Championships, '53 and '55, and had a really good coach, Coach Johnson. Jay Bob and Curty and I had been at DeBremond Stadium in early December when they won state by beating Las Cruces, 19 to 14.

I had been able to go to several football games during the regular season—El Paso Jefferson, Albuquerque Highland, and Artesia, which had been homecoming. I even got a ride to the homecoming bonfire with some of the high school kids in charge of gathering wood. They found out through Gerald that there was an old outhouse behind my house. I asked Mom if they could have it, and she said yes. Then I said I'd give it to them if they would give me a ride to and from the bonfire Wednesday night. One of the boys, Adam Choate, didn't seem too happy about it, but a pretty girl named Debbie said sure. They'd pick me up at six.

The pit beneath the outhouse had been filled in before we ever moved to our house, likely when the owner installed indoor plumbing. The outhouse was just sitting there ready to fall apart. The teenagers loaded it in a pickup, and that night it was on top of the bonfire with a dummy of an Artesia Bulldog sitting in it.

Adam Choate drove us to the bonfire. I sat shotgun next to Debbie, who was in the middle. There were two other girls and a guy in the backseat. Everyone was nice to me except Adam. He kept saying things like, "Finally, we see what the little moron who went to high school looks like." Debbie told him to be quiet. I was cute and she liked me.

After the bonfire wood caught fire, we had to move back. It was so hot no one could stand to be close. The pep squad and the cheerleaders led yells for a while, and then Coach Johnson introduced the players. I couldn't wait to grow up and play football for the Coyotes! I daydreamed about playing fullback and scoring touchdowns, or about playing defensive end and tackling the quarterback for a loss. When I got old enough to play for the Coyotes, then I'd know what it felt like to be a champion.

I wasn't so sure about basketball. Bob Cousy of the Celtics was my hero, but so far I wasn't very good at dribbling or shooting. My primary skill was fouling kids so hard they stayed away from my area of the court. Curty refused to play basketball with me anymore. He said I played basketball just like I played tackle football.

Jay Bob asked, "Did Mr. Connell play sports growing up?" Mr. Connell was his favorite teacher too.

"I don't know. I've never heard him say. He's not very good at softball—we know that—but he's still the best teacher we've ever had."

"I wish I could draw as good as he does. He's a great artist."

"Me too," I said.

"You too? The only thing you can draw is flies. You're the worst

art student in the world! How anyone can make A-pluses in everything else and be so bad in art is beyond me."

"Enough," I said. "Want to go to the movies next Saturday?" I
wouldn't have to pay admission because the Chamisa Theater
started out 1956 giving free admission for six weeks to kids who
had made the honor roll. Jay Bob would have to pay, but he had
plenty of money. "It's *20,000 Leagues Under the Sea*!"

"Really! We've never seen it! How did you find out?"

"I read the newspaper just like Curty. You ought to try it." Even
though we were poor, Mom refused to give up our telephone and
our newspaper subscription. We didn't have a dog, though, because
we didn't have enough table scraps. At least that's what Mom said.
My hoodlum cousin Greg said it was because Mom would get
attached to it, and then it'd die like Dad did, breaking her heart
again.

"Is it a double feature?"

"Single." Most often the Chamisa Theater showed double fea-
tures. Jay Bob would meet me after I got off from Whitman's Auto
and we'd watch two movies and a bunch of cartoons from one
o'clock to suppertime. Then his mom would pick us up.

"Sure I want to go! And did you hear the latest about the Martians?"

Oh man, not the Martians again. Growing up in Roswell was
weird because the Martians had either landed or not, and if so it
was in Roswell's backyard in 1947. Jay Bob was a true believer. I
was skeptical, but mainly because I believed in Eisenhower and
Truman. To be a true believer you had to maintain that Truman had
the whole thing covered up, and I couldn't believe he'd do that.
Truman had fired MacArthur and saved us from World War III. He
was a great man. The buck stopped on his desk. Eisenhower was a
square shooter too. Believers said that he had ordered J. Edgar
Hoover to have FBI agents kill anyone from Roswell who tried to

tell the story to outsiders. I didn't believe he would do such a thing.

"There are Martian survivors of the crash, and they're living at the old gravel pit."

"You're lying like a rug," I said.

"No I'm not. Gerald told me. Guys in high school have seen 'em. They go out there at night and hide. The Martians can't see humans and walk around right in front of them. We could see 'em too if we went out there."

I didn't know what to say. Gerald pretty much told the truth, unlike Curty's brother Darrell. Darrell was a thespian. "By the way, where is Curty?"

Curty lived two houses away from Jay Bob. I lived three blocks away. Curty and I took turns sleeping on the spare bed in Jay Bob's room. Whoever didn't sleep on the bed slept on a cot that we'd set up between the beds.

"Darrell is in some drama thing at the high school. Curty had to go watch and can't make it. So what do you think?"

"I don't care what Gerald says. There aren't any Martians at the old gravel pit."

"How about some night we go look?"

"Okay," I said, not at all wanting to go to the gravel pit after dark. It would be spooky.

"How about let's sneak out tonight?"

Jay Bob was bluffing, and so I bluffed in return. "No, tonight let's ride our bikes to Whitman's Auto. There's a *Playboy* magazine in the trash bin."

"You're lying! A *Playboy*?"

I told him how I had found it that morning, and how Allensworth's had dumped a mountain of trash on top of it. "I couldn't get it out, but I know which corner it's in."

At that point Jay Bob became inspired. He was ready to make like the Lone Ranger, "Hi ho, Silver, away!" and because I was still under the spell of naked ladies, I was crazy enough to make like Tonto and go with him.

Jay Bob's robbery planning experiences served us well. He raised his window while the TV blared in the living room. His parents were watching *Perry Como* and couldn't hear us. He unlatched the screen so we wouldn't make any noise undoing it later when it was quiet. He practiced opening and closing the window. It was remarkably not noisy.

We went out to the garage and found batteries for the lights on our bicycles, as well as a flashlight that he would carry. I didn't have gloves with me, and so he liberated a pair from Gerald's closet. It would be cold. And his solution to the mountain of trash that we needed to move was to get out the little shovel he had bought at the Army-Navy Surplus Store, one used by GIs for digging foxholes. We were ready!

At nine thirty Jay Bob went in and told his parents we were going to bed. "Nighty night," his mom said. His parents would stay up and watch the news. On her way to the bedroom Mrs. Jones would open the door and stick her head in to check on us like she always did. We would be pretending to be asleep, and she wouldn't be able to see that under the covers we were fully dressed. The minute she left and headed toward her bedroom, we'd be on our way out the window to Whitman's Auto and the *Playboy* magazine!

We got into bed and waited for what seemed like forever. We waited for *Perry Como* to be over. We listened for the news to start and then waited for the news to end. We listened for Mrs. Jones's footsteps on the hardwood floors in the hall. The next thing we heard was her saying, "Jay Bob! Joe Don! What on earth! Why are you sleeping in your jackets and gloves?"

Darn. It was morning.

4

CHURCH

THE JONESES WEREN'T BREAKFAST PEOPLE. Mom and I were, although I preferred cold cereal to eggs and bacon. Eggs made me gag, but Mom didn't care. Mom was a firm believer in starting the day with protein. She didn't buy the claim that Wheaties was the "breakfast of champions." To her it was eggs, bacon, toast, and a slice of cantaloupe.

Whenever I slept over on Saturday night, I'd ride my bike home Sunday morning in time to have breakfast before Mom and I had to leave for church. The Joneses were Presbyterian. Mom and I went to the First Baptist Church. Sunday school was at nine thirty, worship at eleven.

Jay Bob made fun of me because Baptists couldn't drink or dance. As though he did! My Granddaddy Miller had lived around Presbyterians growing up. He said they weren't against drinking or dancing. They just couldn't enjoy either one. He also said that Presbyterians were not a happy bunch. Most looked like they had been weaned on a dill pickle.

Curty was a Catholic. Mom didn't tell any of the relatives in West Texas that I had a Catholic friend. They wouldn't approve. They worried about people who were under the influence of the pope.

None of my classmates from Missouri Avenue were in my Sunday school department, which was against the odds. There were more Baptists in Roswell than starving kids in Armenia. But it did give me the opportunity to make a friend that I would never have had otherwise, John Hall. John was a fourth grader at Valley View Elementary. And although it was unnatural for a fifth grader to be friends with a lowly fourth grader, I liked John a lot. Our Sunday school department consisted of fourth and fifth graders, both grades mixed together in sex-regated classes. There were three classes for girls and two for boys. The minute Sunday school let out, John and I would race down the street to Ford's Pharmacy and get a nickel bottled coke out of their machine. It was a treat even though they only had Coca-Cola, which burned going down.

Adults griped that it wasn't right for Ford's to be open during church, but after worship a crowd always stopped in to make a purchase on the way home. And there was a crowd between Sunday school and the worship service, ten thirty to eleven. John and I weren't the only ones buying cokes. Men came in to smoke and talk and drink coffee.

John was different from any boy I had ever known. He was a listener, much more so than Joe Don and Curty. After I told John about my week, which consisted primarily of finding the *Playboy* magazine, I asked him about his dad, a distinguished man of intrigue. All the adults had wanted to know more about him ever since the Halls moved to Roswell last summer. "My dad is older than most, lots older than my mom. His first wife died. They had one daughter, my stepsister. That's why we moved to Roswell. She lives here with her husband. They go to the Methodist church."

"What does your dad do?"

"He's retired. Used to be a famous judge."

"He must be really old if he's retired."

"Yeah, but he's in good shape. He plays tennis and goes on hikes with me. He was a high jumper in college. Set the record and still holds it."

"Where did he go?"

"I don't remember, but I'll ask him and tell you."

"I wish I had a sandpit so I could practice high jumping at home," I said.

"Me too. I do the scissors like my dad did. We have this room in the basement of our house in Maryland. Dad invites famous people over to 'kick his ceiling.'"

"What do you mean?"

John explained that as a young high jumper his dad constantly stood around kicking his right leg above his head. It was his lead leg, the first part of his body over the bar. Although his best jump was six feet, five inches, his goal had been higher. He would kick the tops of door frames to practice getting his leg up in the air seven feet. The practice of kicking his leg above his head became so identified with him over the years that he built a special room in his basement with a ceiling painted white.

When the judge admired someone, regardless of what he or she had done, he would invite this person over to "kick his ceiling." Several athletes had done this, as well as a couple of Rockettes from Radio City Music Hall. If they couldn't reach the ceiling, he would let them lie on a couch that could be lifted up by four men, bringing the person within range. By the scuff mark each person signed his name and the date.

"Like who?" I asked.

"Rocky Marciano."

"You're lying! Really?"

"Really. And there's a lot more than his. You should see all the names. My dad knows lots of famous people."

"Sounds neat!"

"It is. I miss our house; we still own it. And I miss my friends.

But Dad wants us to be close to my stepsister, which is why we're here. Did your dad know lots of famous people?"

"Some, but I'm not sure how many. I was young when he was killed."

"What would you do with him if he was alive?"

"Play catch for hours and hours, until it got too dark to see. Same with shooting baskets. And you know what I can't do that other kids can? Say, 'Daddy, look at me!' He'd look at me clown around and try things. Dad went to Texas Tech. He played football and basketball, but not baseball. And I never heard anything about track. I don't think he ran track."

"Are you going to play football and basketball?"

"Yeah, when I get to junior high. All I can play for real right now is Little League baseball."

"Me too. Dad and I went to Del Beene's and got a glove yesterday."

"Me too! I picked out a big brown Rawlings for an early birthday present."

"I got the black one! How much did yours cost?" John asked.

"I don't have it yet. It's on layaway. It cost me all my birthday presents, but it's worth it. It's a great glove."

Another kid in our Sunday school department, a rich snot from Military Heights Elementary, overheard us talking. "If you had a daddy like everyone else, you wouldn't be so poor. Baseball gloves aren't expensive."

His remark caught me off guard. I didn't know what to say, and so I didn't say anything. But John stuck his tongue out at the kid. We put our empty bottles in the return case and headed up the block to go to worship.

• • • • • • •

On the way home after church Mom asked me what I thought of that morning's sermon. Last year, when we sat together, she never asked. But ever since I started sitting with other kids in the balcony, she asked most every Sunday.

I told her it was all right, had lots of good stuff about the matriarchs of the Bible—Grace, Hope, and Charity. Mom knew I was kidding. What she didn't know was that I daydreamed through most the service about getting the *Playboy* magazine. But even then my thoughts weren't that far removed from God.

I had wondered if God would help me get a ride from my house to Whitman's before the trash was picked up and the *Playboy* magazine lost forever. God had helped the men of Jabesh-gilead march all night so they could retrieve Saul's body when it was nailed to the wall at Beth-shan. Or would God strike me blind for looking at a *Playboy*, like he did Paul on the road to Damascus? Being a Baptist and having to compare your life to Bible stories was confusing.

I also spent sermon time wishing that Mr. Connell went to our church. I liked seeing him every day, and from Friday to Monday was too long not to be around him. But he was Methodist, probably because he liked to dance. He said that dancing was his favorite form of recreation. I imagined that he and Miss Tower went out to O'Brien's Night Club every Saturday night and danced until dawn.

Mom said, "The sermon made me realize that I need to clear something up. God loves us because he chooses to, not because we deserve it. And like God, I love you just because I do. I'm going to love you all my life long."

"That's good," I said, not having a clue what she was talking about.

"I'm afraid I sometimes give you the wrong impression, like when I make a big fuss over your report card. And I am proud of you, but I wouldn't love you any less if you brought home C's."

"Really? Then can I play hooky and just show up for tests? That'd average out to C's."

"No, you can't. What I mean is if C's were the best you could do. For example, who doesn't make good grades in your class?"

"Raymond Spencer. His dad knocks him across the room when he brings home his report card."

"I would never do that to you. If C's were the best you could do, I'd hug your neck."

"Then why bother making A-pluses? All you do is hug my neck. How about some of that filthy lucre Reverend Harper talks about? Fifty cents for an A-plus!"

"Get serious, Joe Don. I'm being serious now."

"Okay . . . You got all that outa the sermon this morning?"

"Sure did."

"Then I'm not sure I agree."

"What do you mean?"

"I love you, Mom, but I'd love you more if we had a TV."

"Even if none is the best I can do?"

"No excuses."

"Liar," she grinned. "You are such a kidder, just like your daddy was. Here's a word for you to look up when we get home, 'prevaricator.'"

"And here's a joke I heard in Sunday school. What's the moral of Jonah and the whale?"

"I don't know. What?"

"You can't keep a good man down."

"That's a good one," she smiled.

"But while he was in the whale's stomach, he watched TV. For three nights he got to watch Sergeant Bilko, *Perry Como, Lassie,* and all the other good shows. And he ate off a TV tray. He ate fried chicken, mashed potatoes, dinner rolls with grape jelly, and chocolate pie just because his mother loved him and waited on him. Even though he didn't go to Ninevah when he was supposed to, she still loved him."

"Good Lord, Joe Don! You are full of it! The word is 'prevaricator.'"

"But like Jonah's mom, you love me anyway."

5

MISCHIEF

FRIDAY NIGHT THE HOBBS EAGLES were coming to town to play the Coyotes. Hobbs was one of New Mexico's better basketball teams, and the gym would be packed. I hadn't seen a basketball game all season and was glad when the Joneses invited me. We would go early to see Gerald play for the B-team, and then have good seats for the varsity game.

Gerald scored eight points in a losing effort. The B-team lost by twenty. The varsity game was going to be more exciting, and Jay Bob wanted us to move to the high school section. He said that he liked to root louder than the parents did in their section, but I knew the truth. He wanted a seat so he would have a better view of the cheerleaders.

Before the varsity game started, we went to the snack bar. I got an RC Cola and a Baby Ruth, courtesy of Mr. Jones, who had given Jay Bob money. Jay Bob got popcorn and an orange drink. While we were waiting for the change, I recognized a voice coming from my right.

"If it ain't the little moron who went to the basketball game!" It was Adam Choate. He sneered at me like I was something stuck on the bottom of his desk.

"If it ain't the big jerk who smells like an outhouse."

"You got a mouth on you that needs closing, kid! How'd you

like a knuckle sandwich?" I should have kept my mouth shut. Adam turned mean. He moved in close and held his fist in my face. I just stood there and took it.

After Jay Bob got the change, we turned and went to our seats in the high school section. Adam made fun of me as we walked away, but he didn't follow or bother me anymore.

The first half was close. At halftime the Coyotes were behind by three points, so everyone rooted like crazy as the third quarter began. The gym was so loud you could hardly hear what the person standing by you was saying. But then Hobbs pulled away, and by the fourth quarter it was all over but the shouting. People in the stands were just trying to be supportive. There was no hope.

Jay Bob and I were sitting next to each other not saying much. I was daydreaming about playing basketball for the Coyotes. I'd have a killer jump shot that would put Hobbs in its place, and I'd constantly steal the ball when the other team was dribbling.

Jay Bob started talking to a kid, Roger Jamison, who had just moved to a seat below us. Roger was in the other fifth grade class at Missouri Avenue. He had heard about my secret whistle and wanted to see it. Jay Bob asked me if I had it on me. I did. It was in my blue jeans pocket.

My hoodlum cousin Greg had given me the whistle. It was the only one like it I had ever seen. It was a thin cylinder, half an inch long. You put it in your mouth, shut your lips, but not tight, and made a hissing sound. The air hitting the whistle made a loud, high-pitched sound, and no one could easily tell where it was coming from.

I had pulled a joke on Mr. Connell using the whistle. I was in the cloakroom getting ready to go home after school and started blowing it in secret. The kids didn't know I was the one whistling because my mouth looked like it was closed and I didn't have anything in my hand. Mr. Connell came walking in from the classroom

36 · SUMMER of CHAMPIONS

with a puzzled look on his face. He looked at all us kids, and then looked at the floor and the ceiling, but couldn't figure it out until I showed him. He had never seen a whistle like it.

"Give it here," Jay Bob said. "Let me show Roger."

I made sure no one saw me hand it to him. "Be careful and don't drop it."

"Did you wash it off? I don't want your cooties."

"Yeah, but don't blow it!" It had been several weeks, but I had washed it off once.

He let Roger look at the whistle, but didn't let him hold it. Jay Bob put it in his mouth and was showing him how to blow it even though he had never actually done so. Roger whispered, "Blow it so I can hear."

"No, Jay Bob!" I whispered, but I could tell that he was going to anyway. He was just waiting for the crowd's sound volume to go back up, so that when he did hardly anyone would hear. Soon enough Hobbs turned the ball over, and Roswell ran down the court for a layup. The crowd roared. But on the way in for the basket, the legs of the Roswell player got tangled up with the legs of a Hobbs player and both crashed to the floor. The crowd gasped! There was absolute silence as people waited to see how badly the two boys were hurt. It was just then that Jay Bob, who had been having difficulty making the whistle work, finally got it to blow.

It was loud and made the officials mad. They didn't like competing whistles in the gymnasium. As soon as both boys got up—they were okay—a referee went to the scorekeeper's table and spoke into the microphone. "I want that whistle turned in now! The game will not continue until I have it and the Roswell High principal has the name of the student who blew it!"

The referees knew the section of the bleachers that the sound came from, and it wasn't the Hobbs side. And although many could point to the vicinity of the sound, no one could pinpoint the perpe-

The light was better there than anywhere else in the house, except the light by Mom's bed. Mom had read to me a lot as a kid, and then one day I took over and had been reading on my own ever since.

There were two New Mexicans I had been reading about for years. Both of them were from around Lincoln, which was just up the road from Roswell: Smokey the Bear and Billy the Kid. Everyone liked Smokey the Bear. You'd have to be some kind of a villain not to like a baby bear who miraculously lived through the Capitan Mountains forest fire. With badly burned feet, he climbed a tree and hung on until he was rescued by a firefighter. I read everything I could find about Smokey, who at the time was living at the National Zoo in Washington, D.C.

Not everyone liked Billy the Kid, but for some reason I was drawn to him. If he had killed men, they had most likely needed it, which was something adults said about sorry people. Plus Billy lived during the Lincoln County wars. It was kill or be killed, just like World War II and Korea, only closer.

Who I had no use for was Pat Garrett, the sheriff who tracked Billy down and killed him at Fort Sumner. He had been a buffalo hunter before he was a sheriff, and it was a sorry excuse of a man who killed thousands of buffalo for fun. I considered it an embarrassment to my home town that he had once been a resident. I did like the song his daughter Elizabeth wrote, though, "O, Fair New Mexico," which became the state song. I updated the words to

O fair New Mexico,
We love, we love you so.
Home of Curly, Joe, and Moe,
O fair New Mexico.

On Saturday Mom had to work late helping change a display. That gave me half an hour after working at Whitman's to run down the street to Cobb's. They had a whole section of valentine cards, but they were for grown-ups. I liked Janet, but I couldn't tell her "You're My First Thought When I Wake, And The Last Before I Sleep. Don't Cause My Heart To Ache, Or Cupid Sweet to Weep. Be My Valentine." Too mushy!

After looking through the cards for several minutes, I found one that was just right. It said, "Roses Are Red, Violets Blue, But Nothing So Lovely Is As Special As You." I could say that. She would like that.

I had that morning's quarter with me, as well as two dimes, a nickel, and three pennies. As I reached into my pocket, I had an idea. Last Fourth of July I had made the most money in my life when my older West Texas cousin Stanley saw an angle. I had been on a visit to Grandpa Snider's farm in late June. We were shooting off firecrackers, blowing up anthills and cow paddies. I said I wished I could do the same at home, but Roswell had a fireworks law that prohibited firecrackers. There were some baby fireworks you could do—sparklers, glow worms, and smoke bombs—but that was about it.

My cousin Stanley said, "Why don't you buy a bunch here, take 'em home and jack up the price? Kids'll pay whatever you ask just to have 'em." And he was right!

I had a dollar at the time, and I used it to buy Black Cats for a dime a pack. I sold them in Roswell for fifty cents each, five dollars, which I blew almost immediately. Money burned a hole in my pocket.

I bought a new blouse for Mom. For myself I sent off for a bathtub submarine on the back of a comic book. I also got a bunch of little green army men and stationed them on my fort in the backyard. The rest I just squandered, except for the fifty cents I gave as my tithe to Jesus.

Mom had been happy about the blouse. She said, "Joe Don, I can't believe you're so generous!" But then she gave me a headache. "I figured you'd save that five dollars for a TV, start a TV account."

Oh man, I hadn't thought of that! I was sad for a whole morning. I needed to remember to look before I leaped.

Big valentine cards were ten cents at Cobb's, and I was pretty sure that I'd be the only kid in my class to shop there. Cobb's had four other cards like the one I had chosen for Janet. There were bound to be four other boys who liked girls in our class as much as I liked her. I'd buy five cards for fifty cents, keep one, and sell four for fifty cents each. Two of my three pennies would cover the tax.

It was harder than I thought the next Monday finding four guys who would spend half a dollar for a valentine card, but I did. By Tuesday morning I had turned fifty cents into two bucks!

Monday night I daydreamed about Janet, how she would fall in love with me at the Valentine's party. In my daydreams she was wearing a gold tiara and a baby blue ball gown with long white gloves. She would reach into her valentine's sack, pull out my card, and open it with the gold letter opener that she kept in her pink purse. She would read it, and when she got to my name at the bottom of the card, her face would glow with excitement. She'd turn and smile at me and say, "Oh, I had hoped it would be you!" I'd be sitting there looking cool in my new flour sack shirt.

She would fill a picnic basket with cupcakes, and we would leave the party to go riding in a coach like the one in *Cinderella*. We would hold hands as we walked to get in. The driver would take us to Tilden's Roller Rink, where when it was "ladies' choice" Janet would choose to skate with me, which was different from what had happened back in the fall at our class party. Not only did she sit out the "ladies' choice," but I couldn't muster the courage to ask her during "gentleman's choice." Walter Garcia, who was the best skater around, asked her, and the two of them glided around the rink. It was just as well. I wasn't much better at skating than I was at art. We probably would have crashed against the sideboards, and she would have hated me forever.

Then came Valentine's Day for real. First thing Tuesday morning we dropped our valentines into one another's sacks, which were thumbtacked to the wooden chalk rail. The stupid little valentines I gave to everyone but Janet. In her sack I dropped the big one.

The party was the last thing that afternoon. We couldn't open valentines until then, and the suspense was terrible. We were going to have to wait through geography, spelling, history, music, and math. It was going to be a long day.

The Valentine's issue of the school newspaper had been distributed first thing that morning to each student in fourth grade and above. Sherry Watson, editor, followed up with an announcement midmorning on the PA system. Each copy of the newspaper had been numbered in ink in the top right-hand corner. The numbers were for a drawing. The principal had been asked to pick a number, and the winner was going to get two passes to the Chamisa movie theater. Sherry called out the winning number, two hundred fourteen, and I won! I had two fourteen!

I went to the principal's office to claim my prize. I didn't need the tickets myself since I was an honor roll student and got in for free. But maybe Mom could go with me for free, applying both children's tickets to an adult ticket.

Sherry Watson was sitting in the chair across the desk from the principal, who looked at me and smiled. "You lucked out, Joe Don. Sherry asked me to pick a winning number. I said, 'Let's see. Valentine's Day is on the second month of the year, fourteenth day of the month. How about two fourteen.' And so here you are!"

I was always uneasy in Miss Sherelle's presence. Kids called her Miss Sherelle, but adults sometimes called her Belle Sherelle. Adults didn't do that with other teachers. Something important was being said by using her first name. Curty said it was because she was from the South, but I figured it was how adults paid respect to a really strict person, which she was.

I didn't dawdle in Miss Sherelle's presence. I thanked her, took the tickets from Sherry, and left. Sherry excused herself and hurried after me. She caught me in the hallway and said, "You know, Joe Don, I wouldn't say no if you asked me to go to a movie on those tickets."

Oh man, not again. Would this girl never leave me alone? Sherry Watson was one of the prettiest girls in the grade above ours, but sixth grade girls weren't supposed to acknowledge the existence of fifth grade boys. They certainly weren't allowed to talk to us in public. It was a federal law, maybe even a lesser-known commandment. Yet Sherry time and time again went out of her way to get mushy with me.

I was just about to say, "My mom won't let me date girls," when a teacher's voice boomed out.

"Sherry!" It was Mr. Davidson, her homeroom teacher, calling to her from the doorway of his classroom. "We're waiting for you so we can start the test. Hurry up!"

She turned toward her homeroom and didn't say anything else. I walked on to Mr. Connell's room, saved not by the bell, but by a teacher.

• • • • • • •

It had started on a hot day last summer at the Cahoon Park Swimming Pool. Jay Bob and Curty had been bugging me for weeks to go swimming with them. Any other summer and I would have gone every time I had a dime for admission. But Mom had gotten a bargain on a swimsuit for me. It was orange and tight-fitting, which was okay, but it had a diamond-shaped cutout with two strands of cross-webbing on each hip. My bare hip was exposed to public view! Mom said it was no big thing. It wasn't like people could see my rear end or anything. But it was a big thing to me. I hated it.

Jay Bob and Curty had taken Mom's side without seeing the suit. They had told me for weeks that no one would notice the cutouts. "Let's just go swimming!" But once they saw my suit inside the locker room, they changed their minds.

"Smoly hoke!" said Curty. "I didn't know it was like that. You're a naked nudist."

I was ready to turn around and go home. A champion didn't expose his butt, but I had already paid my dime and couldn't get it back. I kept my towel around my waist as we walked to the pool, and quickly jumped in. So long as I was in the water, a person would have to swim up to me underwater to see through the cutouts, which they had better not given the mood I was in. We were in the water for maybe an hour. Swimming was usually impossible. Cahoon Park wasn't so much a swimming pool as it was a body of water in which kids splashed, stood, jumped, and dove. The pool was so packed with kids that day we could hardly move. We couldn't even play our usual water tag. If that many people had been in a public building, the fire marshal would have closed it down.

We did get into a water-splashing fight with some kids. It was so much fun that a lifeguard penalized us by making us get out of the pool for ten minutes. My mind was still having fun when I jumped out, and so I forgot about my swimsuit. The three of us lay down on our towels to sunbathe. We were less than ten feet from the edge of the pool, enjoying the sun on our lily white backs and legs, when I heard some girls in the pool giggling. I turned to see what they were laughing at and discovered that it was me!

They were pointing at the cutouts in my swimsuit! I quickly sat up facing them and put my towel over my lap. I turned my eyes away and gazed off into the sky as though I was watching a bird or a plane or Superman and had no idea why they were giggling.

I didn't know what else to do when suddenly an older girl swam up and shooed the younger girls away. I didn't recognize her in her pink suit and bathing cap, but Jay Bob did. He whispered, "It's Sherry Watson!"

Oh, man, what if she had seen the cutouts in my swimsuit? What would I do? She'd tell sixth graders, or worse, she would write an article about my swimsuit in the Back to School issue of the school newspaper!

My worries were for nothing. She leaned against the side of the pool, arms crossed on the deck, smiled at me, and said, "I think your suit is sexy. I saw one like it in a magazine and loved it. It takes a cool guy to wear a suit like that."

I couldn't believe my ears. I made like a zombie. I couldn't move a muscle. I couldn't say a word. A pretty girl in the sixth grade was talking to a lowly, almost naked worm like me, and she had used a word that Jay Bob, Curty, and I didn't even use when we were alone, "Sexy!" Then she splashed water on me, caught me in the face, and said, "Can't catch me on a grandpa's knee!" She turned and swam through the swarm of kids. It was miraculous! Kids parted to make way for her as though her middle name was Moses.

When my body came out of its trance, I got up but didn't follow her. I walked with my towel around me to the locker room and was getting dressed to go home when Curty and Jay Bob came in. "Are you crazy?" Jay Bob asked. "Why didn't you go after her? She said you're sexy! She said you're cool! What do you want, an engraved invitation?"

"It's too weird, Jay Bob. She's going to be a sixth grader."

Curty took my side. "Yeah, guys don't date girls older than they are. It's not right."

"And we don't even date," I added, "not until we're in junior high or high school. How many times have we had this discussion?"

Actually never—I was getting ahead of myself. But we had known of kids at Missouri Avenue who went on dates, and we thought they were silly. They mainly went to formal dances, but some went to movies.

"Who cares what grade she's in?" Jay Bob said. "And it's not a date. It's horsing around. She likes you. She's beautiful. Go chase her! She's waiting!"

I didn't go after her. I went home. And ever since she had chased me. Whenever she caught me inside the school store across from the playground, she bought me candy. She'd share her Dr. Pepper with me and not even wipe off the mouth of the bottle after I'd taken a swig. And after we got our school pictures, she handed me a big envelope on the playground. It was her picture, but not the small kind that kids traded. It was a big one like you give your parents, and it was signed, "To Joe Don, With All My Love, Sherry."

· · · · · · ·

Last thing Valentine's afternoon we had the party. Gilbert's mom, Mrs. Bertrand, provided cupcakes and Kool-Aid. She glared at me when I got mine and said, "It would be nice if your mom could provide refreshments for a class party."

"She'd be happy to. But I'd have to bring them because she has to work."

"That simply will not do!" she snapped. "The mother has to be present to serve the refreshments. We cannot put that burden on the teacher."

After each of us ate a strawberry cupcake and drank a cup of grape Kool-Aid, we started opening our valentines. I watched as Janet took several small ones out of her sack and opened them. Finally she pulled out the big one! She opened it, looked really pleased, then turned to Terry Adair and said, "Thank you, Terry. It's a really special valentine!"

What was she doing with the valentine I sold Terry? In astonishment I watched as she then pulled out and opened two other big valentines, saying nothing.

Darn. Who would have thought that three out of five of us liked Janet Mitchum? Dismayed, I had another cupcake and cup of Kool-Aid.

After the party, I walked out on the playground and pulled my bicycle out of the bike rack. I was ready to ride home when Sherry handed me a valentine as she ran to get in the car with her teenage sister. Her sister Becky, who was Gerald's heartthrob, picked her up every day. The high school got out earlier than elementary school. I didn't open her valentine on the playground, but carried it with me inside my spelling book. Mom wasn't home yet when I got there, so I sat at the kitchen table and opened it. I had seen it at Cobb's. It was the one I hadn't bought for Janet because it was too mushy. She signed it "With Hugs and Kisses, Sherry!" and with little hearts over the two i's.

Reading it embarrassed me, but at the same time made me feel good. I had felt the same way when I saw how she signed her picture. I liked Janet Mitchum more, but I didn't dislike the way Sherry made me feel. I took the card and put it next to her picture in the ammo box beneath the floor of my fort.

7

HONORS

THE THURSDAY NIGHT AFTER VALENTINE'S I gave Mom exciting news!
Miss Tower had asked me to be the editor of the school newspaper,
the *Missouri Avenue Magpie*! She asked me even though I
wouldn't officially start until September, when I was in the sixth
grade. Miss Tower taught music, spelling, and reading, and was the
newspaper sponsor. The reason she asked me early was that if I
accepted, which I did in my quest to be a champion, I needed to
spend the rest of the school year learning how the paper was put
together.

Being named editor made me study even harder for another
honor I wanted, winning the school spelling bee. It was held on a
Wednesday in the library after lunch. I was confident that I could
beat the other fifth graders, but not knowing how good the sixth
graders were, I had studied a copy of their spelling book. It turned out
they weren't much competition. There were three of us fifth graders
still standing when the last sixth grader went out. I won on the word
"impairment," which was easy compared to some of the other words
we had to spell.

That night I ran outside to greet Mom when she drove up from
work. I opened her door and said, "Mom, I won!"

We hugged while she was still sitting behind the steering wheel.
"Joe Don! I'm so proud of you!"

"But you'd be just as proud had I lost?"

"Yes I would, but not nearly as happy for you!"

We went inside for a supper of fish sticks, which was one of my favorites. Afterward we practiced for the city spelling bee. Miss Sherelle had given me a special word list. Mom would pronounce the word and tell me what it meant, most often without having to look it up in the dictionary. Mom graduated from high school, which had only eleven grades at the time, but was never able to go to college like she wanted. Still, she was good at reading, spelling, and pronouncing. She checked out books from the Carnegie library on her lunch break and sometimes read until late at night. We practiced until it was my bedtime.

The next morning when Mom left for work, she said, "Joe Don, we didn't celebrate your victory last night. How about we do it this evening after supper?"

"As in go buy a TV?"

"No, as in go to the Dairy Queen for an ice cream. I think it's back open."

"Okay, but I'd love you more if you bought us a TV."

"No you wouldn't. Here's a word for you to look up, 'fabricator.'"

"But you're smart, Mom. If you'd watch *The $64,000 Question*, then you could go on the show and make enough money to quit working at Allensworth's."

"You're full of prunes, Mr. Fabricator. I'll see you tonight. We'll go to the Dairy Queen. Bye."

I never let up for long about a TV. I'm surprised Mom didn't tire of it and slap me halfway across Chaves County. Many parents would have. But she knew that I knew it was out of reach. It was all she could do to keep food on the table and clothes on a growing boy. Even then she had to have as much help as her pride would allow, like from my grandparents or Mr. Kyle Rodman or Uncle Charlie. That's why helping her was one of my New Year's resolutions.

I was expensive. One day my new blue jeans would have a four-inch cuff, and then a few months later no cuff at all, no knees either. Mom spent many a night patching my jeans. Or one day there'd be room in the toes of my Buster Browns, but soon enough my toes were ready to bust through. One day the icebox and kitchen shelves would be full, a few days later empty. It seemed like I was always hungry.

I didn't know how much money Mom made, but I knew it wasn't enough for luxuries. Still, I dearly loved TV—*I Love Lucy, Dragnet, December Bride, Jack Benny, My Little Margie, Rin Tin Tin*, and *Sergeant Preston*. The list went on and on, although I had little use for Mr. Wizard, Sid Caesar, Milton Berle, Arthur Godfrey, Jane Wyman, Bishop Sheen, Ted Mack, and Mike London, a wrestling promoter from Albuquerque. Mom wasn't much interested in any of it. Every once in a while she watched TV at Uncle Charlie and Aunt Elvis's house, but said all she needed was a good library book and an occasional 78 on the turntable.

Jay Bob's mother knew I loved TV. She told Mom that after I finished my homework I was always welcome to come watch TV at their house. Mom didn't let me go every night, but did a couple of times a week. Mrs. Jones also admitted that there was method in her madness. The knowledge that I was in the living room might make Jay Bob, who was forbidden to leave his room until his homework was done, stop dawdling and finish. Jay Bob stretched out his homework like he was pulling taffy.

Because Roswell had only one channel, KSWS, Channel 8, Mr. Jones would never want to watch something other than what I was watching. In no way would I interfere with his evening. In fact, Mr. Jones planned his TV viewing. He watched only those shows he was interested in, and even then seemed to feel guilty because he was taking time away from his reading. I guessed that a librarian had to read every book in his library, which would take a lot of time no matter how fast a reader he was.

Nineteen fifty-six was the first time I was aware of it being a leap year. On February 29 I was in the Jones living room watching *The Phil Silvers Show.* I loved it. Sergeant Bilko was the funniest guy on TV, but just after it started Jay Bob motioned to me from his room. "Mom," he said, "I need Joe Don to help me with some homework."

"Will you, Joe Don?"

"Sure," I said, hoping that it wouldn't take long. It didn't seem polite to say, "Wait until Sergeant Bilko is over."

Jay Bob closed the door behind me. He sat on his bed, and I sat on the spare bed facing him. "Did you hear what happened to me after school?" he asked.

I had not.

"I got depantsed." And then he started crying.

"No! How did it happen?"

The weather had been warm, so Jay Bob and Curty decided to stay after school and play basketball on the concrete outdoor court with some other kids. While they were playing, a gang of chukes rode up on bicycles, about a dozen of them.

"Chuke" was short for "pachuco." There were several pachuco gangs at South Junior High School, where we would have to go to school in the seventh grade. We were not looking forward to it.

Chukes fought with switchblades, box cutters, bicycle chains, and in my opinion the most frightening weapon of them all, neon light tubes! Neon light tubes were scary. In addition to the glass shattering and cutting you when it hit your head, what would the stuff inside do? Burn your face off? Get in your mouth and poison you? Blind your eyes?

The chukes had snuck up on Jay Bob, Curty, and the other kids playing basketball. Curty was on defense, playing against Jay Bob's team, and saw them coming. He and most of the other kids were able to make themselves scarce. Jay Bob was taking the ball in from half-court, going from side to side showing off his dribbling skills. His back was to the chukes, and he couldn't figure out why everyone was running off until too late. They caught him and one other kid, Ronnie Green.

The chukes pushed Jay Bob and Ronnie around for a while. Then they depantsed them, taking their shirts and shoes also, leaving the two in their underwear and socks.

As the chukes rode off with their clothing, Jay Bob and Ronnie ran for their jackets, which were piled on a bleacher along the sideline of the basketball court. They wrapped their coats around their middles so no one would see their underwear. But kids were already returning as the chukes rode away. Kids saw Jay Bob's and Ronnie's underwear!

Walter Garcia, our classmate, lived across the street from the school. His room was on the second floor, with a window that looked out on the playground. He was working on his stamp collection and saw what happened. He had seen depantsings before and knew that chukes sometimes threw clothes into a trash barrel down the block. Walter ran outside and yelled for Jay Bob and Ronnie to run to his house. His parents owned a feed store and weren't home yet from work. Jay Bob and Ronnie waited in Walter's room while Walter dashed down the street. Sure enough, the clothes and shoes were in a fifty-five-gallon garbage drum. He took them back to his house. Jay Bob and Ronnie got dressed and went home.

"Did you tell your parents?" I asked.

"No. I don't tell them nasty stuff." Jay Bob was still whimpering, his face a snotty mess.

"Did you tell Gerald?"

"No, he'd just tell our parents. And I threatened Curty that I'd shoot him like a dog with rabies if he told anyone."

Jay Bob was upset. He wanted to kill the chukes dead, bury them in sand up to their necks like in a pirate movie, and laugh as the tide came in and drowned them.

"Or how about like in a Tarzan movie," I said, "when the bad natives tie a good one between two bent-together palm trees, one leg to each tree. Then they cut the ropes and split him in two. That'd smart."

I was in pain over what had happened to Jay Bob. He had been embarrassed, humiliated, and shamed. It didn't seem fair for me to be basking in the glow of winning the school spelling bee, not to mention being named editor, when the worst thing that could happen to a kid had befallen Jay Bob. Kids saw him in his underwear! I didn't know what to say. Whenever Mom had a bad day, I could give her a hug and make it better. But guys didn't hug each other.

I moved over and sat beside him on the bed. I punched him lightly on the arm. If I was him I'd never want to go back to school.

8

MARTIANS

JAY BOB'S MOM FOUND HIS RIPPED SHIRT in the laundry hamper—the chukes tore it pulling it off—and made him tell her what had happened. She felt sorry for him, and let him have a sleepover Saturday, even though she and Mr. Jones were going to be at a banquet and dance until midnight. Gerald was put in charge.

Jay Bob and Curty figured that Saturday night would be our best chance to sneak out to the old gravel pit. With Gerald in charge we wouldn't actually have to sneak out. We could just make like mountain men and hit the trail. I didn't want to go, but there was no way I could get out of it without being called chicken.

Gerald drew us a map of the gravel pit and showed us where to stand so we'd have the best view of the Martians, which was along the back wall or cliff. The gravel pit had been dug out years ago so that the back wall was about as high as a three-story building, straight up and down. The rest of the walls were also clifflike, the front side being lower and broken by a dirt road that led down into the pit. We would have to walk down the road and across the pit to get to the wall where we were going to stand.

"Proud of you, Number Two Son," Gerald said to his brother. "You guys like bug stains on car grill. It take guts."

"You can't kid me, Gerald," I said. "There aren't any Martians. I'm just going so I can prove it once and for all."

"You see hundreds of them if you not chicken out."

"We're not chicken!" said Jay Bob.

"Number Two Son brave, but be sure you stand in right place. If you do, it like looking at prairie dog village. Many come up out of holes in ground."

"Holes in the ground?" said Curty. "You mean they come up out of trap doors? They live in camouflaged cellars?"

Gerald had grown tired of his Charlie Chan impersonation. "I'm not sure. All I know is that they're like prairie dogs, but you can't see any holes. How they get in and out of the ground is weird. There's this squishy sound, and suddenly they're there. Maybe the squishy sound is the sound of a trap door opening. I don't know. I've never figured it out."

"You've seen Martians?" I asked.

"Sure."

"Then why didn't they shoot you dead with their ray guns?"

"I don't know that either. Some guys think that it's because they don't see that well at night. Others think that something happened to their antennas in the crash. Whichever, they won't bother you. These Martians don't have ray guns, and they can't detect human beings. You'll be safe. When you hear squishy sounds, you'll be able to see them, but they can't see you. Sometimes you hear lots of squishy sounds before you see any."

Gerald took off from the house to go to see his buddies about fifteen minutes after his parents left, around seven thirty. He wasn't supposed to go out, but he said he wouldn't tell on us if we didn't tell on him. The Martians didn't come out until nine o'clock. It would take us half an hour to hike out there, and so we had an hour to kill.

"Do you know why the little moron took a ladder to school?" I asked. "Because he wanted to go to high school!" We laughed.

"I've got one," said Jay Bob. "Knock, knock."

"Who's there?"

"A goat."

"A goat who?"

"A goat tell Aunt Rhodey, goat tell Aunt Rhodey, goat tell Aunt Rhodey the old gray goose is dead!" We laughed. A goose that died with a toothache in her head. We wished we had a dime for every time we had sung that song in music class. We sang it almost as often as we did the one about Benjamin Franklin. *"Benjamin Franklin inventive was he. Out in a storm with a kite and a key. Poor Ben Franklin, wise Ben Franklin. Poor Ben Franklin . . ."* And then we changed the ending to, *"What a shock's waiting for him!"*

Curty had one. "A little girl asks her mom, 'Mama, some boys by the swing set in the park asked if I could hang by my legs from the trapeze. Why did they do that?'

'To see your panties, silly!'

'Well I fooled them. I didn't have any on.'" We laughed so hard that Jay Bob had to go to the bathroom. That was the funniest joke we had ever heard.

When he came out he said, "Since Gerald's not here, let's listen to his records!"

We went into Gerald's room. He had two new ones, "See You Later Alligator" by Bill Haley and the Comets and "Tutti Frutti" by Little Richard. We liked them and played them twice. Gerald had lots of records, and we played the others too.

At eight thirty we grimly went out the back door. If this was going to be fun, we didn't act like it. We cut down the alley toward Sunset Road. It seemed colder than usual. We had on jackets and gloves. Jay Bob and I had on stocking caps. Curty wore his Davy Crockett hat. Jay Bob took a bow and a quiver of eight arrows in case the Martians weren't as friendly as Gerald claimed. I carried his camping ax, and Curty took along his dad's hunting knife. Jay Bob and Curty both had a pair of binoculars around their necks so

we could see better when we got there. All three of us had flashlights.

On Sunset Road we headed south. It was a longer hike than we
thought, and we didn't get to the road that led down into the gravel
pit until nine fifteen. We stood still for the longest time trying to
work up our courage. We had begun whispering because we didn't
want the Martians to hear us.

"It's awfully cold out here," Curty whispered. "Maybe we'd
better go home before we catch cold."

"Yeah, we could get sick in this weather," I said.

"Chickens!" Jay Bob said. "Get your weapons ready and walk
slow."

And so we did. Curty and I held our weapons in one hand while
using the other to shine our flashlights ahead of us. Jay Bob put his
flashlight in his quiver because it took both hands to ready an
arrow in his bow. He followed our lights.

Slowly we crept down the road and across the gravel pit. There
was enough moonlight that we could barely make out the old shack
in the middle of the pit. It wasn't windy, so there weren't that many
spooky sounds, although we did have to stop a couple of times to
listen before we went on. Finally we made it to the back side of the
gravel pit and took a position standing at the base of the cliff. We
were tightly wedged together. I was in the middle.

We were terrified. I desperately hoped we wouldn't see any
Martians. I prayed that they were going to spend a quiet evening
watching *Buck Rogers* and *Flash Gordon* on the TVs inside their
burrows. Anything but come outside to play. We looked and looked,
seeing nothing, especially through the binoculars. All we could see
through them was solid black. Just as I was getting ready to suggest
that we leave, we heard some *splats,* the squishy noise that Gerald
told us about!

"What's that?" Jay Bob whispered as he drew back an arrow.

There were more *splats*. They were getting closer, but we still couldn't see any Martians. *Splat, splat, splat* . . . and then something that sounded like a bugle went *Da Da Da Dot Da Dah*, followed by an evil Martian voice saying, "Charge! Kill the earthlings, fellow Martians! Shoot them with your ray guns!"

By the time the voice got to "fellow Martians," the three of us were racing for the road out of the gravel pit, screaming our heads off, zigging and zagging in an attempt to be hard-to-hit targets. Jay Bob, who was the fastest, dropped his bow and quiver because they were slowing him down. I was close behind with the axe, and Curty, who was by far the slowest, was running as if his feet had grown wings! I could hear him breathing alongside me as we ran for our lives.

At first it was dark, but then there was light coming from above and behind us. I figured it was from a spaceship. Not a lot of light, but enough that the Martians could spot us with the sights on their ray guns. We didn't look back. We ran up the road and turned left on Sunset before the light started to fade. I was a little ways behind Jay Bob, and by then Curty was falling behind. We ran until we could run no longer, hoping we were safe as we stopped to take a breather. Jay Bob and I pulled up together. A couple of minutes later Curty arrived.

Jay Bob was in tears. "Oh God! There are Martians and they're not friendly! Gerald is wrong! They can see us! They've even got light!"

Curty and I weren't crying, but we were so scared that we were shaking. We agreed that we had to get home as fast as we could. The Martians might be following us. Who knew how far a ray gun could shoot? "But stay together!" Curty said, not wanting to be left behind again.

We jogged awhile and then walked awhile, all of us too tired to hustle for long. We had just made our way across the intersection of Sunset Road and McGaffey Street when two cars came up behind us and stopped at the stop sign. A familiar voice rang out from the lead car, "Number Two Son forget something!"

In the streetlight we could see that it was Gerald in his old heap, and that he was holding Jay Bob's bow and quiver outside the rolled-down window. High school guys then jumped out of both cars and threw things at us. They went *splat* when they hit the ground. Water balloons!

"Suckers!" Then both cars drove off, turning right on McGaffey.

We'd been had. Gerald and his friends had been waiting for us, hiding on top of the cliff to which we had our backs pressed. Once we were in place, exactly where Gerald knew we'd be, they started throwing water balloons, faster and faster, getting closer and closer. Then someone blew a bugle, and when we started running they turned on the headlights of their cars.

"I can't believe they fooled us," Curty said. "I wish I could think of a practical joke like that."

"I can," said Jay Bob. Jay Bob was upset, angry, and ready to prove he was no one to be trifled with. On top of his getting depantsed earlier that week, Gerald's practical joke had made him vengeful. "I'm going home and sail all Gerald's records out in the street from the roof. Let's see what they sound like when they land!"

It was almost ten thirty by Jay Bob's watch when we dragged into his backyard. We had slowed down as soon as we realized there were no Martians chasing us. Curty was so tired he just wanted to go inside and go to bed, but Jay Bob called him a coward. Said if he wasn't man enough to get revenge, he could go to bed like a sissy. I was tired too, but figured I'd better stay up and help Jay Bob. Curty decided he'd help too.

We got the ladder out of the garage, took it into the backyard, and leaned it against the roof. Then we went inside, which really felt good because it was warm. After we used the bathroom, Jay Bob put all of Gerald's 45s in a box, and Curty found three blankets. We went back outside to climb on the roof.

Jay Bob climbed up first. I carried the box of records in one arm and handed it to him. He carried it to the other side of the roof. The Jones house had a gable roof, the front yard side sloping down toward Deming Street, where Jay Bob wanted to splat Gerald's records.

Curty threw the blankets up to me. After he was on the roof, we pulled up the ladder so Gerald couldn't climb up and stop us when he got home. Then we joined Jay Bob on the front yard side of the roof, which wasn't so steep as to be dangerous. Granddaddy Miller's roof was so canted you couldn't walk on it without a rope holding you, but the Jones roof was easy walking. And if you slipped and fell, Jay Bob said to go feet first—your heels would catch on the gutters. My house didn't have gutters.

We sat down, pulled our blankets around us, and waited at the top of the roof. Gerald had to be back soon if he was going to beat his parents home. Curty asked Jay Bob if he wanted to take a practice shot. It was a long way across the front yard to the street, and if the records landed in the grass, they might not break.

"No," said Jay Bob. "I want Number One Son to watch every Number One song shatter into a million pieces. I want to torture him record after record!"

I was glad he didn't throw a record for practice. Maybe something would happen and he'd change his mind. Maybe some adult neighbor would see us and make us get down. Jay Bob would get in big trouble for breaking Gerald's records. If Gerald didn't kill him, his parents would. This was not good, but I didn't try to talk Jay Bob out of it. When he got mad and made up his mind, nothing I said would make any difference.

We were going to tell jokes to pass the time, but we couldn't remember any. We decided to recite state capitals, but sometime after California we stretched out on our backs to rest our eyes. By Louisiana we were asleep, and so we weren't aware that Gerald didn't arrive home first.

Gerald had intended to come home after he razzed us at McGaffey and Sunset, but he ran into some guys who had a couple of cases of beer. Becky Watson was one of the girls riding with them. Gerald had it bad for Becky, and so when she invited him to go back to the gravel pit for a beer bust, he went. Gerald got drunk and lost all track of time, not to mention every lick of sense he ever had. He was sitting by a campfire trying to sing "Tutti Frutti" with Becky when the cops raided their party.

Mr. and Mrs. Jones didn't get home as early as they planned. It was almost one o'clock when they pulled in the driveway, put the car in the garage, and noticed that Gerald's old heap wasn't in its usual place. They made a beeline to Gerald's room. Not finding him there was worry enough, but then they checked Jay Bob's room to see how we kids were doing. Our not being there sent them into a panic!

They called Curty's house. We weren't there, but they'd be right over. They called Mom. She was on her way. They were about to call the police, when Mr. Jones noticed a police car stopping in front of the house. Two officers got out and opened the back door. Out came Gerald, wobbling like a top about ready to topple.

Mr. and Mrs. Jones knew immediately what he'd been doing, and ran out to the car. Mr. Jones grabbed Gerald by the shoulders and looked him in the face. "Where's Jay Bob?!"

Pointing upward Gerald said, "Number Two Son having camp-out on top of house. Hey guys, what's going on up there!"

After that Gerald threw up in the flowerbed and passed out. No one paid him much attention until later. Everyone was focused on the roof, trying to figure out how to get us down. Mom and Curty's parents had showed up by then, and Mrs. Jones was embarrassed half to death. She felt responsible.

The adults were afraid to yell loud enough to wake us, even if that was possible. We might wake with a start and go off the roof. Curty sometimes had a problem with sleepwalking, and we had already moved from where we started out, especially Jay Bob. He was about three feet lower than Curty and I. Looked at clockwise, he had fallen asleep at straight up twelve, but his head was now pointing toward three. Mr. Jones went to get his ladder, but couldn't find it. Curty's dad said he'd go get his, but a policeman said no. This was work for the fire department. He called the fire station and told them to come as quickly as possible, but not with their sirens on.

It was almost two o'clock by the time they got us off the roof and everyone cleared out. The fire truck had come with sirens blaring. The sound roused us boys, fortunately without our walking or rolling off the roof, as well as most everyone else on the block. Neighbors came outside and watched the firemen climb up a ladder and carry us down one by one to safety. They carried me down last, and when I was on the ground the crowd applauded.

Mom ran to hug me, as did Mrs. Jones. Through my sleepy-headed fog I heard her say to Mom, "I am so sorry about this. I can't tell you how embarrassed I am."

Mom wasn't upset with Mrs. Jones. She had called Mom earlier about the sleepover, telling her that she and Mr. Jones were going out and that we boys would be supervised by Gerald. That was okay with Mom, and it was all right with Curty's parents too. We were good boys, and Gerald had never gotten into any trouble.

And he hadn't. I didn't know he had such mischief in him, and maybe he didn't either. For sure he didn't think about the conse-quences. Although the junior varsity basketball season had ended,

the coaches found out about the beer party. Players weren't allowed
to drink alcohol ever. The coaches would have to decide if he could
go out for the varsity team next year.

Gerald's parents grounded him for the rest of the school year.
He could drive back and forth to school, but that was it other than
when they sent him on an errand. Jay Bob was grounded for two
weeks, with no TV or playing with Curty and me after school. And
Mom was upset with me for sneaking off to the gravel pit. My punishment was that I couldn't watch TV at Jay Bob's house for two
weeks, or go to movies on Saturdays during the same period. I had
to come straight home after school.

· · · · · · ·

Noon the next Saturday I was surprised to find Jay Bob and Gerald
waiting for me after I got off work at Whitman's. They were still
grounded, but their parents had given them a brief reprieve for
hamburgers. While Mr. and Mrs. Jones attended a library luncheon,
Gerald had their permission to drive Jay Bob to Green's Drive-in on
the north end of Main Street to get burgers for lunch, nowhere
else, then straight back to pick them up from the luncheon. They
were to stop and ask me if I wanted to go along and to pay for my
lunch. Did I want to go?

Mom was still in Allensworth's, and so I ran to ask her. I didn't
think she'd agree, but she was distracted and said yes. She would
meet me at home in an hour.

Gerald was driving Mr. Jones's '52 Buick, which was a fine car.
Earl, the deliveryman, had one just like it. Gerald pulled into
Green's Drive-in so that he was sitting next to a car with some of
the guys who had been with him at the gravel pit. They were in a
'51 Ford. They razzed Jay Bob and me, "Hey guys, shot any Martians lately with bows and arrows?" They didn't bother me, but
they made Jay Bob mad.

After the carhop took our order, one of them said, "Hey Gerald, we're driving out to Comanche Hill. Going to see how fast we can get it going by the time we hit bottom. Want to come?"

"No!" yelled Jay Bob. "He's grounded, splat-brains!"

"Shut up, pip-squeak!" Gerald checked his watch. "I don't have much time, but yeah. That would be fun. Can we go as soon as she brings our order?"

Comanche Hill was long and steep. It would have been a much better place to hold the annual soap box derby than the hill on North Main, but it was quite a ways out of town going east, past the Pecos River and almost to the turnoff to the Bottomless Lakes. Gerald and the guys in the '51 Ford, as well as some guys in a '50 Studebaker, drove like maniacs getting there. Jay Bob gave Gerald a hard time for being such a dope, but Gerald ignored him. He'd do as he pleased.

All three cars stopped at the base of the hill. I got out. I wasn't about to ride in a car going as fast as it could down Comanche Hill. So did Jay Bob. We had far better sense than teenagers. We went over and sat down on a rock to finish our hamburgers and cokes while the guys decided what they were going to do.

"Skunk car!" said Jay Bob, as he slugged me in the shoulder. A skunk car was any black car with a white stripe or white top. The first person to see one and call it got to slug all the others with him. Jay Bob was uncanny. He could smell a skunk car before it was even in sight.

Gerald would go down Comanche Hill first. A guy from the Ford would ride with him to keep an eye on the speedometer. What he wanted to know was how fast Gerald was going when he hit bottom and passed the Studebaker on the side of the road.

What no one had thought about was the dip at the bottom of the hill. The road did a strange thing going down. There was a rise and then a shallow dip just before the road reached the bottom and flattened out on level ground. The guy who was riding in the back-seat watching the speedometer said that Gerald was going a hun-dred and ten when he hit the rise and went airborne. When the car came down, he got thrown into the front seat. That was about the same time that the bumper was knocked upward by the impact with the pavement and both headlights knocked out.

Amazingly the tires didn't blow and we were able to drive back to town. Gerald was remarkably calm for a condemned teenager. He was going to be grounded until his hair turned gray and he walked with a cane. But he lost his temper and punched Jay Bob in the arm to make him stop saying, "Man, are you going to get it!" He hit him so hard that Jay Bob cried.

· · · · · · · ·

That night Mom and I went to Uncle Charlie and Aunt Elvis's for supper. After we finished, I went with my hoodlum cousin Greg into his room. He had stolen a bunch of comic books and asked me if I wanted some. I didn't. He lit up a cigarette and offered me one.

"No thanks."

"Best you not start. I was already up to a pack a day when I was your age. With me it's a bad habit."

"Greg, do you think there are Martians living around Roswell?"

"Naw. The gravel pit is just a stupid story. I think there were Martians back in 1947, but they all died. What do you think?"

"Most of the time I don't believe it, but sometimes it's hard to tell."

"Tell me if it's true about Gerald Jones." Greg was a year older in school. I had never thought about him knowing Gerald.

"What do you mean?"

"I hear he went down Comanche Hill doing a hundred and ten today, and you were there."

"Yeah, that's what the guy in the backseat said."

"But he knocked out his headlights?"

"And the bumper got bent upward," I said.

"Lucky he didn't lose control and flip the car. I never thought about that dip at the bottom. I was going to see how fast I could take Dad's car down Comanche Hill, but now I'm glad I didn't. A '56 Oldsmobile is a lot faster than a '52 Buick. I'd probably have totaled the car and killed myself."

I listened as Greg went on and on about how fast he had driven his dad's car in drag races. When Mom and I left to go home, the family had agreed that we were going to Ruidoso for an outing soon, all of us but Greg. I was glad that he wasn't going. I was tired of teenagers and their stupid games.

BOOK II

LIFE HAPPENS

9

GETTING JUMPED

MR. CONNELL WAS PROUD that I had won the spelling bee, but seemed even prouder that I had been asked to be the editor of the *Missouri Avenue Magpie*. He said he would work with me. He had some ideas about how we could improve the artwork. Mr. Connell and I talked a lot in class while other kids were finishing their geography homework. I would go up and sit in a student's desk by his desk.

Monday morning Miss Tower asked him if I could be excused from homeroom for fifteen minutes to help plan the next issue. Mr. Connell said sure. Miss Tower didn't have a homeroom period, and so the two of us went to her classroom where we were joined by editor Sherry Watson. There were only four issues a year—Back to School, Christmas, Valentine's, and End of School. The next one was the End of School issue, and it pretty much took care of itself. All the sixth graders would write their "wills."

"I leave my desk to Julie." . . . "I leave the gum under my desk to Ronald." . . . "I leave my spelling book to Sam, if it doesn't fall apart before the end of the year." . . . "I leave Mr. Connell's art class to Regina. I hope she appreciates his bad jokes."

Mr. Connell joked around a lot. I liked that about him. He asked us one day, "If people come to the arid Southwest for sinus problems, where do artists go? The Painted Desert."

And he liked us to tell him jokes. I was proud that he thought one of mine, that I had gotten from my Uncle Gerald, among the funniest he had ever heard. "Did you hear about the butcher who backed up into the meat grinder? He got a little behind in his orders."

Sherry said that she would make an announcement in both sixth grade homerooms telling the kids to write their wills. We set deadlines for receiving them and for printing the paper. Then Miss Tower excused us to return to our classrooms. I was reluctant to go out in the hall with Sherry. No telling what sort of mushy stuff she'd pull, so I dawdled. I asked Miss Tower a question about the music assignment that was due later in the day. Sherry left.

After Miss Tower answered my question, I walked slowly to the door. Miss Tower was busy at her desk and paid me no mind. I stuck my head out to take a look. There was no one in sight, so I headed toward homeroom. But I hadn't checked behind Miss Tower's propped-open door! In two steps Sherry was on me like wax lips on a fourth grader. She handed me a fancy invitation. "You can't ignore this," she said. "You've ignored me so far, but this demands a reply! And if you don't, I know where your mama works. She and I are going to have us a long talk about you!"

A long talk? Sherry Watson talking to my mom about me? Oh man, I'd never live that down!

Sherry turned and headed for Mr. Davidson's room. I opened the envelope. It was an engraved invitation to a formal dance at the Women's Club, music provided by the Pioneers of the Pecos Valley Dance Band. Sherry was a member of the Young Women's Club. Their dance was less than two weeks away on a Saturday night.

I didn't know what to do. I thought about getting Jay Bob's advice, but remembered how he had acted at the swimming pool. He'd just tell me I should go and then tell everyone I had a "date" with a sixth grader. With friends like him, who needed a gossip columnist? So I said nothing about Sherry when he and Curty came running up at recess.

"Let's ride our bikes to the craft store after school," said Jay Bob. "I want to get a model. Then we can go to the Army-Navy Surplus Store and see what new stuff they have."

I loved going to the Army-Navy Surplus Store—even had a dime in my pocket. Although it wasn't that great a distance, I had never ridden my bike there. Neither had Jay Bob or Curty. We had only stopped in when we were already downtown for some other reason. I wasn't sure this was a good idea. "But we'll have to ride through chuke territory. You're the one who just got depantsed."

"I know, but we don't have to ride by South Junior High. I just figured out another way. We can take Deming to Main Street, and there'll be enough grown-ups along the sidewalks that chukes won't bother us. Then we can come back the same way."

Deming Street, which ran east-west along the south side of the school, seemed a safe enough bet if we pedaled fast the last few blocks before Main. That was a neighborhood too close for comfort to South Junior High. Still, I wasn't sure how safe we'd be on Main Street. We'd have to pass La Bonita Bar.

Almost every night I would read in the *Roswell Daily Record* about how many people had been stabbed, shot, beaten, mugged, or robbed at La Bonita Bar. Mr. Connell used to say that rather than risk a full-scale war with the Russians, the United States ought to issue a challenge like Goliath did with the Israelites. "Tell them that if their top regiment can take La Bonita Bar on a Saturday night, they can have America. If not, La Bonita gets to keep all the rubles taken in the brawl. No one wants Russia." It was the meanest place in southeast New Mexico, but hopefully only so at night.

After school we set out from the playground. We biked the five blocks east on Deming with no problem. When we turned north on Main Street, no chukes in sight, I had the feeling that things were going to be okay.

The three of us were casually riding along the edge of the slow lane when I noticed La Bonita to my right. The door was closed and no one was on the sidewalk. I guessed when it came to safety that there was a big difference between day and night. Jay Bob and Curty were riding ahead of me when I saw both of them look behind us. Their faces looked like they had just seen the Creature from the Black Lagoon! They took off pedaling as fast as they could. I turned and saw a gang of chukes on bicycles coming up behind us! I stood on the pedals, pumped for all I was worth, and outran them for a block.

Jay Bob and Curty were way ahead of me on their Schwinns. The chukes would never catch them, but they would overtake me. I was on a J.C. Higgins, the slowest bicycle known to modern man. Superman on a J.C. Higgins couldn't outrun Howdy Doody on a Schwinn. My bike was so bad it might as well have been made in Japan.

I could hear the chukes yelling, "Get the gringo!" as they gained on me. I knew I couldn't outrun them much longer, and so I looked for a building to duck in. To my right was an old driveway, cut into the curb and sidewalk. It was just to the south of Del Beene's. I took it, pedaled my bike up on the sidewalk for most of a city block, and was ready to jump off and run inside. But just as I dismounted, a chuke crashed his bike into mine. He lunged forward across both bikes and grabbed my right leg as he and the bikes fell on the sidewalk.

I struggled to get away, but he was older and stronger. I couldn't break his grip on my right ankle, and the rest of the gang was closing in. In a panic I kicked him in the mouth with my left foot.

He let me go and grabbed his mouth, crying out in pain. I ran into Del Beene's. As I looked back through the glass pane in the front door, he was spitting out blood and teeth.

I wouldn't be safe by the door, so I moved to the back of the store and made like one of their stacks of tires. If the chukes looked in, they couldn't see me. Del Beene's was one of Roswell's major stores. It sold appliances, furniture, sporting goods, and automotive supplies—much like Whitman's, except a lot larger. Mom said it was upscale compared to Whitman's. Normally there were customers all over the place, but I saw no one other than the clerk.

I eyed him for evidence of hospitality, hoping he wouldn't kick me out. He wasn't very old, mid-twenties maybe, probably a flyboy stationed at Walker Air Force Base. Flyboys worked part-time jobs in town to make ends meet—that is, if they were married and had bills. At night single flyboys got into fights with the "rocks," guys from Roswell High, or with *flatheads,* cadets at New Mexico Military Institute. According to Gerald, there was a rumble every weekend. The three groups hated each other.

The clerk would look at me for a moment and then divert his eyes. He had both his hands placed on the counter, arms straight, fingers drumming. He seemed uncomfortable, like he didn't quite know what to say. Probably from the North. Yankees weren't friendly like us Southerners, but that was okay. I just hoped he wouldn't let the chukes slit me like a tire if they came in. I waited for what seemed a sermon length, but the bell on the front door never jangled. Finally, the clerk walked to the door and went outside to take a look. He came back in and said, "They're gone."

"Thanks," I said, and left.

I was afraid that the chukes had stolen my bike, but what was I thinking? No self-respecting chuke would be caught dead on a J.C. Higgins. I picked it up off the sidewalk just as Jay Bob and Curty rode up. They had been watching from catty-cornered across the street at Craft Store. They had stayed outside on the sidewalk, but were prepared to dart inside should the chukes take after them. "Did you kick that guy's teeth out?" Curty asked.

"Yeah. I think I saw him spit out two."

"You must have kicked him just right. I think it's hard for a kid to kick a guy's teeth out."

"He didn't cry," said Jay Bob.

"He's a tough guy, the way he crashed into your bike. That would hurt," said Curty. "What are you going to do now?"

"Go home as fast as I can. Which way did the chukes go?"

"They rode back toward La Bonita."

"But I haven't bought a model yet!" Jay Bob whined. "And we haven't been to the Army-Navy Surplus Store!"

"Go if you want, but I'm going home."

"I'm with you," said Curty.

"Okay, fine!" Jay Bob said. "We're going to have to cut through South's territory."

By then junior high school had been out for more than an hour. All the gangs were off elsewhere getting in trouble. None were hanging around waiting to chase us, and so we rode home without getting jumped a second time.

That night for supper Mom and I had macaroni and cheese with tuna fish in it. Before we finished I started whimpering, which turned into full-blown sobbing. "What on earth is the matter?" Mom asked.

I couldn't answer.

"Did something happen today at school?"

"No," I sobbed.

"Did something happen after school?"

"Uh huh," I nodded.

"What?"

"I kicked a chuke's teeth out." I could hardly talk, I was sobbing and heaving so hard.

"You did what? Wait a minute. Let me get something for your nose." She returned and gave me a handkerchief. She pulled her chair around the table and sat beside me, her arm around my shoulders.

I wiped snot off my mouth and chin and explained what had happened on the way to Craft Store, how I was about to get clobbered in front of Del Beene's.

"So it was self-defense?" she said.

"I guess, but I kicked his teeth out, Mom! His teeth! There was blood all over his chin! I'm pretty sure I saw two teeth on the sidewalk!" That I had hurt another human being so badly weighed heavy. I was inconsolable. This was not the sort of thing I ever imagined doing.

"Hon, it's okay, really it is. I know it seems terrible, but these things happen. You have to defend yourself."

Maybe so, but I shouldn't have had to kick his teeth out. There should have been another way. I cried in bed several nights. I couldn't get out of my mind what I had done. And I felt alone. Mom, Curty, and Jay Bob had no idea how bad I felt. Whenever I had the chance, I was going to talk to Mr. Connell. He'd understand. He'd make me feel better. All I needed to do was to catch him when no one else was around.

the UNIMAGINABLE

SUNDAY MOM AND I RODE TO RUIDOSO with Uncle Charlie and Aunt Elvis. Mom didn't like to miss church, but Sunday was the only day of the week she could get away.

Since the women were with us, Uncle Charlie and I wouldn't get to do any fishing, which was okay. I loved to fish, but fish acted like I had made my bait in art class. They turned up their noses in disgust and left my line alone. Both Uncle Charlie and Greg almost always caught their limit. They were good fishermen. We wouldn't go to the racetrack either. Uncle Charlie liked to bet on the horses, but the racetrack was closed for the season. Besides, Aunt Elvis said that betting was a sin.

Ruidoso was seventy miles west of Roswell, through the Hondo Valley. Mr. Connell said a great artist named Peter Hurd lived in the Hondo Valley, but I didn't know where his ranch was. He painted pictures of windmills and stock tanks. He was the son-in-law of the great illustrator N. C. Wyeth.

Most kids got bored going on car trips, but not me. I daydreamed, which was one of the things I did best when I had time on my hands. Sometimes daydreams just came out of nowhere and took over my mind. Or sometimes I would pick a topic, much like punching a button on a jukebox. But however it happened, there was never any shortage of things to daydream about.

I liked having cowboy adventures. I'd have six-gun shootouts and ride horses just like Gene Autry, Roy Rogers, and Hopalong Cassidy. Or I'd be a knight of the Round Table like Sir Lancelot. I'd have sword fights and jousts. Or I'd be Superman and play all the positions on a baseball team. I'd pitch the ball so hard the batter couldn't see it, yet arrive behind the plate in time to be the catcher who caught the pitch. Then I'd throw the batter a slow one and jump high in the air to rob him of a homer. After the game I'd use my X-ray vision to see through Lois Lane's dress.

I also had daydreams about making touchdowns, scoring the winning basket, spiking tops, winning at marbles, and bowling a perfect game. Uncle Charlie was a good bowler. Sometimes he would take us bowling in Ruidoso. The pinboys didn't like to see him coming because he threw the ball so hard. It was like he hit the pins with a hand grenade! They exploded! Even though the pin-boys sat up on a ledge, they would get hit. I didn't understand how he did it because Uncle Charlie wasn't very strong. Mom said he was "slight," which was the reason he never got drafted into the army.

On the way to Ruidoso I daydreamed about playing pool. Uncle Charlie had bought his hoodlum son Greg a full-sized pool table. For years Greg had a small pool table that I liked playing on, but then he got rid of it. Said it was for kids. He was going to make a living hustling pool, and so he spent hours every day at the Eight Ball Billiard Parlor practicing. He told his parents that he needed a regulation table at home so he could get in even more practice. They gave in, bought him one, and put it in their den.

Greg said that I could play pool on the big table whenever he wasn't there, or I could play with him when he was there and his friends weren't. He'd be happy to teach me some things. The one thing I couldn't do was dig the tip of the cue into the table and tear the felt. If I did, I'd be in big trouble. Greg had killed people for less.

It was hard making the transition from the little pool table to the big one, but after a while the big table was more fun. Greg was good. I liked playing with him and learning from him. Most of the way to Ruidoso I daydreamed about mastering Eight Ball and Rotation. I would sink long shots, bank shots, and put English on the cue ball. I'd beat champions named Willie Mosconi, Minnesota Fats, and Southwest Slim.

It was a sunny day in Ruidoso. We walked along the stream until lunch. It was the same stream that Uncle Charlie liked to fish, but he preferred upstream on the Mescalero Apache Reservation. After we spent a couple hours unwinding, we went to Uncle Charlie's favorite restaurant for lunch. He sold life insurance, and one of his policyholders owned cabins and a restaurant called the Alamo Court. The reason the owner named it that was because of all the people from Texas. Most of the time there were more Texas license plates in Ruidoso than New Mexico plates.

Lunch was good—rainbow trout, French fries, salad with French dressing, red beans, Parker House rolls, and cherry pie. Uncle Charlie was up and down the whole meal, shaking hands and greeting people. Not only did he know the owner, but he knew half the people who walked in. Mom said that he was a people person, ought to go into politics.

After window shopping at a couple of curio shops that were closed because it was Sunday, we drove home midafternoon so everyone could get a nap. Being in the mountains not only improved your appetite but also made you sleepy. I started my nap in the car, but only after I daydreamed about Mr. Connell.

Ever since my conversation with Mom about remarrying, I had been daydreaming about her marrying Mr. Connell. The reason I hadn't thought about it before was that I had just assumed he would marry Miss Tower, both of them being single and teaching across the hall from each other. Alea Ritchy had assumed the same thing, but one day she asked me why it was that time marched on without the two of them marching down the aisle. Where was the ring?

Alea had a point. Mr. Connell had never proposed to Miss Tower, so he must be unsure about her. She wasn't right for him, but maybe Mom was. Mom was prettier and a better cook than Miss Tower. Miss Tower was always talking about how she hated to eat her own cooking, which may have been why Mr. Connell didn't propose. Jay Bob thought she was pretty, but he thought the same about any woman with curves.

Mom marrying Mr. Connell would be a change for the good. I daydreamed about them having the wedding at the church. I'd be the best man. And when they walked outside the church afterwards there would be soldiers in dress uniforms holding crossed swords for them to walk beneath. The wedding cake would be the largest one that Small's Bake Shop had ever made, twenty layers of choco-late cake and chocolate frosting with a bride and groom on top.

We'd dance the "Hava Nagila" at the reception at the Elks Club and drink champagne. Dancing and drinking were permissible because Mr. Connell was Methodist. After the honeymoon at Nia-gara Falls, we'd move into a bigger house. Mr. Connell lived with his mom in a house that wasn't much bigger than ours. That wouldn't do. We'd get a big house so that Mom could have a sewing room and Mr. Connell could have a studio. I'd need a den with a TV and a pool table. My room would have twin beds, a big closet, and a chest of drawers. We'd have the greenest lawn in Roswell.

There was just one problem. How was I going to get Mom and Mr. Connell together? I was just getting to that when Mom said, "Joe Don, wake up. We're home."

• • • • • • •

I was lucky to have Mr. Connell for homeroom teacher. I had had female teachers through the fourth grade, which hardly could have been otherwise. Missouri Avenue Elementary only had two male teachers—Mr. Bill Davidson, sixth grade homeroom, social studies; and Mr. Pete Connell, fifth grade homeroom, art and geography.

Mr. Connell had taught my class art in the fourth grade. Even though art was my worst subject, I had liked him a lot and was excited to be assigned to his homeroom for fifth grade. He also taught us fifth grade geography, including his personal experiences in Mexico. An art gallery in Mexico City had stolen one of his paintings. A lawyer was trying to get it back for him. Before moving to Roswell he had lived in New York. He called us his little "nudniks," which was a word they used there. I couldn't find it in the dictionary, but assumed it meant children.

He thought that a good profession for me when I grew up would be marine biologist, and so he gave me articles to read. He also made jokes about it. He said that when I became a marine biologist he wanted me to solve a problem about Wisconsin that had always bothered him. Namely, why is it Green Bay instead of Blue?

Since I didn't have a dad, Mom thought I was lucky to have a male presence like Mr. Connell in my life. She liked my being around him. All I had to do now was get her to like being around him, and vice versa. And the chance immediately presented itself!

The Monday night after we went to Ruidoso, Mom said that her boss, Mr. Franks, had finally agreed that they needed to hire someone part-time to draw and paint signs. Easter was coming, and they needed some pictures of bunnies and ducks and springtime, not to mention prices on signs that didn't look like they had been painted by a first grader. No one at Allensworth's was much better at art than I was.

I suggested Mr. Connell, and Mom liked the idea. Tuesday

morning Mom was going to tell Mr. Franks to phone Mr. Connell, and I was going to tell Mr. Connell to phone Mr. Franks. Hopefully the two would connect. But Mr. Connell wasn't at school that morning, which was unusual.

He was never sick. Miss Tower had missed three weeks straight in November and December with an ailment no one would tell us about. But Mr. Connell never missed school, not until that Tuesday.

We were surprised to find Miss Tower in his place for home-room. After the playing of the Lord's Prayer song and the principal's announcements, she introduced Mrs. Pfleugger, saying she would be our substitute for the rest of the term.

"The rest of the year?" Jay Bob whispered from the seat behind mine.

"Where's Mr. Connell? Is he in the hospital?" I asked in a low voice. My stomach was starting to hurt. I was worried and had questions, but it didn't appear that Miss Tower was going to tell us anything more. She had already turned to leave the classroom. I could see a tear in her eye. Something really bad must have happened.

I was going to raise my hand and ask Mrs. Pfleugger what had happened to Mr. Connell, when Walter Garcia whispered from my left: "The cops arrested him after classes yesterday." From Walter's house across the street he had seen it. He had been changing a flat on his bike in his driveway. "Three cops took him away in hand-cuffs."

At recess we boys huddled to see if anyone knew why Mr. Connell had been arrested. No one knew anything other than what Walter had seen. Who would know? Jan Browning's dad was on the school board. We looked to see where she was on the playground. All the girls were gathered around her near the swing sets. We boys circled them.

She knew what we had come for and blurted out, "He was arrested for molesting sixth grade boys. It will be in the paper this afternoon."

"What does 'molesting' mean?" Curty asked.

"Doing something nasty," she said. And with that she and the rest of the girls walked away with their noses in the air. It was like they didn't want anything to do with us boys.

That night at the supper table neither Mom or I mentioned Mr. Connell. We didn't talk about nasty things like the facts of life or molesting people, neither of which I understood. It was too embarrassing. I did read the newspaper before supper. On the back page there was a tiny article saying that Mr. Pete Connell, a teacher at Missouri Avenue Elementary School, had been arrested Monday afternoon for molesting minors. He was to appear before a judge Tuesday morning. The *Roswell Daily Record* was an afternoon paper. It must have gone to press before there was anything to report about his court appearance.

I looked up "molest" in the dictionary. All it said was, "to annoy, interfere with, or meddle with so as to cause harm." That was about as clear as mud.

I had a hard time falling asleep. I lay in bed wondering what molesting minors really meant. How could Mr. Connell annoy or interfere with or cause harm to sixth grade boys? How bad was whatever he did? I tossed and turned, wondering what had happened when he appeared before the judge. Would he be put in jail or would charges be dropped? And if charges were dropped, why wouldn't he be back in school tomorrow? Why did Miss Tower say Mrs. Pfleugger would be our substitute for the rest of the year? How did she know what the verdict would be? And did the police think he'd try to escape? Why did they take him away in handcuffs? It had to be a BIG MISTAKE! Surely he would be freed and back in school by morning.

She did ask what church Sherry went to. I said Episcopal, which was information that had come up at a school newspaper meeting. Mom didn't seem too excited about that, but she didn't comment. She had once heard a preacher say that Baptists used grape juice for communion, but Catholics used real wine. Episcopalians were even worse. They passed out a wine list so worshipers could choose what kind of communion wine they wanted. Episcopalians also held bake sales to benefit church members whose vacation homes had burned down. That preacher had a lot of information about Sherry's church.

Mom arranged with a friend of hers at Paul & Ray's, a men's clothing store, to buy me a sports coat at wholesale. I needed it anyway for church. I had grown out of my old one. She also talked to a florist friend about a corsage. I didn't know how she did it, but somehow Mom came up with money for both. I didn't have to spend any of mine.

I had expected Mom to tease me unmercifully about my "date" with Sherry, like she had about the valentine for Janet, but she didn't. She got me scrubbed and polished, and then we sat quietly in the living room waiting for Sherry's mom to drive up to our house.

Mom had determined that the polite thing for me to do was not make Sherry walk up to our door like some teenage boy would do to pick up his date. Instead I stood watching out the living room window so I could see them drive up. When they did, I hustled to the car so Sherry wouldn't have to get out. But she got out anyway so we both could sit in the backseat. Her mom had a white '53 Plymouth. I didn't sit close, but I didn't crowd the door either.

Sherry thanked me for the corsage, which had been delivered to her house, and she introduced me to her mom, a tall lady who was smoking a cigarette in a cigarette holder. She was a blond like

Sherry. Her breath smelled of alcohol. Mom didn't drink, of course, but Curty's parents did. That's how I recognized the smell. Curty's dad liked Hamm's beer, and his mom liked whiskey sours.

Sherry had on a perfume that I really liked. Man, she smelled good! I didn't have any cologne, so I just smelled normal, which I felt bad about. We drove to the Women's Club without much conversation. When her mom let us off, she said she'd pick us up at nine thirty, when the dance was over.

Once inside I picked up my cues from the other guys, just as Mom said to do. There were sixth and seventh graders from all over town, guys who seemed to know what they were doing. I checked Sherry's wrap, a waist-length mink coat, with the hatcheck girl, a funny name given that none of us wore hats. Then I was drawn into the frenzy of filling out dance cards. Guys were hustling from one to another, writing down names for their dates to dance with during the evening, which seemed like a strange thing to do if you liked the girl you came with. Had I been with Janet Mitchum, I would have written my name in for every dance and been done with it. Mom must not have known about this practice because she hadn't given me any advice. Still, I managed to fill Sherry's card without disgracing myself.

The dance began. It was impressive! A big room with a hardwood floor and a high ceiling, filled with guys in sports coats and girls in fancy dresses. At one end of the room the Pioneers of the Pecos Valley Dance Band was making such good music that I thought they must be friends of Lawrence Welk. I kept expecting bubbles!

Mom had never been to a dance and couldn't tell me about dance steps. I had no idea which leg to shake or how, although I had seen people from the shoulders up dancing in movies. Sherry sensed my problem and quickly helped me pass for someone capable of a slow dance. I was a fast learner and didn't step on anyone's feet the whole evening. The jitterbug, though, was something else! I had no idea what I was doing. I just went through the motions and hoped for the best. It seemed like whenever a girl felt like doing a twirl, she did. All I had to do was stand there and hold onto her hand as best I could. No one seemed to be jitterbugging in the same way, so maybe I was doing better than I thought.

I danced with several girls, and I was having a good time when a red-haired girl I was dancing a slow dance with said, "You came with Sherry Watson, didn't you?"

"Yes."

"My parents would never let me date someone from a divorced family. You do know that her parents are divorced and that her mom is an alcoholic?"

"Yes," although I didn't know about the alcoholic part.

"Your parents don't mind that you came with a girl like her?"

"I don't have parents, just a mom."

"Oh? Are your parents divorced too?"

"No. My dad was killed in the Korean War."

I didn't like this girl. She seemed snotty in general and hateful in particular. As we danced I suddenly remembered a joke that Uncle Charlie told about a private in the army. He had been told by his sergeant to think of something nice to say to every girl he danced with at a USO dance. So when the music ended, I gave her the punch line. "Thank you. You sweat less than any fat girl I've ever danced with."

It was intermission. I got cups of punch for Sherry and me, and then refills. We were thirsty. She suggested that we drink the second cup in the basement where it was cooler. She took my hand and led me down the stairway. There were several couples standing around in an area that matched the lobby above in size. She turned my hand loose when she stopped and leaned back against the wall. We finished our punch. So far so good; I hadn't spilled any on her or my new brown sports coat.

"Talk to me," she said.

"What about?"

"Do you like Elvis?"

"He's all right." I assumed she didn't mean my aunt. Actually he was kind of silly with all his shaking around, and what kind of a guy had a woman's name?

"I love him. Would you vote to reelect Ike if you could vote?"

"Yes." I hoped that Eisenhower would be reelected.

"I hate Eisenhower. I'd vote for Adlai. Do you ever read grown-up books?"

I had to figure out what she meant. I read the newspaper and *Life* magazine and *Reader's Digest.* I read library books from the Carnegie library. Most were for kids, but if Jay Bob's dad saw me, he always loaded me up with grown-up books. "I guess so."

"I do," Sherry said. "I'm reading one of my mom's books called *God's Little Acre.* Ever hear of it?"

"No."

"It's probably banned from the Carnegie library. And did you go see the movie *Blackboard Jungle?* It's what high school is going to be like."

"No, I didn't see it."

"Have you heard of a new play called *Cat on a Hot Tin Roof?* My sister is trying to get a copy for us to read because it'll never be presented in Roswell. Too sultry."

I hadn't. I didn't even know what "sultry" meant. Oh man, was I striking out! Sherry and I didn't agree on much anything, and the rest of it I hadn't even heard of.

A buzzer sounded, calling us back from intermission. I started to walk toward the stairway, but Sherry pulled me back. "Shh!" she whispered, her left index finger to her lips. "I want to show you something."

I didn't know what was so important, but I waited with her until all the other couples had gone upstairs. They were so interested in each other that they didn't notice Sherry and me staying behind. When no one was in sight, she pulled me in the opposite direction of the stairway to a locked door. She pulled out a key from her little black purse. The lock turned and we were inside before I had the presence of mind to ask where we were going.

She turned on the light. It was a janitor's closet! There was a desk along one wall and a pinup calendar above it. The lady had on more clothes than the women in *Playboy*. On the other wall were mops and brooms and dustpans. Sherry kissed me on the mouth. "Want to make out?" She turned off the light.

I guessed I did because I didn't try to escape.

We kissed standing up for a long time. When we finally came up for air, I asked, "Is it okay for us to be here? What about your dance card and the girls I'm supposed to be dancing with?"

"If anyone asks where you were, tell them I was in the restroom sick. You were waiting to see if you needed to take me home." She kissed me again.

We kissed standing up and sitting side by side on the desktop. We kissed like bosses and secretaries, me in the janitor's chair and Sherry on my lap. We kissed until I had pucker fatigue. We kissed throughout most of the second half of the dance, sneaking back up to the dance floor just as the music started for the next-to-the-last dance. I was on Sherry's card for the last two dances, and we danced close. I asked her where she had gotten the key. She said it belonged to her big sister. Becky had stolen the original and made a copy.

When the music stopped, I was sorry that the dance was over. I could have stayed there forever with the girls and the smell of their perfume and the sounds of the dance band. Dancing with girls was fun, and the punch was good, although some cookies would have hit the spot. Cake would have been even better. It was strange that a place called the Women's Club didn't have anything to eat.

Sherry's mom was waiting for us across the street as we walked out. We drove home much as we had driven to the dance. No one said anything, although Sherry and I held hands in the backseat. I thought about how kissing with Sherry had been fun, but how it wasn't worth missing out on so many dances. I felt that Sherry had gypped me out of the second half of the dance.

"How was it?" Mom asked as I walked in the door. She was sitting on the couch reading.

"It was okay." I kissed her on the cheek, mustering from deep inside the strength for one last pucker.

"Umm, perfume. Since when did you start wearing perfume?"

"I don't wear perfume, Mom. I've been drinking martinis. You smell booze. Is there anything to eat?"

"You didn't get anything to eat? What color was Sherry's dress?"

"Nope. No caviar, no sandwiches without the crust, no half-oysters in a shell, nothing. It was green."

"Good, then the corsage would have looked nice. Check the icebox. Did you like dancing?"

"It was fun. I don't see why preachers say that everyone who dances is going to hell." I went into the kitchen. There was a bowl of butterscotch pudding. I gulped it down and headed off to bed before Mom could quiz me further. It was a good thing I hadn't danced a leg off. Mom would talk it off tomorrow with a jillion questions.

I looked at myself in the mirror of the medicine chest as I brushed my teeth. My face looked the same, still didn't need a shave. My hair hadn't changed, a butch haircut with a doe's tail held in place with Butch Hair Wax. And my biceps were still no bigger than hens' eggs. I looked the same as I always had, but I was different in a way that made me long for my Big Chief tablet.

I had kissed a girl, which once or twice would have been cool, but there was something wrong with me spending half the dance getting lockjaw in a janitor's closet. It wasn't something a champion would do. A champion would be out on the dance floor dancing with all the girls, getting wholesome exercise. I needed to do better.

• • • • • • •

Good Friday, March 30, was a Roswell Public Schools holiday. Granddaddy Miller had sent Mom bus money so I could go for a visit. Mom asked Mrs. Pfleugger if it would be all right for me to miss Wednesday and Thursday too, which was okay by her since my grades were fine. Mom put me on the bus for Lubbock early Wednesday morning.

Granddaddy and Grandmama Miller lived in Abernathy, Texas, just north of Lubbock. According to Uncle Charlie, Granddad was a legend in West Texas. Granddad had grown up in the olden days before schools had sports, else he would have been a champion for sure given how strong he was. Since there were no sports for him to play, he put all his energies and skills into manual labor. For years he had boasted that he could outwork anyone in West Texas, and for years he had taken on all comers.

Uncle Charlie remembered a time when he was just a boy of eight that Granddad bet two fellows that he and the kid could top more grain than they could. He and Uncle Charlie then beat the two men. He had also challenged men to contests of shoveling grain, chopping wood, and loading lumber, never losing a one. And then there were those contests that Uncle Charlie said to never tell anyone about because Grandmom disapproved and wanted as few people to know about as possible.

Granddad used to fight men bare knuckles by the train tracks in

Lubbock. He had several matches over the years, and men bet big money on the outcome. He lost only one fight, and that was to a famous fighter from Kansas City. Granddad was in his late forties at the time, the other fighter in his thirties. Now in his seventies, Granddad worked full-time at the lumberyard where I would also be working during my visit.

Grandmom picked me up at the bus depot in Lubbock in their big black Nash, a car so roomy in the backseat that my cousin Newley said you could run out for a pass. Grandmom, who had cooked three meals a day seven days a week all her life, had recently developed a taste for store-bought hamburgers. Her sons, whom she thought didn't know, were tickled by her secret runs to the new Dairy Mart where we had lunch. We each had a hamburger, fries, Big Red, and a "cream cone."

Mom said that Grandmom wasn't aging as well as Granddad. She was becoming a Granny Grunt, an old lady who made grunting sounds when she did her work. But calling her Granny Grunt wasn't disrespectful. Everyone loved her. If Granddad was the hardest-working man in Lubbock County, Grandmom was the hardest-working lady. She just grunted more than he did.

It was one thirty when she dropped me off at Strube's Lumber Yard. Granddaddy was grinning as he waited for me in the yard. He was six feet tall, with a barrel chest and big biceps. I couldn't wait until I had muscles like his. He lifted me off my feet in a bear hug. "Boy, you're getting too big for me to lift like this! But I need a big, strong kid to help me stack two-by-fours. Feel up to it?"

I did, and we started stacking lumber. I spent Wednesday afternoon through Saturday noon helping at the lumberyard during the day, and then listening to Granddaddy tell stories at night. He told me why he walked with a limp, which he really didn't unless someone was looking. He said it was because one leg was shorter than the other, which was what happens when you grow up in

Arkansas plowing behind a mule around the sides of hills. There weren't any hills to speak of in West Texas.

He told me how my Uncle Jerry, when he was about five or six years old, couldn't talk right. He had a dog named Buster. Instead of saying, "Buster, you want a biscuit?" he'd say, "Buh-er, you want a bi-it?" Uncle Jerry spoke just fine when he grew up. He was a salesman like Uncle Charlie. Granddad said both of them could sell milk nickels for a dime.

He told me how my dad, when he was about my age, got into trouble riding calves when he had been told not to. Granddad was going to whip him for disobeying, but had mercy when he saw that Dad didn't have but a few patches of skin left on his whole body. The calves had bucked him off time after time on hard-packed dirt. Granddad figured Dad had been punished enough.

Then he said, "The only other time I ever saw your dad skinned up like that was after a football game at Tech." Dad had played end. "Someone had split his lip. He had one black eye, and the other was red from being gouged. His chin was cut and bleeding, his face skinned raw.

"I asked him if it hurt. He said, 'Not as bad as losing.'" Granddad laughed. "Not as bad as losing. That was a great answer! Your dad was a competitor."

Mr. Strube was going to pay me off-payroll for helping at the lumberyard. Noon on Saturday we were waiting outside his office for our pay. Granddad said to me, "Joe Don, you've worked hard this week, but that's who we Millers are. A man pays you for a day's work, you be sure you give it to him."

Granddad said that to me almost every time I was around him. It was like he forgot from one time to the next.

Saturday afternoon my Uncle Caleb, who lived in Abernathy and taught high school, took his son Newley and me into Lubbock to see a movie, *The Ten Commandments*. Afterwards we got malts at a drugstore. They were so thick that the soda jerk slid them down the counter upside down.

I spent Saturday night at Uncle Caleb and Aunt Rose's house. Newley and his little brother James had a room together. James was spending the night with a friend so I was able to sleep in his bed. I had never smoked a cigarette, but took one from Newley, who was two years older. We opened the window and blew the smoke outside so his parents wouldn't smell it. I hated the taste, but for some reason felt like going along. Several times before kids had offered me smokes, but I had always turned them down.

Newley wasn't old enough to dress like my hoodlum cousin Greg, but he had always seemed meaner than Greg. He lost his temper more than any of my other relatives, and oftentimes it got him in fights. He was mad at some kids who lived a few blocks away, and so around eight thirty he told his parents that we were going outside to walk around. That was fine with them. We were to be back in a few minutes.

We walked three blocks to where the kids lived. There were no streetlights like in Roswell. It was really dark. We could hear the TV coming from the living room, but the curtains were pulled so we couldn't see any of the family. The car was in the driveway, and three bicycles were lying on the lawn. I didn't think we'd actually go through with what Newley had in mind, but he pulled out two ice picks from inside his jacket. Newley took the bicycle tires and let me have the car tires. He showed me what to do, and every time I plunged the ice pick into a tire it felt good. It felt like I was saying to Mr. Connell's pets, "Take that, you dirty, rotten liars!"

No one saw us. Afterwards we walked back to Newley's house, happy that we had taught those stupid kids a lesson. We played with the Ouija Board for a long time. We asked it all sorts of questions. It said that my girlfriend was Janet Watson.

After we had turned in for the night and I said my prayers, I questioned what we had done. It was clearly wrong to have punctured the tires. Yet, just as I had gone along with Sherry, I had also gone along with Newley. Oh man, was I messing up!

Easter morning I went to the Nazarene church with my grandparents, which was different because they knelt on the hard tile floor when they prayed. Also strange because it was much smaller than the Baptist church in Roswell. During the sermon the preacher said, "Easter is about new life, and we farmers know about new life. Arthur, what did you lose during the Depression?"

Arthur was my granddad. He said, "I lost my farm."

"And what did you learn from that?" the preacher asked.

"That the bankers were against me, but God wasn't. God had a new life for me here in town. And it's been a good life working at the lumberyard and doing odd jobs for people who need my help."

The congregation responded with amens. The preacher called out two more names. Two more examples of new life, and two more rounds of amens. I joined in the amens each time, but I didn't think that I myself would ever be called on to give witness. New life was one of those blessings that didn't seem to apply to everyone. Ever since Dad died, all my life had done was go from bad to worse. It was PU life, not new life.

Granddad drove me to Lubbock after Easter dinner to catch the bus back to Roswell. He said, "I hear you had some trouble with a gang."

"Yeah, they tried to jump me. I had to kick one of 'em in the mouth. Kicked out two teeth."

"And you feel bad about it?"

"I did, but I don't think about it as much as I used to."

"Your dad and I got in our share of scraps and worse. And I don't think you should feel bad if it was self-defense. Hurting people goes against Jesus, of course, so you gotta be careful. Don't go around beatin', people up. Don't be a bully, but defend yourself when you have to. Knock the tar out of 'em so they leave you alone."

Granddad put me on the bus, and three hours of daydreaming about Mr. Connell later, I arrived home to a late supper.

BOOK III
FEELING BAD

LASHING OUT

THE SATURDAY AFTER I RETURNED FROM ABERNATHY, we had a sleepover at Jay Bob's. Curty was there, and the two made my life miserable.

"You know what I hear," Jay Bob said. "I hear that you kissed for an hour with Sherry Watson at the Women's Club dance."

"Where did you hear that?"

"Where didn't we hear it?" answered Curty. "Jan Browning was there and Alea Ritchy and some sixth graders. Last week when you were gone to Texas, it's all anyone talked about on the playground. 'K-I-S-S-I-N-G. First comes love, then comes marriage, then comes Joe Don with a baby carriage!'"

Oh man, I had not seen Jan or Alea! I had not recognized anyone from Missouri Avenue other than Sherry. How could I have missed them and they seen me? Why weren't they on my dance card if they were there? "They're lying," I said.

"I don't think so," grinned Jay Bob. "They know, 'Ooh la la!' that you went into the janitor's closet and didn't come back upstairs until the dance was almost over."

"Why didn't you tell us?" asked Curty. "Why do we have to learn this from others?"

"Because Jay Bob made fun of me at the swimming pool."

"I didn't make fun of you! I told you to go after her. And so you finally do, and you don't even tell us about it."

"I didn't go after her! I didn't even want to go. Mom made me. There was an invitation and I got forced into it."

"Worse things have happened," said Curty. "How was it? How many times did you kiss?"

"I don't know. I didn't count."

"Come on, Joe Don!" Jay Bob said. "Dad just made me learn a new word, 'vicarelessly,' but it's neat. 'Vicarelessly' means Curty and I can experience kissing with Sherry if you will tell us what happened."

"Really? You can do that?"

"Yeah."

"I learned a new word too," said Curty. "I got it from my brother Darrell. He says that the polite way to say you're going to the bathroom, number one, is to say you're 'reliving' yourself. I gotta go relive myself. So wait for me before you say anything." He left for the bathroom.

"You go to the bathroom to relive yourself?"

"Guess so," said Jay Bob. "But I never heard anybody say it."

"My Uncle Charlie says, 'I gotta go see a man about a horse,' or 'I gotta go drain my radiator.' I guess there are lots of ways of saying it."

Curty came back. "Did you kiss a whole bunch, or was it like one really long kiss all the time you were in there?"

I spent a long time answering vicareless questions such as how did I position my lips, where were we standing or sitting, did I get lipstick all over me, did she run her fingers through my hair, and did we kiss in the backseat of the car going home. And then we spent time wondering how many hours a week teenage guys spend smooching with their girlfriends.

"But she's not my girlfriend," I said.

"She's more yours than mine," Jay Bob answered. "When are you two holding your next kissing session?"

"Never."

"Sure," said Curty. "If it was me, I'd be over at her house right now, except she's a sixth grader. I keep forgetting that. She ought to have a sixth or seventh grade boyfriend, not a fifth grader. This is weird, Joe Don."

"But not as weird as what Curty's dad heard about Mr. Connell down at the Grill," said Jay Bob. "Tell him, Curty."

"You know how he was arrested on a Monday afternoon and we found out Tuesday morning? That was when he admitted to a judge that he was guilty. By the time we got out of school Tuesday afternoon, he was already in the state prison at Santa Fe. It was the fastest trip to prison in Roswell's history!"

"He's in prison in Santa Fe? But what about his trial?"

"You don't have a trial when you plead guilty. You don't get any habeas corpus or statues of limitation or anything. You don't even get to stop at Vaughn to relive yourself." Vaughn was ninety-five miles north of Roswell, the closest town on the road to Santa Fe.

Curty continued: "People from the courthouse say he pled guilty to keep from embarrassing his mom with the details in the paper. He didn't want her to have to go through a trial. In less than twenty-four hours after being arrested, he was in prison. It's a record."

"Did they ever say what molesting means?"

"No one has ever told me," said Jay Bob. "Just something nasty."

"If I have to kill those sixth graders, I'm gonna make 'em tell the truth! We gotta get him out of prison!"

"What are you talking about? He admitted he was guilty!" said Jay Bob.

"But only because he didn't want to embarrass his mom! No one wants to talk about nasty stuff around their mom, even when it didn't happen. Do you have an ice pick?"

Jay Bob looked puzzled. "Sure we have an ice pick. What for?"

"Tony Fritch and Donny Small live three blocks away." They were two of Mr. Connell's pets. I told Jay Bob and Curty what my cousin and I had done in Abernathy. "Let's go put some holes in those liars' tires."

"Have you gone crazy?" said Jay Bob. "I'm not going to do that."

"Me either," said Curty.

"Then you're both chicken!"

"No we're not! Mr. Connell's pets aren't liars! They're telling the truth," said Curty.

I slugged him in the nose with my fist. He fell on the bed crying.

"Go ahead and believe their lies! That's okay! I don't need your help. I'll get him outta prison by myself!" I got my jacket and went home. The sleepover was over.

· · · · · · ·

Little League had begun. What I had wanted was to be put on Malco Oil Company's team, which had some of the best players in the league, including the very best, Tommy Jordan. Any team but Cathey-Jacobs Pharmacy would have been an improvement, but for the second year in a row I was put on Cathey-Jacobs. Jay Bob and Curty were once again placed on Pecos Valley Ford.

Cathey-Jacobs had wound up in the cellar at the end of the 1955 season. If all the returning kids in the league were assigned to the same teams as last year, we likely wouldn't do much better in 1956. But I was determined to be a champion on the baseball diamond, hustle and play my best whoever I played for. As it turned out, we got a few new kids, including one of a handful of Negroes in the league, Herman Newton.

Mexican kids in Roswell were like white kids. Some were nice, like Walter Garcia, Rudy Otero, and Eddie Cordova in my class.

Some were rotten. But Jay Bob, Curty, and I had begun being wary of Mexican kids in general because of our experiences with chukes. They didn't like us and were going to pick fights every day at South Junior High School. There were no Negroes at Missouri Avenue and few in Roswell. The three of us had no history with Negro kids and were fascinated by them.

Herman not only was a good fielder, hitter, and base runner, but he was funny. His answer to almost everything was, "Ask yo granny." And he constantly went up to kids to measure their arm length against his. He wasn't very tall, but had the longest arms I had ever seen on a kid. He would say, "God made me so's I can catch grounders without bendin over." Herman lived in the Little Chihuahua neighborhood of Roswell, not far from La Bonita Bar, with his eleven brothers and sisters. He was so skinny that he made Jay Bob look fat.

Herman thought that I talked funny. One day he overheard me say, "Well, honk my tonk!" He thought that was the funniest thing he'd ever heard. "What do it mean, 'honk my tonk'?"

"I don't know. It's just something grown-ups say."

"Well, it got to mean something. Ask yo granny. She'll tell you what it means to honk yo tonk!"

Herman and I had fun talking on the bench as we waited our turn at bat. We always sat together. I told him about how we had started calling Mrs. Pfleugger by the name of Hally Bo Pink. It stood for halitosis, body odor, and pink toothbrush. He liked that, even though I couldn't explain what pink toothbrush was. I also told him about her huge hinee. "It wouldn't fit on this bench if she was sitting here all alone."

The day I told him what it meant to relive himself, he laughed so hard that he had to go relive himself. "You white boys talk funny!"

There were two Little Leagues in Roswell, the Optimists on the north side and Lions Hondo on my side. The Optimists had a nice ballpark, but we had the worst field north of Mexico. There was no grass, just hard-packed clay. A line-drive foul ball down the third base line would bounce halfway to Carlsbad before it could be retrieved. And we only had one game ball. I brought pocketbooks to read while we waited for foul balls to be returned to play.

At the start of the season, the outfield fence was a rickety picket fence, but then someone stole most of the pickets, probably to stake tomato plants. From then on all we had was a strand of wire attached to what few pickets were left, and it wasn't stretched taut. It had a droop in mid left field and mid right. On occasion our wire fence was the cause of heated arguments. The batting team would claim that the ball went over the fence (wire), while the fielding team said that it had gone under the fence (wire), thereby reducing a homer to a ground rule double.

The dugouts were just wood planks, no covering. The backstop was made of chicken wire, and there were no restroom facilities other than behind a dilapidated old shed fifty yards away. We got good at holding it until we went home. One of our rules was, "Don't drink anything after lunch on game days."

As the season progressed, occasional rains relocated the chuckholes, and the strange infield bounces that we had become used to changed pattern. The field was a mess, but after playing on it for a season, All-Star games out of town would be easy. Adults said that any cow pasture in America was better than our ballpark.

Our coach, Mr. Gilbert, was an ambulance driver, and he drove like it even with a pickup full of us players on our way to the ballpark. He put a shell on the bed of his pickup, which he'd get up to eighty miles per hour going across town, always slamming on the brakes when he came to a stop. The whole team along with the equipment fit inside the shell. I could tell which of our players were Catholic by the way they crossed themselves whenever we took off. We practiced close to where most of us lived, in the park across from Missouri Avenue Elementary School. On game days we'd meet at the practice field, and Coach Gilbert would drive us to the ballpark.

There was no backstop where we practiced, and so we spent hours each week chasing wild pitches and foul balls. Another team, Davis Paint & Glass, practiced at the park too. We constantly invaded each other's area shagging balls. One day Herman Newton hit what would have been a homer if we'd had a fence. It hit a kid playing centerfield for Davis Paint & Glass in the shoulder. He couldn't stop crying and so they let him go home.

Chukes sometimes hung around our practices like wolves looking for a stray calf. They didn't try anything so long as there were adults around, but after practices they depantsed a few kids as they walked home.

The afternoon that Herman Newton hit the kid in the shoulder, Mom was waiting for me when I got home. We practiced late and she had supper ready. After I cleaned up, we sat down and she said grace, finishing with, "And help me do what I have to do. Amen."

"What does that mean, Mom? You never said that before."

"It means that I got a letter from Uncle Caleb in Abernathy. It seems that you and Newley took ice picks to some tires."

"Says who?"

"Says Newley, who admitted it!" Her voice was stern. "He's going to pay for their tires out of his allowance since it was his idea. And because you went along, you're going to get five licks with your dad's belt."

"But I didn't mean to do it! I was just there when he handed me an ice pick. It just happened! You don't understand!"

"I do so understand, young man! The road to hell is paved with that exact excuse. You damaged people's property, and it's a sin. It's against the law! You could go to Springer for such a thing." Springer was New Mexico's reform school.

"But I didn't think we'd really do it!"

"Makes no difference. You're going to be punished."

I was seething. Never before had I been so mad at Mom. When she punished me for sneaking off to the gravel pit, it hadn't been my idea either, but I accepted my punishment without complaint. I shouldn't have been so upset about being punished for what happened in Abernathy. I had done wrong, yet I was terribly mad. "I hate you," I said, hardly believing my own ears.

"That's ten licks! You don't talk to me that way! Want to try for fifteen?"

No, I didn't. I no longer wanted to talk to Mom at all, and so I pretty much stopped. I dropped helping her from my New Year's resolutions, and from one day to the next said no more to her than I had to. Dad's belt hurt, but not nearly as much as my silence was going to hurt her.

· · · · · · ·

When the season began, the other teams were of the opinion that Cathey-Jacobs was such a bad team that Mr. Gilbert ought to be driving us to the hospital rather than the ballpark. But an amazing thing happened. We beat Malco the first game of the season, and we just kept winning! Not every game, but almost twice as many as we lost. We weren't that bad!

After every game, win or lose, Mr. Gilbert drove us to the Dairy Queen. Parents would chip in and he'd buy us small cones or Dilly Bars. That was the choice. I'd alternate between the two, never quite figuring out which one gave you the most ice cream.

I played second base, where I stayed busy with grounders and pop-ups. One Wednesday we were playing S&J Pecan Company, which called itself "The Nut House." My church friend John Hall played for S&J, and he grounded out to me three times, every time he came to bat. The game was close, and even though I hit a home run, "The Nut House" won. After the game John said, "Good game, Joe Don. See you at Sunday school."

I was a sore loser and didn't speak to him.

That Sunday morning the car wouldn't start. Mom and I caught a ride with a family on Summit Street, the McAllisters, who were always late. I missed the opening convocation of Sunday school, which was when all the classes in our department gathered for a devotional and a couple of gospel songs. I walked in just as my class of fourth and fifth grade boys would have been ready to begin our lesson. John wasn't there. Mr. Haynes, a mechanic at McNeely Hall Motor Company, was our teacher. He closed the door to our classroom, and with a serious look on his face said, "Guys, as Mrs. Whitman announced during the devotional, we gotta be men here today and face up to what has happened to John."

"What happened to John?" I asked.

"He was putting gasoline in a lawn mower yesterday and didn't take it outside in the open air. There was a hot water heater in the storage shed, and the pilot light ignited the fumes. He was burned over ninety percent of his body."

I felt tears pooling in my eyes. My stomach hurt. "But he'll live, though, right?"

"No. He's going to die." Mr. Haynes's voice choked as he spoke, and he looked at the floor as if he was about to cry.

The rest of us did cry as Mr. Haynes handed out Kleenex. "Don't ask me to explain why this is, 'cause right now he's alert and knows everything. His mind is just fine. I don't even think he's in terrible pain. The doctors say, though, that he's lost so much skin that his body is going to shut down. He'll die in a few hours or at most a day or so."

"But how do the stupid doctors know?" I argued. "If his mind is okay, maybe he'll be all right."

"I'm with you, Joe Don. I asked the same thing but didn't get much of an answer. I don't know how the doctors know; they just do."

Some kid asked whether John had first-, second-, or third-degree burns. Mr. Haynes said whichever one was the worst. I said third. I knew answers like that, but I didn't know you couldn't gas up a lawn mower around a water heater.

We sat around crying until our tear wells ran dry. Then Mr. Haynes told us about the funeral. Going to a funeral was how we paid our respects to the deceased. Another reason we had funerals was so that family and friends could grieve. Like with a motorcycle, which was what Mr. Haynes rode, a funeral was a kick-start for getting the sorrow out of our systems. We would not sit together as a class but with our parents.

Doak Proctor asked, "Does John know he's going to die?"

"I don't know." Tears suddenly ran down Mr. Haynes's cheeks. "What a terrible thing to have to tell your child. I wouldn't know what to do." He reached for a Kleenex and wiped his eyes.

I spent the worship service and early afternoon trying to figure out what to do. It would be strange talking to a person who knew he was going to die, but it would be better than never seeing John again. I had to see him. If he knew he was dying, I'd thank him for being my friend. If he didn't know he was dying, we'd just talk about stuff, act like he wasn't. In either case it was going to be a hard conversation. I didn't know how I was going to pull off my end.

Mom apologetically called Mr. Kyle Rodman after church to see if he could get her car started. He came over as soon as his family finished lunch. He had it fixed by three thirty. No sooner did Mom thank him and he drive off than she got called in to work. Allensworth's had unexpectedly received a big shipment of goods and had to figure out what to do with it. She said she would be late getting home. I was to fix myself a sandwich and get to bed on time.

"First I'm going to ride my bike to St. Joseph's and see John Hall." Mom and the McAllisters had talked about John on the way home from church, how tragic the loss of a child was and how hard it was on his parents. Mom didn't know that John was my church friend. I'd never said much about him, even back when I talked to her. But I had thought she would be supportive of my visiting him simply because he was in my Sunday school class. She had gone to see people from her Sunday school class when they were in the hospital. It was what church people did.

"No. You have no business out there. They won't even let you in the hospital. You have to be twelve."

"But I'm eleven and big for my age. I'll be twelve in four months. I can pass."

"Joe Don, it's nice of you to think about him, but promise me you'll stay here. There's nothing you can do at the hospital but get in the way."

"But Mom!"

"No, promise me! I don't have time for this now. I've got to go."

I promised, but with fingers crossed and the intent of not keeping my word. Shortly after Mom left I hopped on my bike and headed toward St. Joseph's. It took about twenty-five minutes, dusk settling in as I arrived. There wasn't a bike rack, so I laid my bicycle in the grass to the right of the main door.

No sooner did I walk into the lobby than a man asked what I needed. I told him I needed to know what room John Hall was in. "How old are you, kid?" he asked.

"Twelve."

"I don't think so. Sorry, you can't come in here."

"But I really am twelve, almost thirteen." I subtracted a year from my birth date and said, "I was born August 28, 1943."

"I don't believe you. Go on home. It's the rules."

I was getting mad, but I kept my head and tried a strategy that I had learned from Curty's dad. Mr. McDonald was a man who didn't take no for an answer, and he had shared some of his secrets with us kids. Remembering that St. Joseph's was a Catholic hospital, I said, "Can I speak to your Sister Supervisor?"

The man laughed. "My Sister Supervisor? Yeah, right. Nice try, kid, but tonight I'm in charge. No appeal." With that he grabbed me by the arm and led me toward the door.

I jerked my arm away and walked out myself. I was looking in through the plate glass trying to figure out what to do when the man got in the elevator and disappeared, leaving no one at the reception desk. Sensing my chance, I dashed through the lobby and ran up the stairs to the second floor. I stopped, caught my breath, and approached a nurse in the hallway.

"Pardon me, ma'am. I had to go to the restroom and got separated from my parents. They're visiting John Hall. Can you tell me what room he's in?"

"Why certainly," she said. She talked with a Texas twang, which I recognized because everyone in our family talked the same, although Mom was trying to soften hers. The nurse picked up a clipboard, looked at it for a moment, and said, "John is in room 307. You can go up the stairs or take the elevator. It's the last room to your right."

I took the stairs to the third floor. Room 307 was the corner room. The door was closed and there was a sign on it. I was trying to make out what the sign said when someone grabbed me from behind and lifted me off the floor.

"Hey! Let me go! What's the deal!"

"The deal is you're trespassing, kid!" It was the guy from the lobby, and he spoke in my left ear. "If I catch you in this hospital one more time, I'm turning you over to the police. And Sister Supervisor will file trespassing charges, you can bet on it. You'll go to Springer."

He put me down when we got to the elevator, got in with me, and punched the button for the ground floor. The man glared at me. He was mad, but not nearly as mad as I was. I was so mad that I was about to break into uncontrolled crying, as was my habit when someone was unfair. But for some reason I didn't.

In the lobby he walked me to the front door. "Don't come back," he said as he nudged me out of the hospital.

"Sure thing, Lloyd."

The man couldn't figure out my remark. He said, "That's not my name. Why did you call me Lloyd?"

"Because you're a mongoloid idiot."

The man looked shocked, as though no kid had ever called him a name. I myself had never called an adult a name, but I didn't regret it. The man shook his head and "tsked" me as though he was fed up, turned, and went back inside. I walked across the street and sat down on the curb between two parked cars.

It was getting dark. If I tried to make it to John's room again, I'd likely get caught and have to go to Springer. I decided not to try. I determined which of the front windows was John's, the last one to my left on the third floor. If I couldn't be with him, I'd keep watch over his window. That's what a champion in the Greek army would do for his king, and so I did. I sat on the curb crying because it was unfair not being able to go to his room, but even more so because he was dying and there was nothing anyone could do about it.

Officer Brothers, an acquaintance of Mom's who went to our church, found me sleeping at six thirty the next morning, just after it started getting light. I had moved from the curb to a nook in a nearby block fence. There was a trashcan in the nook, but it didn't smell bad. I snuggled in behind it and got under a pile of old newspapers and leaves to stay warm. That way I could still see John's room but be out of the way of the cars that pulled in and out along the street. "Let's go home, Joe Don," he said.

"Am I under arrest?" I asked, remembering the man from St. Joseph's.

"No. I'm giving you a ride home."

"Let me get my bike."

"No need. I found it and took it to your mama around midnight. I just couldn't find you. What were you doing out here?"

"I was keeping watch."

Officer Brothers seemed to understand. "Are you cold?"

"Freezing."

He got a blanket out of the car trunk and wrapped it around me. He radioed in and had the dispatcher call Mom. Then he drove me home.

Mom was sitting on the couch when I walked in. She looked old, like Grandma Snider. She didn't say anything for the longest time, but then said, "Joe Don, I have never been so worried about you as I was last night."

I didn't say anything.

"But then again, I've never been as upset with myself either. You know why?"

I still didn't speak.

"Because as I called around trying to find you, I found out something I would have known if I could only get you to talk to me anymore. Namely, that John Hall was your best Sunday school friend. Had I known that, I'd have gotten you inside that hospital."

"I'm sorry."

"You should be. And I'm sorry he's dying, but what else haven't you told me?"

"Nothing."

"How about your slugging Curty the other night? Why did you do that?"

"I don't know. It just happened."

"It just happened? You punched one of your best friends in the nose! It just happened? Slugging Curty has to do with Mr. Connell, doesn't it? I know you liked him a lot, Joe Don, but he did a bad thing and has to be locked up. That's the way it is!"

"Don't you need to get on to work, Mom?" I didn't feel like getting into an argument about Mr. Connell.

"Yes I do, but come sit with me a minute."

I sat down by her on the couch. She hugged me tight for a long time. Then she said, "Pee-yew! You smell like you've been in the garbage. You need a bath."

"Now?"

"Yes, hurry. I've got to get to work and you to school."

Just then the phone rang. It was Mr. Haynes telling us that John Hall had passed at six fifteen that morning.

• • • • • • •

That night Mom punished me for disobeying her in a way that I had never imagined. She said, "Go get me all your work money, every cent, so I can safekeep it."

"Why?"

"Because your punishment is no cokes or candy bars or movies for a month. Every Saturday you will give me your quarter from Whitman's. I'll keep it for you. You can have it back at the end of the month."

"That's not fair!"

"Neither is your not talking to me. Nothing for a month."

"Okay . . . four weeks, twenty-eight days."

"No, thirty-one days, the longest month of the year."

No cokes, candy, or movies was more painful than ten licks with Dad's belt. Whatever else Mom was to me, she was a worthy opponent.

I told Mom that I was old enough to go to John's funeral by myself, but she wouldn't hear of it. She took off work Wednesday afternoon to drive me. Mr. Franks docked her pay.

The sanctuary was filled. Men were standing alongside the walls so women and children could have seats. Mom and I were seated in the front row of the balcony. She looked at the railing and then looked at me. I knew what she meant.

I didn't remember him saying it, but Dad had thought that the railing of the balcony was the stupidest thing he'd ever seen. To keep you from stepping off, there was a low wooden restraining wall, about eight inches high. Then there was a brass railing mounted to thirty-inch-high brass posts. Dad and Mom had once sat in the front row of the balcony when I was a toddler. Dad looked at the two and a half feet of space between the top of the restraining wall and the brass railing and made us get up and move. There was nothing but vigilance to prevent a little kid from going over and falling to the main floor.

All the members of my Sunday school class were there with their parents. Team members of S&J Pecan Company wore their uniforms and sat together. There were lots of kids from Valley View Elementary where John had gone to school. The front of the sanctuary was lined with sprays of flowers. John's body was in a grayish-silver casket.

Ballard's Funeral Home had brought John's body to the church, and they would take him to the cemetery. Ballard's was the funeral home that some people believed had taken the bodies of the Martians to Walker Air Force Base, or as it was called back then, the Roswell Army Air Field.

John's was not the first funeral I had been to. I had gone to the service for Dad, although I didn't remember anything about it other than the flag on the casket. And I went to Mr. Rowland's funeral last year. He was Mom's first boss at Allensworth's. He was a kind man, and she liked him a lot more than Mr. Franks, who took his place. We had to walk by Mr. Rowland's open casket at the end of the service, paying our respects. John's service wasn't going to be open casket. Doak Proctor said it was because we would vomit if we saw how badly he was burned.

Curty and I had made up from my slugging him. He told me that the people at Jake's Grill had been talking about John. They said that he had been put in a hammock instead of a bed in the hospital because had had so much of his skin burned off, including his face. The hammock made it easier on him than a bed.

I was glad that the casket was closed. I wanted to remember John as he looked before the fire. It would be a nightmare to see a badly burned face sticking out of his blue sports coat, white dress shirt, and red bow tie. One thing bothered me a lot. I wished I hadn't been so mad about his team beating mine. We could have talked after the game. As it was, his last memory of me was my acting like a baby. That made me sad.

Mr. Haynes had told us that the funeral was for paying our respects. I listened closely, but I never heard any respects paid. Rev. Harper didn't mention anything about John other than the "tragic accident" that ended his life. He was happy that John had been baptized, which meant he was in heaven. That was most important, but I got mad that Rev. Harper never mentioned what a great kid John was. He could have said that he was a great listener and was interested in sports and movies and made good grades. It seemed to me that if we were going to pay our respects, the preacher ought to at least mention why we liked and respected John.

Mr. Haynes had also told us that a funeral was for John's friends and family. That it would help kick-start our grief, help us get the sorrow out of our system. Grief was how nature healed a broken heart, but no healing was kick-started for me. I listened closely for what Rev. Harper might have to say about my sorrow, but he never said anything. All I heard was: "What if an accident like what happened to John happened to you? Would you be ready to meet your Maker?" The preacher seemed more interested in saving us than easing our sorrow. He made me so mad that I wished I had kicked him in the mouth rather than the chuke.

After the service we went outside on the lawn to wait for the family to lead the way to the cemetery. They came out last, following the coffin. Six men carried it. I wished that I had been asked to be a pallbearer, but guessed kids weren't eligible. I didn't know how much a coffin weighed. Maybe I wasn't strong enough, or maybe it was just another deal like St. Joseph's Hospital. No kids allowed.

I had expected John's mom to be crying her head off, and she was. What I didn't expect was the look on his dad's face. His was the saddest man's face in the whole world. I'd never thought much about grown men and sorrow. Men weren't supposed to cry, I had supposed because they didn't feel pain like we kids did. And he didn't cry, but I had never seen a man in such pain. Neither had the men standing by me. One said, "How can that poor man ever face a lawn mower again? I couldn't. I could never mow a yard again."

Some of the mourners followed in cars as the procession headed to the cemetery for the graveside service. I didn't care anything about going. The main event was enough. Mom said she needed to get back to Allensworth's so she could get in another hour or so of work. School was almost out for the day. I went with her and browsed the Army-Navy Surplus Store a few doors down until quitting time.

the RUBBER BOOT

IT WASN'T UNTIL THE FIRST PART OF MAY that Mom realized I hadn't shown her my April report card. Miss Sherelle called her in for a conference on Mom's lunch break.

I didn't know about their meeting until that evening. Cathey-Jacobs practiced late, and I got home after Mom. We were having Swiss steak, mashed potatoes, and lima beans for supper when I asked Mom if I could have some more potatoes. She reached into the serving bowl and threw a spoonful in my face.

"How does that feel, Joe Don?"

I was so shocked as to be speechless. I wiped the glob of mashed potatoes from my face and put it on my plate.

"I'll tell you how it feels, young man! It was how I felt this afternoon when Miss Sherelle and your teachers filled me in on you. It was like a slap in the face, 'Wake up, Lurleen! You're in the dark about your son!'"

I was in big trouble.

"Where to begin? How about two days ago when Miss Sherelle called you into her office? Was this to give you an honor? No. It was to tell you that if you picked a fight with another of those sixth grade boys, she didn't care if it was off the school grounds, she was going to suspend you.

"Joe Don, the man is guilty! You should feel sorry for those boys, not beat up on them. Yet, Miss Sherelle thinks you've fought all but two."

Right. I had fought four of the liars. There were two left when Miss Sherelle threatened me. None had confessed. I beat up the first three, but the fourth kid's dad taught judo at Walker Air Force Base. He flipped me every way but loose. I spent more time flying through the air than Superman in that week's television episode. He threw me down so hard that I could hardly breathe. I was lying on the ground pretty much unable to move when he walked away. But first he had looked me in the eye and said, "Leave us alone or I'm going to hurt you bad."

I looked up the word for what I was facing. It was "conspiracy." Mr. Connell's pets were conspiring to get rid of him. It would take more than my beating them up to get them to confess. It would take something like tying them to the railroad tracks.

Mom continued. "And then there was the City Spelling Bee. Not only did you not tell me when it was—I thought it was coming up in May—but you didn't go either. You let your alternate, the girl who came in second, represent Missouri Avenue."

"I lost interest."

"You lost interest! We just practiced hour after hour until you lost interest. Well, here's something that you will be interested to know. This afternoon we figured out that you forged my signature to your April report card. Miss Sherelle is going to give you five licks for that one."

"No big deal."

"No big deal! No big deal was your report card. I saw it."

"I made A's and A-minuses."

"But not A-pluses, and only because you're book smart. Your teachers say you aren't turning in your homework. They just can't stump you on a test."

Mom picked at her food for a minute and then said, "Was it because you didn't want me to see your deportment grades?"

Bingo.

"All unsatisfactories. In one grading period you went from being one of the best-behaved kids in the class to the worst. I couldn't believe my ears! You talk back to your teachers, you never stop talking to other kids, and you stuck a porcupine quill in Terry Adair's bottom!"

Not exactly. Dan Corfield, whose parents owned a ranch north of town, had found a dead porcupine on the road. He collected a pill jar full of quills and brought them to school. He was showing them to me as we stood in line waiting to go in the building. Terry Adair was standing in front of me, and even though he deserved a kick in the rear for being Janet Mitchum's boyfriend, all I was doing was pretending to jab him. Kids were laughing, but then someone shoved him back into the quill. I tried to get it out before the teachers saw, but he was jumping around so fast I couldn't. He finally pulled it out himself and laughed. It hadn't hurt that bad, but I had to stay after school as punishment.

"And tell me this. What do you know about what they think you did?"

"What?"

"Peeing in the boy's rubber boot."

Yes, I had done that, but he deserved it. It was one of the few days that it rained in Roswell, and it had started early in the morning. The streets were filled with water and the ground was muddy. We kids wore our rubber boots to school. And because of the rain we didn't have to wait in line outside before going in the building. Kids went straight inside when they arrived, but there was no law that said we had to go in until the bell rang. There was a lull in the rain when I got there, and although most kids were inside, some boys were spinning tops on the driest part of the big sidewalk. For some dumb reason I decided to spike tops with Tommy Chrisner.

Tommy was new to our school that year. He was from Chicago and had some hardwood tops the likes of which we couldn't buy in Roswell. He was very good, and split other kids' tops right and left. No one had ever spiked one of his, and although I myself had never spiked any kid's top, hope sprang eternal. I'd be the champ if I could get one of his. But I missed, and he didn't. He split my light blue in two.

The bell rang. Tommy and I went in the building and walked through our classroom into the cloakroom. We were the last kids to arrive. The class was playing eraser tag and paid us no mind. We hung up our jackets in the cloakroom and were taking off our rubber boots when the idea came to me. I wouldn't hurry to my seat. I'd let Tommy go ahead of me while I "relived" myself in one of his rubber boots. That'd teach him.

It was one of the riskiest things I had ever done, but I was lucky. No one walked in on me, and no one heard the tinkling sound because it was a "rain day." On rain days Miss Sherelle did silly things to help the teachers maintain control of us unruly kids. Instead of starting with a recording of the Lord's Prayer on the PA system, that morning she asked the whole school to join Mitch Miller in singing "The Yellow Rose of Texas." The sing-along-with-Mitch was my cover.

It was raining when school let out. Most of the class was in the cloakroom getting on their rain gear when someone knocked Tommy's boot over. The contents spilled on the floor. Kids were puzzled as to what it was, but they caught on quickly. Girls screamed and the boys ran away. Mrs. Pfleugger sprang from her desk to see what was the matter, and as she rounded the corner into the cloakroom hit the puddle full speed. She slipped and fell, knocking down a girl and a boy as she slid along the floor on her humongous bean honker. It was impressive!

I figured we'd have to stay after school while Mrs. Pfleugger got to the bottom of it all, but we didn't. She stood up, adjusted her glasses and her dress with the pee stain on the hip, and gave us her best dignified look. "The class has been dismissed. Gather your belongings and leave immediately." And we did, all of us but Tommy Chrisner.

The next morning the principal herself launched the investigation. Miss Sherelle stood before our class saying that someone had urinated in Tommy's rubber boot. The right thing for this person to do was confess. As was her habit, she began looking each of us in the eye.

Everyone knew what had happened, but few had ever heard the word "urinate." They turned to those of us who had for confirmation. I knew what it meant because one day I had skimmed through a sixth grade health book that some kid had left in the hall. I read the explanation, but I'd never heard anyone actually say the word. Urination wasn't something we were supposed to know about until next year.

There was a brief period of whispering back and forth, followed by suppressed giggling. Kids were trying to hold their giggles, but "urinate" was the funniest word many had ever heard. Alea Ritchy could hold it no longer. She exploded with laughter, which then set off Terry Adair. And although I didn't like Terry for being so cute that Janet Mitchum liked him, I loved it when he laughed. He was so funny! Just looking at him giggle convulsed me with laughter, as it did the rest of the kids. We were in stitches!

Miss Sherelle didn't know what to do with us. In her most serious voice and face she had asked for a confession, and within a couple of minutes the class was laughing hard enough to bust a gut. This had never happened to her before. Mrs. Pfleugger rapped on her desk with a ruler, "Class! Stop your laughing!"

And we did, for about ten seconds. But then Alea lost it again, followed by Terry, followed by the rest of us. We knew that we had wandered into dangerous territory. We were in trouble! You don't laugh when the principal visits your classroom. But the fear of punishment was nothing compared to the word power of "urinate."

Miss Sherelle was furious, but she knew kids. She could have threatened Alea or Terry within an inch of their lives, but knew that once they got started they couldn't stop. Neither could the rest of us. To settle us down, she would have had to punish the whole class, all of whom were innocent of the original offense but one. She decided against it. She walked out the door slowly, staring holes in each of us, saying, "Laugh all you want. I will get to the bottom of this." Mrs. Pfleugger went with her out into the hall. She stayed gone for several minutes, probably in the hopes that we would settle down. And we eventually did, but for weeks afterwards all I had to do to send the class into gales of laughter was whisper the word "urinate."

No one remembered that I came in late with Tommy Chrisner. They were too engaged in eraser tag. Tommy didn't even remember. Some kids said that they had seen him drinking whiskey and that he was drunk all the time. I didn't know about that. All I knew was that he wasn't too bright when it came to things other than tops.

Miss Sherelle thought she had seen Tommy and me on the playground spinning tops. And she had. She stood at the top of the steps for a while as though she was the teacher on playground duty that morning. Spiking tops was against the rules, so Tommy had to wait until she went inside before he spiked mine. The day after launching her investigation, she stopped me as I was walking to the restroom. She asked what I knew about Tommy's boot.

"Nothing," I said.

"Didn't I see you playing tops with him out in the rain that morning?"

"No, ma'am."

She didn't press me any further, just gave me a look that said, *You'd better not be lying to me, young man!*

I said pretty much the same to Mom at the supper table. "I don't know anything about the urine in Tommy's rubber boot. May I be excused, please?"

Mom seemed tired and disgusted. "Yes, but we aren't finished. We'll talk about your punishment tomorrow. You're going to straighten up and fly right, or else!"

• • • • • • •

Because of my misbehavior, Mom added another month to keeping my money. She came to school on her lunch hour in support of Miss Sherelle when I got five licks for forging Mom's signature. She signed me up for weekly progress reports. Then to top it off she tricked me into getting in the car late Sunday afternoon and took me to Rev. Harper's study. I had thought we were going to Uncle Charlie's for supper.

In addition to being mad at Mom for tricking me, I was hungry and ready to eat. So was the pastor. He needed his supper before the evening service, but Mom couldn't have cared less about our stomach rumblings. She was ready to rumble. "What's the problem, Lurleen?" Rev. Harper asked. "And please, both of you speak up. Remember I have a hearing problem."

Rev. Harper couldn't hear worth a flip—everyone knew that. But he already knew what the problem was. I was sure that he and Mom had had a talk beforehand. Adults liked to gang up on kids like that.

Mom broke into tears. "I used to have a sweet boy. I don't anymore, and I want my sweet boy back."

"What's he been doing?"

"What hasn't he been doing!" She spoke loudly. "He's been picking fights. His deportment in school is terrible. He forged my signature on his report card. And he lies. He won't admit that he urinated in a boy's rubber boot in the cloak room."

"He did what?" Evidently Mom hadn't mentioned that one.

"He urinated in a boy's rubber boot," Mom shouted.

"Really?" Rev. Harper grinned and laughed.

"It's not funny!" Mom snapped.

"Oh, I know it's not, Lurleen. I just never heard of such. Why did he do it?"

Mom didn't know. She didn't know why I was misbehaving. I just was.

"Joe Don, is this true?"

I didn't say anything. I looked away.

"You answer him, young man!" Mom said.

I still didn't say anything.

"That's another thing," Mom said, tears flowing down her cheeks. "He used to visit with me at the supper table. Now he doesn't say two words all evening. And he won't listen to reason about Mr. Connell."

"Mr. Connell?"

"His teacher, the one who went to prison. Joe Don beat up some of the boys involved, even slugged one of his best friends in an argument about Mr. Connell. And you know what else? John Hall was one of his best friends and he never told me!"

"Is all this true, Joe Don?"

"What's true," I shouted, "is that you didn't pay your respects to John Hall when you preached his funeral! You just tried to save us. And because of you I'm going to be an atheist."

That set them back further than a fifteen-yard penalty. They looked at each other trying to figure out what I was talking about. They tried to get me to explain, but I just sat there silent, sometimes staring at the two of them, sometimes looking off. Nothing either one could do or threaten me with would make me talk.

Rev. Harper suggested that Mom go outside. He would like to talk to me alone. She went out in the hall. "Joe Don, I'm sorry I let you down at John's funeral. But something else is bothering you. Would you like to tell me about it? I won't tell your mom unless you want me to."

I didn't say anything.

"Sometimes things happen to us that cause us to act in ways we never would otherwise. It's happened to me before. I'd like to know, son, what it is that's bothering you so."

"I'm not your son."

"Okay, you're not my son, but I'm still worried about you."

"And I wasn't your son back when you had your precious Father-Son Banquet." I exaggerated the words "Father-Son Banquet" to make fun of it. For three weeks from the pulpit he had gone on and on about what a great banquet it was going to be. And after it was over, all the kids who were there said it was. The great Roswell football player Tommy Brookfield was the speaker, and I missed out because I didn't have a dad.

"Oh my, I'm sorry! I never even thought about your not being able to go. Forgive me, Joe Don, I simply wasn't thinking."

I looked at him for evidence of sincerity.

"But it wasn't my precious banquet," he said. "I didn't even go. Know why?"

I was surprised. "Why?"

"I have three daughters, no sons. Boy, did I want to hear Tommy Brookfield speak! But I wasn't eligible. The music director was in charge . . . So tell you what. Let's you and I go together next year. It's going to be an even better banquet than the last one."

"That'd be weird. You can't do that, can you?"

"Sure we can. I'm the boss around here, at least sometimes, and I declare that for any purpose around First Baptist Church you and I can be a father-son team, although we'd better do some father-son type things between now and then, just to make it legit."

"Like what?"

"You like baseball, don't you? I hear you're really good."

"Yeah."

"Do you ever watch the Roswell Rockets play?" The Roswell Rockets was a Class C professional team that played at Fairground Stadium.

"Yeah! Joe Bauman is my hero. I want to hit homers like he does." Joe Bauman hit seventy-two home runs in 1954, a world record. He owned a filling station where Mom bought gas.

We talked about Joe Bauman and the Rockets for a while. "I try to make most of their games, but I have to go by myself because my wife and the girls aren't interested. The Rockets are in town next week. Want to go to a game? I'd love some company."

"Yeah." Maybe Rev. Harper wasn't as bad as I thought.

"I'll call you and tell you when. You can go now, Joe Don. I've got to get ready for the evening service, and I'm really hungry!"

Mom was waiting for me in the hall. We rode home in silence.

14

FIELDING INSULTS

ALTHOUGH SCHOOL WASN'T YET OUT FOR SUMMER, I had started sleeping in my fort beneath the elm tree. It was hot in the house, and my room didn't have a window like Mom's. Out in the fort it was nice and cool, some nights even cold. I slept on Grandma's quilts on the floorboards.

A year earlier I had gotten interested in building a tree house, but wasn't able to do so even with Jay Bob's help. The tree wasn't right. Instead we built a fort with one end against the tree. It was built out of scrap wood we found and dragged home.

The fort wasn't very big. I could walk around inside on my knees, but couldn't stand up. It was about eight feet long and six feet wide, with boards that I could pull out to catch a breeze. We had put tarpaper on the roof, but didn't have enough to cover it completely. If it rained, I'd have to get up and run to my room.

Also, when the nights started warming up, the three of us boys shifted from sleepovers to campouts. These were held in Jay Bob's backyard beneath the pecan tree. We had tried sleepovers in Curty's backyard the previous summer, but we stopped after a drunk crashed through the fence. He plowed his car through the backyard where we had been sleeping on cots a few nights before. The McDonalds lived at the corner of Deming and Lopez. Twice now, drunks going around the corner had wound up in their backyard.

Our first camp-out just happened to be the evening of the junior-senior prom. We had hot dogs for supper, along with baked beans and chocolate cupcakes with sprinkles; and were setting up our cots beneath the pecan tree when Mrs. Jones called out to us. She said we had to come see Gerald.

The Joneses had called off Gerald's rest-of-the-year curfew. They figured he had been punished enough, and so they let him go to the prom. He was in the living room. Mr. Jones was getting his camera ready to take Gerald's picture.

Curty said, "Wow, Gerald! You clean up good." And he did. He was wearing a white sports coat, a red rose boutonniere, a red cummerbund, black slacks, and black patent leather shoes. His hair had about a gallon of Wildroot Cream Oil Charlie on it, slicked back so it looked like Elvis's hair.

"Who are you going with?" Curty asked.

"Ah so, none of your business, twerp."

"I know," I said. "He's going with his true love, Becky Watson."

I knew because I was spending time with Sherry at the school store. Mom had driven me to it. If she was going to hold my money so that I couldn't buy cokes and candy bars or go to the movies even though I could get in for free, I knew someone who would buy me cokes and candy.

The morning after John Hall's funeral I was working during homeroom period with Miss Tower and Sherry on the newspaper. Miss Tower left the room and I said, "My mom won't let me go to any movies for the next month. I'm being punished."

"What did you do?"

"She caught me reading that book you like, *God's Little Acre.*"

"Really! Did you like it?" Sherry asked.

"I would have, but Mom took it away just after I started. That's how come I got two weeks of no candy, cokes, or movies. The next two weeks' punishment I got because I told her I'd vote for Adlai, not Ike."

If Sherry liked me before, now she liked me even more. Every day toward the end of the lunch hour we would meet at the store where she'd buy me a Dr. Pepper or a candy bar. And we were trying to figure out how to go to the movies. Sherry wanted us to meet after I finished work at Whitman's Auto on a Saturday. She would pay her way. But there was no story I had yet come up with to keep from riding home with Mom.

For more than a week all Sherry had talked about was her sister Becky's upcoming date with Gerald to the prom. In Sherry's opinion, going to the prom was the most romantic thing in the world.

Gerald looked at me in disbelief. "How do you know who I'm going with?"

"A little birdie told me," I said. Curty and Jay Bob smiled at each other and at me. They knew who I'd been keeping company with.

"Yes, he's going with Becky Watson," said Mrs. Jones, "and they're going to be the best-looking couple there!"

"Wait a minute!" I said. "You're a sophomore. How come you get to go to the prom? I thought it was just for juniors and seniors."

"Becky is a junior. She invited me."

I hadn't known she was older. Curty whispered in my ear, "The apple doesn't fall far from the tree, does it?"

I wondered if Gerald had spent time yet with Becky inside the janitor's closet at the Women's Club, but I wasn't going to ask him in front of his parents.

Mr. Jones snapped Gerald's picture and Gerald was out the door. But he came back a minute later because he had forgotten Becky's corsage in the icebox.

"Is Darrell going to the prom?" Mrs. Jones asked Curty.

"Yes ma'am; he's got a green cucumber bun and corsage and everything. I guess he's already left. My parents are going to be chaperones later tonight. They volunteered to take an hour."

That gave Jay Bob an idea when we went out to our cots beneath the pecan tree. "Curty, do you think your parents would let us ride with them to the prom so we could see what's going on? We could just stand around outside and watch."

I saw through Jay Bob's plan. "All you want to do is ogle teenage girls."

"So what if I like teenage girls? They're more interesting than girls our age. What do you think, Curty?"

"I guess I could go ask."

Curty went home and came back a few minutes later. His parents said yes, as then did Jay Bob's parents and Mom via telephone. We didn't even clean up. We just climbed in the backseat of the McDonalds' Chevy.

The deal was that we had to stay outside. We couldn't go inside the lobby of the gymnasium. Prom was just for teenagers and chaperones. The McDonalds would serve their shift, and then we'd go home.

But standing outside was okay because there was plate glass at both entrances to the gym, north and south. We made like Peeping Toms and moved from one end to the other. We could see most everything going on in the lobby. At the north end couples were getting their pictures taken by a photographer. At the south end refreshments were being served. What we couldn't see were the kids dancing or how the gym was decorated. Darrell and Gerald had said it was going to be neat. The theme was "An Evening in Honolulu." They even had a beach with sand.

After a while we just stood at the south entrance, watching as couples went in and out the lobby. Jay Bob was in heaven! If he liked the way teenage girls looked in general, they looked great in low-cut prom dresses. And they smelled good! At first we didn't stand too close to the door, but then we moved closer. No one seemed to mind us being there until Adam Choate showed up.

He was with Debbie, the girl who had come with him to get the outhouse for the bonfire. "What are you babies doing here?" Adam said. "Why aren't you home in your cribs with a bottle?"

"Oh, Adam, hush," said Debbie. She smiled at us. "They can be here if they want. How are you boys doing?"

"Fine."

"You don't even know what fine is," Adam said. "You're nothing but a bunch of squirts."

"Oh, go squirt your pimples," I said.

That made him mad. His face turned vicious. "Miller, you'd better not be here when we come back out!" If Debbie hadn't been holding his arm, he might have slugged me.

"Else what?"

"Else I'm going to burn that shack you live in. We should have tossed it on the bonfire and let you move in the old outhouse. You and your mom would be better off." Adam and Debbie walked inside. She was giving him grief for being mean to me.

"Why is he like that?" Curty asked. "My brother can't stand the creep."

"Neither can Gerald. Did you smell alcohol on his breath?"

"Not really," I said. "Did you know he has a brother that plays for Pierce's Creamery? That kid Rodney Choate."

"I know him!" said Jay Bob. "He goes to Valley View. But I didn't know that was his brother."

"I'd hate to be his brother," said Curty. "He's so mean that he makes me appreciate Darrell."

Awhile later Curty's parents came out. They were ready to take us home, and we were ready to go. We spent the night with two blankets because it would get cold by morning.

We were looking at the stars when Curty said, "You may like the way high school girls look, Jay Bob, but have you ever seen them dressed out for PE?"

"Yeah, one time I had to go in the gym to get Gerald so we could leave for my grandmother's funeral. Their gym suits are terrible! You could take the best-looking high school girl in the world and make her look like a skag in a gym suit."

"Why is that?" Curty asked.

"To keep the boys' PE class from looking at them. Even with their stupid uniforms, Gerald says that the girls' PE teacher spends most her time griping. She gives the boys' PE teacher grief, says that they are looking at her girls."

"Then she'll hate you when you get to high school!"

I had never seen a girl's gym suit, and so I changed the subject. "Did Adam Choate really have alcohol on his breath? I didn't smell anything."

"I think it was beer," said Curty. "Smelled like Hamm's. But if you were a teenager going on a date, what would you gargle with, mouthwash or cologne?"

"That's a dumb question," said Jay Bob. "Nobody gargles with cologne!"

"But it has alcohol in it just like mouthwash. You don't swallow, you just gargle. Which would make your breath smell better?"

"Why don't you just brush your teeth for a change?" I said. "Good night. Let's go to sleep."

We were quiet for a while, and so I said my prayers. Then Curty broke the silence, "You really don't live in a shack, Joe Don. It's small, but not a shack."

"Thanks, Curty."

· · · · · · ·

Thursday evening after supper Mom asked if I wanted to go with her to Gizelle's to get some elastic for a dress she was making. I told her I was going to Jay Bob's to watch TV, but Mom said she hadn't seen enough of me lately. I was to go with her to the store. Gizelle's stayed open late on Thursday, and Mom sometimes stopped in to get material for her sewing.

I hated Gizelle's. It was like being attacked by the Sewing Vampire. It just sucked the life out of a kid and left stitch marks. There was nothing to do but stand around hoping Mom would hurry up. It was all cloth and zippers and buttons and doodads for women, nothing interesting to look at, and some of it embarrassing should anyone catch you. I tried not to glance in the direction of their naked nudist womannequins.

I was the only male there, and I tried to stay out of the women's way. I made like a broom and stood in a back corner, daydreaming about freeing Mr. Connell from prison. Jay Bob said that there were books at the library that taught people how to fly a helicopter. I'd read one, and then go out to Causey's Aviation and borrow a helicopter when no one was around.

I'd arrive at the state prison while the prisoners were exercising in the yard, drop a rope ladder to Mr. Connell, and pull him up before the guards knew what was happening. We'd get back to Roswell just after homeroom period had started. All his pets would be in Mr. Davidson's class. We'd burst in and he would make them tell the truth. They'd go crying to Miss Sherelle's office and confess that they had lied. She would call the police, and then tell Mrs. Pfleugger to go home. Mr. Connell was back on the job!

I was caught up in my daydream when I felt someone tapping on my head. "Anybody home?"

It was Alea. "Hi, Alea! What are you doing here?"

"My mom thinks that if I come with her to Gizelle's that it will rub off on me."

"What do you mean?"

"Home economics. That I'll grow up and cook meals, clean house, and sew my clothes."

"You don't want to be a housewife?"

"Maybe, but I think I'd rather be an engineer on a train or a hobo. Did you see my costume at the Halloween carnival? I came dressed as a hobo."

"I guess."

"You didn't notice. You only had eyes for Janet Mitchum, Miss Fairy Princess. If she wasn't such a nice kid I'd hate her guts. Did you hear she's moving?"

"Janet's moving?"

"Yeah. Her dad's in the air force and he's been transferred to Alabama. He's leaving next week. Janet and her mom and sisters are going to stay here, sell the house, and leave before the new school year starts."

Alea lived three houses down and across the street from Janet. She would know. My stomach began to hurt. This was horrible news. I couldn't imagine going to school without Janet, even if she paid me no mind.

"You know who likes you?" Alea asked.

"Who?"

"Jan. She thinks you're cute."

Jan Browning? She was pretty, but she was stuck-up and threw hissy fits. Curty said she held her nose so high that the next time it rained she was going to drown.

"Alea! Let's go!" It was her mom calling from across the store.

"Bye. See ya in the comic strips."

No sooner did Alea leave than Roger Jamison came in. He was with his mom and older sister. I hadn't seen him much since he and Jay Bob had cost me my secret whistle at the basketball game. Roger also hated Gizelle's and was glad to see me.

We talked about what we were going to do that summer. He

wasn't playing Little League because in June he was going to a four-week camp for boys along the Guadalupe River in Texas, Camp Rio Vista. He was going to play tennis and ride horses and go canoeing. There was no end to the sports that he and the other boys were going to do at Camp Rio Vista. It sounded great! Ten boys were going from Roswell and eight girls to its sister camp, Mystic.

I asked him how come I had never heard of Camp Rio Vista. He said because it was an exclusive pleasure camp. It cost about five hundred dollars. Rio Vista knew who the Roswell families were that would be interested and was in touch with just them.

"Five hundred dollars!" I said. "I can't imagine paying that much."

"That's because you're a bastard. If you had a dad who was in the oil business, you could pay that much easy."

What I really couldn't imagine was his calling me a bastard! I didn't know exactly what the word meant, only that it was a cuss-word insult. I slugged him in the jaw with a right.

He started crying. "Why'd you do that!"

His mom raced over and stepped in between us. "Stop that! Leave my son alone!"

"He called me a dirty name!"

"He most certainly did not!" she said.

"Did too!"

By then Mom had muscled in between Roger's mom and me. "What's going on here?"

"Your boy was beating up my son!"

"He called me a dirty name!"

"What?" Mom asked.

"He said I was a bastard."

Mom winced and the woman's attitude changed. "Did you call him that?" she asked Roger.

"Yes, but he is one."

"He most certainly is not!" Mom said. "Who told you that!"

Roger's mom blushed. "Ma'am, let me see if I can get to the bottom of this. Rebecca!"

The boy's sister answered, "Yes, ma'am."

"Come here! Have you been teaching your brother dirty words again?"

She grabbed both kids by an ear and led them a few feet away for a family conference. There was fierce whispering on her part and quiet answers from the kids. Then there was a look of disgust on the mom's face. "You're both going to get it when we get home!"

She came back and said, "Ma'am, I sincerely apologize. My daughter keeps teaching her little brother cusswords, and this time he didn't understand. He thinks that the word means anyone who doesn't have a daddy, no matter what the reason. He meant no disrespect. He likes your son and says your husband was killed in the war."

"Apology accepted." Mom wasn't one to easily hold a grudge, and she seemed relieved that the situation was settled. Then she looked around and saw all the women staring at her. She seemed embarrassed. "Come on, Joe Don, let's go. I have what I need."

We had parked a block away because there were no spaces closer. We hustled to the car and got in. Mom put the key in the ignition, but didn't turn it over. Instead she leaned her head on her hands on the steering wheel and started crying.

After a minute or so I asked, "Mom, are you mad at me?"

"No," she said as she sat up straight and wiped the tears away. "I'm just sad . . . Damn that bastard MacArthur!"

• • • • • • •

Because Memorial Day was a holiday, Mrs. Taylor, our history teacher, decided to have a special lesson the day before. Any student who had lost a relative in a war was invited to give a brief speech. The speech was to include the name of the relative, which branch of the armed forces he served in, and which war. We could bring pictures and personal items that belonged to the person if we wanted—but no knives, swords, pistols, or rifles.

After Dad was killed, Mom gave the good things he had to grown relatives in Texas—an M-1 rifle, a carbine, a .45 pistol, two Marine Corps knives in scabbards, and a Japanese sword. Whenever I would gripe that she didn't keep any of the good stuff for me, she'd say that the relatives would return it all when I was grown. She had kept Dad's leather flight jacket for me. It hung in her closet, but I wouldn't be big enough to wear it until I was out of high school.

I was amazed at how many kids took part in our Memorial Day lesson. We had kids who had lost granddads in World War I, uncles in World War II, and uncles and cousins in Korea. And not just men; Terry Adair had an aunt, a WAC, who was killed in World War II.

Kids brought uniforms and medals and helmets and caps and army blankets and a footlocker and a riding crop. I had thought long and hard about what I should bring. In addition to his flight jacket, Mom had Dad's medals and insignias and patches in a drawer in her bedroom, but I didn't take them. I took the picture of Dad and Joe Foss and Charles Lindbergh.

In World War II Dad had been stationed several places, including California. He wasn't in the whole war. I didn't know everything he had done in the war, but for a long time he had been ground officer for Joe Foss's marine fighter squadron. Joe Foss was America's ace pilot in World War II. Far more kids had heard of Eddie Rickenbacker in World War I, but both pilots had shot down the same number of enemy planes, twenty-six. Dad told Mom that Joe Foss was the best shot with a rifle that he had ever seen. Mom said that was quite a compliment because all the marines she knew said the same about Dad.

The reason that Charles Lindbergh was in the photograph was that he was selling Corsair airplanes during the war. He had come for a visit with Joe Foss, and even went on a mission. Dad said Lindbergh shot down one Japanese plane. There was another man in the picture, a total of four. Mom and I didn't know who the fourth guy was, but the other three were our heroes.

I didn't speak for long when it came my turn. I was the only kid in the class whose dad had been killed in a war, and everyone knew it had been the Korean War. So I just told them the story about his also being in World War II, showed them the picture, and told them a little bit about Joe Foss. Everyone knew about Charles Lindbergh.

My main interest was to get Terry Adair in trouble. Terry had made me mad by bragging at the school store about how Janet Mitchum loved him so much that she would do anything he told her. That made her sound stupid, which she wasn't. I wanted to punch him in the mouth, but that would only get me in trouble with Janet. What could I do? One day at recess I was thinking about Terry when Alea came up. She said, "My grandmother's in the hospital. She has some disease I can't pronounce, but she also has gas real bad. Guess what they call it? Flatulence!"

To Alea "flatulence" was a funnier word than "urinate." She laughed until tears rolled down her cheeks.

I walked over to where Curty was monkeying around on the jungle gym, and said, "Did you know that they put people in the hospital for having gas?"

"No they don't."

"Yes they do, and they call it flatulence. You could die from it. Next time you start flatulating at one of our campouts, I'm going to call an ambulance."

"No you're not."

"Yes I am. It's for your own health."

I often played around with the verses of songs, changing them so they were silly. I had worked on "Tumbling Tumbleweeds" off and on for a long time. It didn't take much effort to change it on the spot to

> *See him tumbling down,*
> *Stinking up the downtown.*
> *Lonely but free he'll be found,*
> *Curty, the flatulent tumbleweed.*

It was always fun to tease Curty, but then I had an even better idea. Flatulence began with the same syllable as did flat feet. Flat feet were the reason Terry Adair's father hadn't served in World War II.

Terry and I had been in the same class at school ever since first grade. I knew all his stories just like he knew mine. Every time he mentioned that his aunt the WAC had been killed in World War II, he also said that his dad had wanted to enlist, but couldn't get in the army because he had flat feet.

The day before the Memorial Day speeches in history class, I got Terry alone on the playground and asked him how his speech was coming. He said fine. I asked him if he knew the military term for flat feet. He didn't. I told him I hadn't known it either until last week when I was reading a book from the Carnegie library. Military doctors called flat feet "flatulence." It was Latin. If you had one flat foot, you were flatulent. If you had two, you had flatulents. Terry was grateful for the information. I wrote the word down so he wouldn't forget it. He would use it in his speech.

And he did, but just barely. He told the class how his Aunt Alice Adair was killed when a bomb fell on the headquarters where she was working. He showed us a picture of her, as well as a cap that she wore. But he forgot to mention anything about his dad, and so I raised my hand as he started walking back to his seat. "Terry, wasn't your dad in the army too?"

"No. My dad had flatulents. He had flatulents so bad they wouldn't let him join the army."

My plan had worked! He had said it in front of the class! I waited for Mrs. Taylor to scream at him and send him to the office. I waited for Janet Mitchum to realize that her boyfriend had just said something nasty in front of the whole class. I'd make sure Alea explained it to her later. I waited and waited, but nothing happened.

Mrs. Taylor just said, "Thank you, Terry. Who's next on the list? Raymond Spencer. Raymond, who are you going to tell us about? And Alea . . . what is so funny? Would you like to tell us why you're laughing so hard?"

· · · · · · ·

The next morning Uncle Charlie and Aunt Elvis drove by our house at nine. Mom and I were waiting and ready to go. We were going to the cemetery to put flowers on Dad's grave. Allensworth's was closed for Memorial Day.

Uncle Charlie was the second of four brothers, Dad the third. He and Dad had been close. Uncle Charlie didn't go to college. He and Aunt Elvis got married several years earlier than Mom and Dad, but couldn't have children. They adopted my hoodlum cousin Greg when he was eighteen months old. He had rickets, which was part of the reason they took him. They figured no one else would.

Mom said that having rickets was why Greg walked like a cowboy. She used to quote a poem that began, *"What manner of men are these who wear their legs in parentheses?"* Greg was in terrible physical shape. He always had a note from his mom, likely forged, as to why he couldn't suit out for PE at school. Lately he had begun to idolize Elvis Presley, but who hadn't? His hair was combed in a greasy DA, and he wore a black leather jacket. He kept one arm of his white T-shirt rolled up so he could keep his cigarette pack in it. He carried a big switchblade in his back blue jeans pocket.

Greg pushed his parents' patience to the limit. The only times I had ever seen Uncle Charlie lose his temper was when he came home from work and Aunt Elvis told him what Greg had done that day. Which wasn't that much different from what he did any day— he just got caught that day. Greg didn't come with us. He was sleeping in from a late night of shooting pool.

There was a crowd at the cemetery. Lots of people had lost relatives in a war. The VFW was handing out little flags to plant on the graves of servicemen. We got one and headed toward Dad's grave. Both Mom and Aunt Elvis had fresh flowers.

At the graveside Uncle Charlie and Mom cried as they touched Dad's headstone. Aunt Elvis would move from one to the other, comforting them. She cried a little bit too. Uncle Charlie said, "It isn't fair that he had to serve in both wars. Two wars isn't fair! He lived through World War II only to be sacrificed by that bastard MacArthur."

There was that word again, and once again modifying MacArthur. It caught the attention of a veteran at a nearby grave. "What did you say about MacArthur?"

"I say he's as sorry as the day is long."

The man got mad. "You can't say that about the Hero of the Philippines!"

"I didn't! I said it about the Clown of Korea! He just sat there with his geisha girls in Tokyo like he was God and sent my brother and a lot of other good men to a needless death."

The man looked even angrier. I stuck my hand in my blue jeans pocket. I had a Boy Scout knife that I had found on the way to school and sharpened at Jay Bob's. The man was stocky and looked strong. I was ready to slash him in the stomach if he jumped Uncle Charlie. I couldn't stab him because the blade was collapsible.

"What service was your brother in?" the man asked.

"He was a marine."

The man eased a bit. "A gyrene, huh? Look, I wasn't in Korea, and I've never understood the squabble between Truman and MacArthur. But I am a survivor of the Bataan Death March. MacArthur is my hero, and I don't take kindly to you running him down."

It was Uncle Charlie's turn to ease. "You're right. We're looking at the man at two different times in his life. How about we just leave it lay?" Uncle Charlie extended his right hand. "I'm Charlie Miller. I should have kept my thoughts to myself. I didn't mean to upset you."

The man shook Uncle Charlie's hand. "I'm Carl Smithfield, and it's okay. Sorry I got riled. You tend to your dead. I'll tend to mine."

• • • • • • •

The last day of school was May 31. Dad's birthday, which Mom kept celebrating, was a week later, June 7. For supper Mom had mercy on my sweet tooth and baked a Mississippi mud cake, the best-tasting cake in the world! And it was just her and me to eat it. The year before, Uncle Charlie and Aunt Elvis had come over, but this year they were out of town at an insurance convention. Greg was probably hosting a hoodlum convention at their house while they were gone. No telling what was going on!

Mom didn't seem as sad as she had been last year. Maybe she had cried dry at the cemetery. In addition to the mud cake, she cooked others of Dad's favorites—fried chicken, mashed potatoes, gravy, red beans, and homemade biscuits. It was a feast! We were going to have great leftovers!

While we were eating Mom said, "I saw Rev. Harper today at the grocery store. He said that you two had a good time at the Rockets game the other night."

"It was all right. Joe Bauman hit two homers."

What I liked about Big Joe hitting a home run was how the men in the stands ran down to hand him dollar bills afterwards. Chicken wire was strung from the roof of Fairground Stadium down to the ground to keep foul balls from going into the stands behind home plate. After Joe had run the bases, he would trot along the grandstands back to the dugout. Men would hand him folded dollar bills through the chicken wire. I always tried to count how many he got, but never could. He made lots of money off a homer.

"What did you and Rev. Harper talk about?" Mom asked.

"Nothing much." Actually, conversation with Rev. Harper was like talking to John Hall. He was a listener, even if he couldn't hear. I liked talking to him. He asked my opinion about everything and always wanted to know how my week was going. We went to a Roswell Rockets game once a week.

One thing I didn't tell him was about Jay Bob. In honor of Dad's birthday he gave me a present, a *Playboy* magazine that he had found under Gerald's mattress. I put it in my second ammo box. Ever since Mom began punishing me by keeping my money, she had been holding surprise inspections. She'd make me go get my ammo box and dump it out. She'd even stand outside my fort looking in so she could tell if I was holding out on her. She searched my fort, my room, and my blue jeans pockets.

Fortunately, Mom didn't raise any idiots, and I saw these inspections coming. One night back in April, she had checked my pants pockets for change. I figured if she was going to do that, my ammo box was no longer safe. I asked Jay Bob what I should do, and he suggested a second ammo box. There had been a sale at the Army-Navy Surplus Store, and the Joneses had several in their garage. He gave me one, and then came over to help me dig a new compartment under a floorboard in my fort. I kept my first ammo box, which had nothing in it, where Mom knew it would be. I kept my second ammo box in the new hiding place. In it was the *Playboy* magazine, Sherry's valentine and school picture, a box cutter I had liberated from Whitman's Auto, and money Mom didn't know I had.

I hardly had the *Playboy* magazine long enough to stash it. Gerald figured that Jay Bob had stolen it and gave him such a painful Indian burn on his right forearm that Jay Bob cried. He told Jay Bob to give the magazine back or he was going to "accidentally" break all his models. Jay Bob apologized for having to take it back, but there was no need for him to feel sorry. I understood what he was up against. I told him it was the thought that counted. Besides, I couldn't imagine my punishment if Mom ever caught me with a *Playboy* magazine.

Mom also didn't know about the money I was getting from Mr. and Mrs. Oldfield, who lived on Deming Street a couple of blocks west of Missouri Avenue Elementary School. One day in May I was walking home after school. An old lady called out to me from her front porch, "Young man! Please come here. I need some help."

What Mrs. Oldfield needed was someone to climb up on a ladder in her living room and screw in a light bulb. I put it in for her, and when I turned to go she handed me a dime. I told her I couldn't take her money. I was just happy to help.

Her husband came walking into the living room with a cane. He was old too and liked me. He said, "Go ahead, take it. We need a lad like you to help out with chores around here. Are you interested? We'll pay you."

I was helping them two or three times a week. I worked in their garden, mowed their yard, and carried groceries from their car and put them inside the house. I made a dime each time. I was making nearly as much or more each week from the Oldfields as I was turning over to Mom from my job at Whitman's. But I always stopped by to ask if they needed me. I didn't want them knowing I had a phone. They might call the house and talk to Mom. Keeping one step ahead of Mom took planning.

· · · · · · ·

The baseball season was down to the last couple of weeks. Monday afternoon we played Pierce's Creamery, which was in second place after Malco. They had some good players, and after each game went to the sales room at Pierce's for free ice cream.

Pierce's ice cream was different from Dairy Queen. Pierce's was hard packed, whereas Dairy Queen was soft. I liked both.

Herman Newton was our starting pitcher. I hoped he wouldn't have one of his wild games. When he had his control, Herman was an okay pitcher. But when he was wild, no one was wilder. Bystanders had better move their cars if they wanted to protect their windshields. Herman would pitch it over the backstop or over our imaginary dugouts. One time he hit a guy on the other team as he sat on the dugout bench

Vic Irwin was Pierce's starting pitcher, and one of the better in the league. I had hit a double off Tommy Jordan, who was the best, but all I had done against Vic was a single. He was taller than Tommy Jordan and threw a blazing fastball.

I had begun to hate our uniforms. Not just the Cathey-Jacobs ones, but the uniforms of every team in the league. All of them were white wool with no lettering. The only way the spectators could tell one team from the other was by the color of the players' caps. Each team had a different color cap, except they ran out of colors. Cathey-Jacobs had the same color as Pierce's Creamery, yellow.

Adults hated our uniforms also. They said that when we ran we looked like schooner ships at full sail, the sleeves of our jerseys billowing. Coaches said that we would play better if we just wore T-shirts and blue jeans. It would be easier to move.

Cathey-Jacobs was home team, and so our yellow caps took the field, while the other yellow caps went to bat. Once in position at second base, I put a piece of Double Bubble in my mouth. I wished I could chew tobacco like major leaguers, but I couldn't. Dan Corfield had given me some before a practice earlier in the season. I got so dizzy I had to lie down. Dan chewed Beech-Nut every day after school. He didn't play baseball. He practiced roping calves.

We were chattering like crazy in the infield. "Hum baby, hum baby, hum baby, SWING!" We were doing all we could to support Herman, but my fears came true. He walked the first three batters. The bases were loaded, and then the fourth batter took a full count before Herman walked in the first run.

Coach Gilbert and our catcher went to the pitcher's mound. They told Herman to ease up on the speed and try to gain control. He did and the fifth batter drove one deep to left field. Two runners came in. It was three to nothing, men on second and third.

Herman struck out the next batter, and then picked off the base runner at third. I caught a line drive, and we were up to bat. It was Rodney Choate who had hit the ball straight to me. His brother Adam was standing behind the backstop. He yelled, "You were robbed, Rod! You're a bum, Miller!"

I batted cleanup and figured Vic was such a good pitcher that I wouldn't get to bat during the first inning. Vic struck out our first two batters, but then George McDaniel got a single. I was up.

I connected with the first pitch and drove a line drive into Vic's left shin. He tried but wasn't able to jump out of the way. I ran to first, and then a timeout was called to tend to his injury. Vic was lying on his back holding his leg and crying. The coaches ran to him.

I liked Vic and felt terrible. I had never imagined hitting a pitcher with a line drive, much less intended to do so. But that's what Vic's mom said.

Vic was on the ground several minutes. After they helped him off the field, they put him on the end of the bench and elevated his leg. His mother came out of the crowd, stood behind him, pointed to me, and yelled, "Kick that boy out of the game! He's a dirty player!"

A new pitcher came in, and play resumed. Pierce's players began thinking about what Vic's mom said. The count was one and one on the batter, but the infield wasn't paying him much attention. I was on first base, and they were looking at me like they were ready to rumble. The second baseman said, "You knocked Vic outa the game 'cause you knew we'd win with him pitching. We're going to get you!"

The mood was turning ugly. It looked like we were going to play tackle football on the base path, which was okay with me. Vic's mom yelled a second time, "Throw the bum out!"

When she did, the plate umpire, Mr. Ferguson, jerked his mask off. He turned to her and screamed, "Lady, be quiet!"

Mr. Ferguson had a really loud voice. You could hear his, "Stee-ee-rike three!" all the way to Walker Air Force Base. But with Vic's mom he was even louder than usual. "It was an accident! He didn't mean your kid any harm. Now be quiet!"

Mrs. Irwin was surprised. She was quiet for a few seconds, but no sooner did Mr. Ferguson put his mask back on than she shouted, "I will not be quiet! Who are you to talk that way to me?"

"I run this field!" Mr. Ferguson said, taking his mask off again. "And if you say one more word, your team forfeits the game for unsportsmanlike conduct!"

Pierce's coaches knew he meant it, but before they could calm down Mrs. Irwin, she yelled, "I'll say what I damn well please, you . . ."

"Game's over! Cathey-Jacobs wins! Lady, you're banned for the rest of the season! If you even think about coming out here again, Pierce's will forfeit the rest of its games. Take mama's boy and get out of here!"

Everyone was shocked, surprised, and dumbfounded. You could have heard a pin drop on home plate. My team had won by the score of 0–3. Pierce's Creamery was so discombobulated that they stopped hating me. They got mad at Vic and his mom and started saying things about them under their breath. No one ever called me a dirty player again, but from then on Vic was stuck with the tag "mama's boy."

Pierce's coaches were so mad that they told their players to just go on home. Coach Gilbert heard them say to forget about ice cream, and so when he gathered our team he said, "Guys, this wasn't much of a victory, and I'm sorry that Vic got hurt. But, if they can't be good sports, then we'll take the victory. We're not going to Dairy Queen, though."

"We're not! Why?"

"We have Pierce's Creamery all to ourselves! Let's go try it out!"

We cheered and ran to get in Coach Gilbert's pickup. On the way, Adam Choate crossed our path and bumped up against me. He said, "Y'all are cheaters, and cheaters get theirs!"

"No, Adam," I said, running on. "We're good sports and good sports get Pierce's Ice Cream!"

the ALL-STAR ROSTER

THE WEEK BEFORE THE ALL-STARS SELECTION, we had a camp-out at Jay Bob's. We had macaroni and cheese with wieners in it, fried okra, lemonade, and watermelon for dessert. I liked watermelon, but I didn't think it should take the place of pie, cake, cookies, pudding, or ice cream. Watermelon, like cantaloupe, should be served along with the main meal, not for dessert. I was going to write Emily Post and share this point of etiquette with her.

After supper Mr. Jones let us shoot his new crossbow. He liked things called "nacronisms"—suits of armor, shields, maces, swords, etc.—the sorts of things found in museums. His crossbow wasn't old enough to be a nacronism, but was like one. He had bought it at the Army-Navy Surplus Store.

Mr. Jones had to help us pull the bowstring back to the cocked position. It was harder than any of us could pull by ourselves, and it was powerful! The first time he shot an arrow, it went through the straw bull's-eye target and stuck in the wood fence. He had to move some bales of hay to behind the target so the arrows would lodge in them. Even at that, it took us awhile to dig them out.

As it started getting dark, we set up our cots beneath the pecan tree. Mrs. Jones came out with Fudgesicles and then went back in the kitchen. I was thankful for some real dessert. As we sat on our cots eating ice cream, Jay Bob told us how mad his mom had gotten at him that morning. He forgot to put the toilet seat down, and in her hurry she didn't notice. She fell in. We laughed. It had happened with Curty and me too. Moms had a hard time holding it. They were sometimes in such a hurry that they didn't look.

"Or you know what's weird about moms?" Jay Bob said. "It's how they all of a sudden start crying for no reason. The other night at the supper table Dad says, 'This is really good meatloaf.' Mom gets up from the table crying her eyes out, goes to her bedroom and locks the door. He said it was good, but we don't see her for an hour."

"The same thing happened at my house a couple of weeks ago," said Curty. "Dad and Darrell and I were watching TV. Mom comes in and says, 'Why don't we turn that thing off and have a family conversation?'

"Dad says, 'Can't. Cost too much. Gotta get our money's worth.' Mom goes off crying to the bedroom and slams the door."

Curty then tried to imagine the situation at Sherry Watson's house. He guessed her mom never fell in the toilet because there were no men or boys at her house. And if there were no men or boys, did her mom ever run to the bedroom crying? Who knew? Life was more than a magazine. It was a mystery.

"What are you doing for cokes and candy now that school's out and you can't meet Sherry at the store?" Curty asked.

"No problem. When Mom's at work, I ride my bike over to her house or meet her somewhere." I didn't tell them about the money I was making at the Oldfields'.

"Like where?"

"Like Saturday afternoon I told Mom we had baseball practice, but we really didn't. She went to Uncle Charlie's house until late. That gave Sherry and me time to go to the movies."

"And did you kiss?" Jay Bob asked.

"I don't remember."

"Sure you remember!" Curty said. "Tell us!"

"All I remember was eating Milk Duds and drinking an orange drink. Why are you so interested in kissing?"

"Because it sounds like fun."

"It is fun, but not that much. After a couple of kisses it gets boring."

"Boring? How could it be boring?" Curty said.

"I can't believe how much money she's spent on you," Jay Bob said.

"So, she's spent some money. She's Episcopalian. She can afford it. Besides, I'm wearing out my bicycle going to see her. It's about to fall apart. Who's going to pay to fix it?"

"I'll work on it for you," said Jay Bob. "But they don't make 'em like they used to. My dad was telling me about this new stuff called 'planned adolescence.' It means that people who make bikes nowadays make 'em to fall apart on us kids by the time we're teenagers. That way we'll have to buy at least one more before we're old enough to buy a car."

What a dumb idea. Mom and I figured that I'd ride my bike through junior high, just raising the seat as I grew. "If I have to buy another one, I'm not buying a J.C. Higgins. I'll buy a secondhand Schwinn."

"I'll sell you mine if I get a new one for my birthday," said Curty.

"Deal! Are you really getting a new bike?"

"No. I just made it up."

"Who do you think will make the All-Stars next week?" Jay Bob asked.

We analyzed the possibilities for a long time. We were in agreement about Tommy Jordan, Ferrell Dunham, Jimmy Valdez, and

Dick Storey. After that we were unsure, although Curty and Jay
Bob thought I had a chance. Curty and Jay Bob didn't think they
would make it, and they weren't interested anyway. They were
homebodies. They didn't want to go on the road to play games,
although Jay Bob would consider going to Akron for the Soap Box
Derby Championship if he won locally and his parents went with
him. Myself, I looked forward to staying in a motel with a closet
and a TV and maybe even a swimming pool.

After we went to bed and I said my prayers, I lay awake for a
long time thinking about my broken New Year's resolutions. Given
how I'd given up on the city spelling bee and helping Mom, my
only hope left for being a champion was to make the All-Stars.

· · · · · · ·

It was three thirty, time to go see if I had made the team. I checked
the crease in my cap using the medicine chest mirror. Then I hustled out the back door and hopped on my bike. *I was off to read the
roster, the wonderful roster of Ros.*

I hadn't told Curty or Jay Bob that I was going to the ballpark. If
I didn't make the All-Stars, I'd be embarrassed for them to know I
had checked the roster. Still, I felt that I had a good shot. Even they
thought so. I'd probably be one of the last ones chosen because I
had one more year of eligibility. There were some really good
twelve-year-olds who were playing their last year, but none played
second base.

Jay Bob, Curty, and I lived about as far away as players could
from the Lions Hondo "all dirt and chuckhole park," as the sports-
writer for the *Roswell Daily Record* called it, almost thirty minutes
by bike. A few blocks north of Curty's house and you were in
Roswell's other Little League district, the Optimists, or Opossum-
ists as we called them. They swung at fast balls like they were
playing possum, with their eyes closed.

As I turned south on Union Street, I stood on the pedals and pumped hard to build up speed. The Darbys' brown chow was less than a block ahead. It had caught me daydreaming a couple of weeks earlier and nipped me on the left ankle as I was going to Sherry's house. The dumb dog broke the skin, but I didn't tell Mom. She'd go into her rabies panic, and I'd rather risk foaming at the mouth than have shots in my stomach. There was no way the Darbys' chow had rabies. It was just mean.

My J.C. Higgins was red and had had silver fenders and a white carrier rack on the back. It also had come with black-and-white exhaust pipes painted on the fuselage, a headlight on the front fender, and whitewall tires. But I had taken off the fenders, carrier rack, and fuselage after I kicked the chuke in the teeth. I didn't think that he or his gang got a good enough look at my face to recognize me again, but they might be on the lookout for my bike, which now looked like a naked nudist compared to before.

The exhaust pipes painted on the fuselage were J.C. Higgins' attempt to imply speed, but anyone who owned a Higgins knew what it really meant: "You will exhaust yourself trying to keep up with your friends on Schwinns." Riding a J.C. Higgins always felt like the back fender was mashed in and rubbing against the tire, even if you had taken the back fender off.

It was hot, one hundred three according to the radio, when I left home. The disc jockey had just played one of my favorite songs, "The Ballad of Davy Crockett," but for some reason it hadn't stayed in my head. I was singing "See You Later, Alligator" under my breath when I came to the Darbys' chow. I pedaled as hard as I could, but there was no need. The dumb dog just lay in the shade of the carport panting and glaring at me. She barked half-heartedly, as if to say, "After while, crocodile."

I sincerely did not like that dog, although I loved dogs in general. I cried reading *Old Yeller* when the boy had to shoot his dog.

Having to put a dog down was so sad that I didn't even like to think about it. Still, I'd pay admission to watch Barbara Darby shoot her brown chow. Or maybe just wing him in a paw so he couldn't chase me.

Who I disliked, detested, and despised were the two high school creeps who lived a block south of the Darbys. Their names were Sam and Bobby Brown. Whenever they saw me go by, they'd jump in their pickup and run me off the road. Most often I would make it to the other side of McGaffey Street before they caught up with me. Union Street had no curb by then, and they'd run me into the bar ditch, where I got goatheads in my tires, and sometimes in my pants leg if I fell off. But they weren't around. I hoped Greg was hustling them down at the Eight Ball.

By the time I got to the ballpark, a crowd had gathered. There was considerable interest in who made the team. I dropped my bike about thirty yards from the backstop where the list was posted and walked toward it. Adam Choate emerged from a group of roster readers and ran to me. "Hey, kid! You made the team! I saw your name on the list!"

I didn't say anything. I continued walking toward the backstop. I didn't want him turning attention my way. My story was that I was just in the neighborhood and decided to see if any of my friends had made the team.

But Adam wouldn't go away. He was walking behind me, talking in my left ear. "Congratulations, kid! You're an All-Star!" I tried to pay him no attention, but I was getting excited.

A place opened up in the crowd around the backstop. I made my way in and stood directly in front of the list. It was handwritten, and whoever wrote it misspelled Ferrell Dunham and Jimmy Valdez's names—only one *l* and an *s* instead of a *z*. But where was my name? It wasn't there! What had happened to it? Adam said he saw it.

I felt a slap on my left shoulder. "Faked you out, hotshot! You ain't good enough to be diddly-squat, much less an All-Star!"

Adam laughed and mocked me as I moved away from the backstop. People were watching, and I could feel my temper getting out of hand when I noticed a pair of track shoes, shoelaces tied together, slung across a high school kid's shoulder. He must have been practicing wind sprints. I pulled them off his shoulder, a shoe in each hand, and swung the one in my right hand into Adam's face as hard as I could.

Blood gushed out of a cleat hole in his face, as well as streamed out a couple more onto his chin and white T-shirt. His face turned from amusement to a horror show. He raised his left hand to wipe his face, but only made a big smear. The one gusher showed no sign of letting up. The blood running off his chin was turning his T-shirt red.

I stood motionless, stunned by the enormity of what I had done. Soon enough I regained my senses, dropped the track shoes, raced to my bike, and headed home as fast as I could pedal. No one stopped me. It seemed like people were yelling at me, but I couldn't make out what they were saying.

After a while I started crying. Not only had I not made the team, but I had committed a crime. Or was hitting a liar with a track shoe the same as stabbing him with a knife? I didn't know, but the track cleats had cut him up pretty good. Cleats were pointy steel. Knives were pointy steel. What if the police were already looking for me? I turned and pedaled down Washington Street, which wasn't as busy as Union. I didn't want to be any more visible than I had to be.

I stopped along the curb to blow my nose, and when I did I came to an unexpected change of attitude. It was like my give-a-hooter suddenly broke. I asked myself why was I crying? Why did I care? Let them send me to Springer. I wasn't a champion. I wasn't an All-

Star. I wasn't diddly-squat. Nothing in my life was like I had hoped. I was a loser.

Mom wasn't home when I got there. I went into my room and pulled out the drawers containing my clothes from under the bed. Then I went and got my suitcase from under Mom's bed. I packed clothes in the suitcase, and then sat down in the living room to wait for the police. I turned on the radio to see if there was an all-points bulletin, but there was only the new song, "The Great Pretender," by The Platters. It was appropriate for a pretend champion like me.

Mom came home within a few minutes. "What on earth are you doing with your suitcase out?"

I told her what had happened.

"You hit a boy in the face with a track shoe! You mean one of those shoes that has the sharp, pointy metal things on the bottom?"

"He deserved it. He made fun of me."

"I don't care if he did! You could have put his eye out!"

"Now I'm going to have to go to Springer. That's why I packed my bag."

A look of panic came to Mom's face. "Who said you're going to have to go to Springer? You have to go to Springer for this?"

"No one said it, but I will. It's like stabbing a person with a knife."

"I'm calling Officer Brothers." Within a minute she had him on the line. Officer Brothers was disappointed in me for doing such a thing. Mom made sure I knew that part. What she didn't tell me was that he was also greatly amused. Adam had been in trouble with the law for several years. He was a bully. He had beaten up several smaller kids really bad, and the Roswell police were just hoping that someday he would pick on someone tougher than he was. They couldn't wait for some football player to knock his block off.

Officer Brothers had never heard of a person being hit in the face with a track shoe, but he didn't think anything would come of it unless Adam's parents filed charges, which he couldn't imagine they would. They would gladly disown Adam if they could get away with it.

Mom thanked him and hung up. "Maybe, just maybe, you won't have to go to Springer. Maybe, just maybe, God does take care of his idiots!"

The phone rang. It was Officer Brothers again. He had forgotten to tell Mom that I needed to lie low because Adam would come after me. He was so much bigger and older that he could hurt me bad. Officer Brothers was so worried about me that he was going to include our house on his nightly patrols.

Mom told me what he said. "How could you do this? Now he's mad and wants to get back at you!"

"Let him come. I'll kill him if I have to."

"Joe Don, shut your mouth!" Mom was beside herself. "Don't you dare talk about killing another human being!"

"But I will. I have the right to defend myself. Granddaddy Miller said so."

"No he didn't! Whatever he said, killing another person isn't what he meant."

I didn't argue with her. It was time to be silent and unpack my suitcase. A few minutes later Mom called Mrs. Jones and asked if I could camp out with Jay Bob. I had gotten in some trouble, and she didn't want me at the house should it come home to roost. The next morning she was going to put me on a bus to Muleshoe, where I'd chop cotton for a week on Grandpa Snider's farm. Hopefully, it would all blow over.

A campout was fine with Mrs. Jones. She didn't tell Mom, but she already knew what I had done. Unbeknownst to me, Jay Bob, Curty, and Mr. McDonald had been there when I hit Adam.

Mrs. Jones gave the three of us hamburgers, cantaloupe, Moon-Pies, and grape Nehis for supper. We ate outside by ourselves on the picnic table while Mr. and Mrs. Jones ate at the dining room table. Gerald wasn't at home.

Afterwards, we shot BB guns at tin cans set up on a sawhorse in front of the archery target. All Jay Bob and Curty wanted to do was talk about Adam Choate, and so we did. Army cots had been set up beneath the pecan tree before I got there. Mrs. Jones had done it for us. After dark, she brought us out some grape Popsicles, which we munched as we sat on our cots.

"When we go to junior high year after next, I want you to ride bikes with me every day," said Curty. "I bet if you hit a chuke in the face with a track shoe, they'd leave us alone."

Jay Bob had a joke, "Knock, knock."

"Who's there?"

"Rita Buck"

"Rita Buck who?"

"Rita Buck this summer, and the teacher will give you a prize when school starts." We laughed.

"How many library books have you read this summer, Joe Don?" At the beginning of the new school year, each teacher gave an award to the kid in her class who read the most library books over the summer. You had to be honest about it because there was no way of proving it other than your word.

"Forty-seven so far. I wanted to read a hundred, but I'm not going to make it. Whenever I go to the Carnegie library, your dad loads me up with books that take too long to read."

"Still," said Curty, "you'll win the prize when school starts. I've only read ten, and Jay Bob hasn't read any."

"But you're writing a book. How's it coming?"

"Pretty good . . . No, pretty slow. That's why I haven't read that many books. I spend all my time trying to get my story right. If I had finished as many pages as I've thrown away, I'd have the biggest book ever written."

"What's it about?"

"About the Martians, how when they burrowed down into the ground one time they went too far and found a lost world that used to be connected to the Bottomless Lakes. All the dinosaurs and cavemen from the lost world come up out of the opening at the old gravel pit and attack Roswell."

"Sounds neat."

"Thanks, but it's hard work. It's taking me longer than I thought, so I haven't had much time to read."

"I don't think I'll win," I said. "You know who reads more than I do? Alea. She reads all day and then stays up late at night reading. I bet she gets the award."

"I've got a joke," said Curty. "Every time I ask you a question, you answer 'Inspector.'"

"Okay."

"What do you call the guy who gives orders to the sergeant?"

"Inspector."

"What do you call the lady who checks your underwear at the factory."

"Inspector."

"What would you do if you saw Marilyn Monroe in a bathtub?"

"Inspector." We laughed and laughed.

"I still can't believe you hit that creep in the face with a track shoe," Curty said, not being able to leave it alone for long.

Curty and Jay Bob hadn't planned on going to the ballpark, but at the last minute Curty's dad decided to drive out with one of his suppliers who was also a coach. Jay Bob and Curty went with them.

Neither acted like there was anything weird about my being there. I guessed I didn't have to be embarrassed. They themselves had looked for my name on the roster.

"POW! Take that, you jerk! And did you see the gusher? Blood spurtin out like you were drillin' oil wells on his face."

"Yeah," said Jay Bob. "I wonder why that one squirted and the other holes didn't. They just ran down his face. His chin was like Niagara Falls cascading blood all over his T-shirt. How many spikes did you hit him with?"

"I don't know. How many are on a track shoe? Four? Five?"

"Adam is going to try to catch you and beat you up," said Jay Bob. "And you can't defend yourself. He's sixteen years old and too big. He's beat up a lot of high school kids."

"But you could order the Charles Atlas course!" said Curty. "Maybe you could build muscles and kick sand in Adam's face. Oh man, that would be neat! You being strong enough to kick sand in the same face you hit with a track shoe!"

"I don't think the Charles Atlas course works," said Jay Bob. "Besides, it takes more time than Joe Don has. He needs to hide out."

Curty said to me, "I made sure that my brother Darrell doesn't slip and tell Adam you're here tonight if he sees him dragging Main Street."

"Maybe he's in the hospital," said Jay Bob. "Maybe they had to stitch him up and hold him overnight. Who knows?"

My stomach hurt at the thought of Adam trying to catch me. "My hoodlum cousin Greg came by late this afternoon and gave me a switchblade."

"Naw!" Curty said. "Gave it to you or loaned it to you?"

"He said it was mine. Said he'd been meaning to take care of Adam Choate for a long time, just never got around to it."

Although I had never known Greg to get in a fight, he did own every weapon known to the modern hoodlum. He didn't give me his big switchblade because I couldn't conceal it in my jeans' pocket. He gave me his smaller, thin, black-and-silver switchblade. It would still do the job, and I could keep it in my pocket without anyone knowing.

"So where is it?" asked Jay Bob.

I pulled it out and popped open the blade.

"Let me see it. That's a mean weapon!" Jay Bob and Curty played with it for a long time and then returned it to me. Jay Bob was most interested. The Army-Navy Surplus didn't sell switch-blades.

"You're going to have girls crawling all over you after this," said Jay Bob. "Gerald says girls like guys who get in trouble."

"Yeah? Why's that?"

"Because they want to save you. It's a religious thing. They want to save you from a life of crime and turn you into someone they'd like to marry and go to church with."

"Think Janet Mitchum will like me?"

"Who knows," Jay Bob answered. "I hear that Terry's no longer her boyfriend. But enough's enough, guys. I'm tired. Let's go to sleep and dream about smooching with Janet Mitchum or, better yet, Marilyn Monroe!"

"First let's sing the Hamm's beer jingle," said Curty. "We haven't sung it in a long time. I'll do the bear walk!"

Curty could do a hilarious impression of the Hamm's bear. Jay Bob suddenly wasn't tired. He ran into his room to get the tom-tom he had bought at Fox Cave, a curio store on the way to Ruidoso. As Curty waddled around our cots pointing his hands and swinging his rump, Jay Bob beat the tom-tom, and we all three sang:

From the land of sky blue waters (waters),
From the land of pines, lofty balsams,
Comes the beer refreshing,
Hamm's, the beer refreshing,
Hamm's.

We sang it several times before going to bed, laughing all the while. I figured I'd lie awake for a long time worrying about Adam Choate and feeling sad about not making the All-Stars, but I didn't. I had laughed so much and felt so good that I fell asleep as soon as I closed my eyes.

· · · · · · ·

Noon the next day my Cousin Jasper picked me up at the bus stop in Muleshoe. Grandpa Snider had filled him in on why I had come for a visit. Mom was afraid I was going to be hurt or get in serious trouble.

On the road to Grandpa's farm, he said, "Joe Don, you hit an older boy in the face with a track shoe?"

"Yeah, did you get this door fixed?"

"Yep, I sure did." A year earlier I had leaned back against the pickup door and fallen out. Cousin Jasper had been doing forty down the dirt road to Uncle Clifford's house. I wasn't hurt at all, but Cousin Jasper was almost scared to death. He stomped on the brakes and jumped out, figuring he was going to have to rush me to the hospital. All that happened was that I had turned a backward somersault. I was on my feet walking back to the pickup by the time he got out. He couldn't believe I wasn't hurt.

"I had to take it to the dealer in Morton, but don't change the subject. Why did you hit him?"

"He made fun of me."

"And now he's going to try and get you?"

"If I don't get him first."

Cousin Jasper grinned. "If you don't get him first? What do you mean?"

"I have a right to defend myself."

"And how are you going to do that?"

"That's for me to know, and him to find out."

"But you can tell me."

"Okay . . . Do you have my Dad's carbine? I need it."

"I have his M-1, but don't even joke about shooting somebody."

I couldn't tell Cousin Jasper about my switchblade and box cutter because he would tell Mom. He was closer in age to her than he was to me, almost thirty, even though he was her nephew. He couldn't be trusted.

"I'll tell you, Joe Don, you have Aunt Lurleen's bowels in an uproar. She told us to work the mischief out of you 'cause you're filled with devilment. You believe that? You believe you got the devil inside you?"

"No, I don't believe I got anything inside me. That's why I'm ready for lunch."

He laughed. "But you are ready to do some serious cotton chopping this afternoon?"

"I was born ready."

For the next several days I chopped cotton with Cousin Jasper and Uncle Clifford. We hoed fields on Grandpa's place and fields on Uncle Clifford's land too. Grandpa was too old to work in the fields anymore, but he would come out and take a look every now and then. Cousin Jasper didn't own any land, but he hoped to one day. Either that or he was going to quit farming and become a crop duster. He'd already taken lessons.

I stayed with Grandpa and Grandma Snider, which was great by me because no one cooked as much good food as Grandma. We had to get up early so we could be at work by daybreak. I'd normally be too sleepy at such an hour to eat gaggy eggs with Mom, but I was excited about breakfasts at Grandma's. My appetite woke up fast!

Putting my elbows on the table was a manners problem I had at home, but not on the farm. There wasn't any room for elbows. Grandma had the table covered with platters of scrambled eggs, fried eggs, ham, bacon, and patty sausage, bowls of chicken gravy and red-eye gravy, pans of biscuits, plates of toast and pancakes, cups of coffee and glasses of milk and orange juice, a tin of Log Cabin Maple Syrup and a little pitcher of Karo syrup. Grandpa always poured Karo in a saucer, chopped up fresh butter in it, and put it on his biscuits. Grandpa was funny about saucers. He drank his coffee out of a saucer too, intentionally spilling coffee over the side of his cup.

I chopped cotton every day until lunch. After we ate I'd take a long nap during the heat of the day. Grandpa loved RC Cola, and so we'd have one after I woke up. We'd play Chinese checkers until I had to leave for the fields around three thirty. I'd take a bag of homemade cookies back with me and work until supper at seven. Uncle Clifford and Cousin Jasper didn't take a nap after lunch. They worked straight through, often until dark.

The supper table was as crowded as the breakfast table: ham, roast beef, roast pork, fried chicken, mashed Irish potatoes, mashed sweet potatoes, green beans, red beans, fried okra, tomatoes, cornbread, homemade dinner rolls, Jello, cakes, pies, and puddings.

I once asked Mom why Grandma Snider's table was so different from Grandmama Miller's. Both were good cooks, but Grandmama Miller never had nearly as much food as Grandma Snider. Mom said it was because the Millers had four boys and the Sniders had two girls and a boy. However much food was set before the Miller boys, they'd eat all of it at one sitting. The Sniders had never eaten nearly that much, and so Grandma got in the habit of keeping on the table what was left from one meal to the next, always adding something fresh.

Hoeing cotton was hard. Uncle Clifford constantly pointed out weeds I had missed. And I had to pull some weeds out by hand else I'd hoe down cotton stalks. One morning while it was still cool, I stopped at the turn row to sharpen my hoe. I placed the head on the tailgate of Uncle Clifford's pickup and carefully ran a file over the bevel, which Uncle Clifford had helped me raise so it would cut better. Cousin Jasper drove up and said he could hoe cotton for an hour before he had to go change the water in another field. A few times a day he hoed with us before going off to do something else.

More than an hour later, after Cousin Jasper drove off, I came to the end of a cotton row. As I was turning the corner to go back the other way, I noticed the rattlesnake, but just barely. I could hardly see it because of the cotton leaves, and I was too late. My foot was coming down right on top of it! I panicked, attempted to fly like Superman, but couldn't! I stepped on the snake, jumped back up in the air with both knees pulled up to my chest, and hit the ground running! It was the most entertaining thing Uncle Clifford had seen in a long while. He laughed and laughed from a few feet away as he hoed another row.

It turned out that my attempted Superman takeoff was not needed. The snake was dead. Uncle Clifford told me that Cousin Jasper had killed it elsewhere. He coiled it up at the end of the row knowing that I couldn't see it until I stepped on it. And it wasn't a rattlesnake. It was a hognose snake, which looked like a rattler but wasn't poisonous.

That afternoon Uncle Clifford told Grandpa what happened, and at the supper table Grandpa Snider teased me. Cousin Jasper's prank had made his day, but I soon gave Grandpa an even better story.

At midnight Grandpa and Grandma were awakened by a scream and a few cusswords coming from the field just north of their bedroom. I didn't have the pleasure because I was sound asleep. After Cousin Jasper came back to hoe with us that afternoon, when no one was looking, I had wrapped the snake around the flashlight inside the glove box in his pickup. He wouldn't need the flashlight until midnight when he left his house to go change irrigation pipe. As I had hoped, he reached across the dark pickup cab, opened the glove box, and grabbed the snake.

The next morning Cousin Jasper was so mad that he drove up to Grandpa's house while we were still eating breakfast. "I'm going to kill him! Where is he?" he shouted as he walked up the walk. He came in the kitchen and told Grandpa and Grandma what I'd done with the snake.

I ran and hid in Grandpa's closet when I heard him coming. I was scared as I listened to him rant and rave and say he was going to kill me. I wasn't sure Grandpa could keep Cousin Jasper away from me.

Then the door to the closet opened, and he was standing in front of me. "Joe Don, you been listening?"

"Yeah," I said, afraid he was going to hit me.

"How do I sound?"

"Mad."

"No, I sound stupid. To say you're going to kill someone is stupid. It's stupid to think about, stupider to say, and stupidest to do. So, I don't know what you have in mind about that kid in Roswell, but figure out something else. You're not stupid, are you?"

"No."

"Good, come on out and finish breakfast. Think I'll have some too. No one makes better breakfasts than Grandma, but don't you ever tell my wife I said that."

I came out. He put an arm around my shoulders and smiled. "I can't believe you put that snake in my glove box. More and more you remind me of your dad."

I stayed at Grandpa's the rest of the week. On the way to the bus depot Cousin Jasper asked me if I didn't want to stop by the fireworks stand in Muleshoe. Grandpa had paid me enough money for chopping cotton that if I loaded up on Black Cats at ten cents a pack, I could make a killing again selling them in Roswell for fifty cents. July 4th was just around the corner. But I told him no.

BOOK IV

FEELING BETTER

the LETTER

JAY BOB AND I PLAYED CATCH IN HIS BACKYARD the afternoon I got back. He told me that his mother had invited Mom over to their house the Saturday afternoon I was gone to Texas. Mrs. Jones had kicked all the men out of the house. It was just Mom and her in the living room for the longest time. They had iced tea and coffee cake. It was serious business.

"What?" I asked as I fielded his grounder.

"I think my mom has an idea how to ease what's bothering you."

"There's nothing bothering me. I'm tired of hearing about it." I threw him a pop-up.

After he caught it, he held the ball in his glove and said, "You may not think so, but I think there is. I can't remember you ever being in a fight until the last few months. You all of a sudden start making A's instead of A-pluses. You hit Adam Choate with a track shoe. And it had to be you who peed in Tommy's boot, which was sorta cool. I would have never had the guts."

"Maybe I did, and maybe I didn't. But there's nothing bothering me."

"Yes there is, and it has to do with Mr. Connell. Nobody else beat up his pets but you." He threw me a line drive.

"It's just that they deserved it for lying, that's all. Just like Adam Choate deserved it for making fun of me." I threw him a grounder.

"Another thing, you don't talk about being a champion like you used to. You're not even trying to beat Alea reading books this summer. Why not?" He threw me a grounder.

"I guess I've outgrown it. It was kid stuff." I threw him a line drive.

We played catch for a while longer and then I went home for supper.

"Joe Don," Mom said at the table, "You know my position about Mr. Connell. He did wrong. But I now realize that you never got the chance to say a proper good-bye to him, and saying good-bye is important. So I've been talking to Officer Brothers. He has permission for you to write Mr. Connell a letter if you want to. He's in the state prison, and it's not easy for a boy to send a letter to a man in his situation. But you can. Do you want to?"

I couldn't believe it. "Sure!"

"But just one, and it has to be censored."

"What does that mean?"

"It means that the prison guards in Santa Fe have to read and approve what you say before they can give it to him."

"That's okay. Can I be excused? I want to start my letter."

"You've hardly eaten anything. Don't you want to finish?"

"No. I'm done."

"Then you're excused, but first let me give you your money back." She went to the cupboard and pulled out a new cigar box. In it was the money she had been keeping for me, including what I had just given her from Grandpa's. I couldn't believe how rich I was! Five dollars and twenty cents!

"Does this mean that the punishment is over?"

"That it does. I even have us two Mr. Goodbars in the icebox for later."

"And way to go, Mom! This is a great El Roi Tan! Where did you get it?" I smelled the inside.

"I just happened to be walking by the cigar store on Richardson on my lunch hour. I don't usually go that way, but did last week. I stopped in to see if they had any empties, and they did."

There was a tear in Mom's right eye.

"Mom, what's the matter?"

"Oh, nothing." Her voice sounded like she was about to cry. "I just got sentimental. That's the last cigar box I'll ever have to get you. When you go on to junior high you'll have lockers instead of cigar boxes."

I worked for the rest of the evening on my letter to Mr. Connell. Mom called out some of her ideas to me from the living room, but I didn't use them. I didn't let her read it either, even though she wanted to. I told her it was personal and, besides, the guards would make sure it was okay. She honored my wishes, and the letter came out like this:

Dear Mr. Connell,

I'm sorry you couldn't be my teacher any longer. You are the best teacher I ever had. You taught me neat things about art and Mexico. Your jokes were pretty good. Things haven't been going too good for me either. I didn't make the All-Stars. I won the Missouri Avenue spelling bee, remember? But I didn't enter the city spelling bee. I've been getting into lots of trouble and fights. I'm not sure I'm a champion. What do you think?

It's hot in Roswell. They say it's lots cooler in Santa Fe.

I hope you have plenty of paint and brushes and an easel and a TV and National Geographics.

Sincerely,
Joe Don Miller.

I sealed it in an envelope and addressed it with only his name. The next morning at breakfast Mom said she would take my letter to Officer Brothers. "And I have some other news! I've met a nice man. We went out for dinner and a movie while you were gone."

Mom went on a date while I was gone? Oh man! Was this a change for the good or a change like all the rest?

"I'm going out with him again Saturday night, so you can have a campout at Jay Bob's if you want."

"What's his name?"

"Harold Parks. He has a real estate business. He sold Mr. and Mrs. Franks a house when they moved to town. He and Mr. Franks have become friends. Harold comes around the store."

A friend of Mom's jerky boss? This did not sound good.

"I know you'll like him. What are you going to do today?"

"I'll borrow the Joneses' lawn mower and mow the weeds." We didn't have a yard, but the weeds and what few stands of Bermuda grass we did have had to be mowed or hoed.

"Do it before it gets too hot. And remember, tomorrow you go back to work at Whitman's Auto. You missed last week."

"Mom, when do you think I'll get a letter back from Mr. Connell?"

"I don't know that you will, Joe Don. But if you do, you'll only get a good-bye note in return. This is not a pen pal correspondence. This is you telling him good-bye, right?"

"Right."

After Mom left for work I went outside and crawled in my fort. I pulled up the loose floorboard and pulled out my first ammo box. Inside I put all the money Mom had returned to me. Then I reached way under the floor and pulled out my second, secret ammo box. There was about forty-five cents that Mom didn't know I had. And for when Adam Choate showed up, there were my box cutter and switchblade. I stored the switchblade at night so I wouldn't risk

Mom finding it, but I carried it with me most days. I didn't know what to do with the box cutter other than leave it there. It hadn't worked out like I thought. I couldn't carry it around in my pocket else I'd cut myself, plus it was too fat to carry without anyone seeing the lump.

I didn't dawdle in my fort. There was mowing to do.

17

COMING to the RESCUE

I NEEDED TO TALK WITH EARL, and did so at break the next morning. Then he needed me to help him move some boxes on the third floor. He said I was a lot stronger than when I first went to work at Whitman's.

I didn't feel like going on a camp-out at Jay Bob's, but I left the house before supper as though I was going to. What I'd do was fake it. I'd return home after Mom and Harold Parks left and make myself a peanut butter and jelly sandwich. I had bought two new comic books after work, and I had four library books I hadn't read. I wanted to stay home that night reading and daydreaming about getting a letter from Mr. Connell. Tomorrow, when Mom figured out that I'd come back home, I'd tell her that I just didn't feel like camping out. I didn't imagine she'd much care.

Alea Ritchy was sitting on the curb in front of her house as I turned my bike up Matthews Street to kill time until Mom left. I stopped. "What are you doing?" I asked.

"Just thinking."

"What about?"

"Lots of things. Like why didn't Terry get in trouble for saying 'flatulence'?"

"Got me."

"You know what I think? I think Mrs. Taylor doesn't know what flatulence is. I think it's interesting what teachers don't know, don't you?"

"I guess. What else are you thinking about?"

"Sixth grade parties." It was a tradition at Missouri Avenue, and one that Miss Sherelle hated, that almost monthly a sixth grader would hold a dance party at her house. It was always a girl who gave the party, never a boy. We hadn't received our invitations to the first one yet, but it was coming up soon. It would be at Barbara Darby's house. I hoped she'd tie up her brown chow.

"We're going to have to make out at those parties," Alea said, "and I'm not sure I want to."

"That's the first I've heard of it. I don't think you have to if you don't want to."

"But everyone knows about you and Sherry. It's a big thing now. It's expected. Besides, I might want to. What if everyone else is kissing but me? I'd feel weirder than I already do. How do you like kissing?"

"It's fun for a while, but if you keep doing it for a long time it gets boring."

"Then why do teenagers do it for hours every night?"

"It has something to do with gonads and hormones."

"I've heard about those, but I don't understand how they work. Do you?"

"Just that they create an attraction between boys and girls. It's like the opposite poles of a magnet."

"How about you and me kiss so I can see what it's like?"

"Right here?"

"No, silly! In my room."

I left my bike in her front yard and followed Alea to her house. This was the strangest thing she had ever said to me, but for some reason I was going along. Her parents were in the living room, both of them reading a section of the newspaper. "Mother, Father, this is Joe Don Miller."

They both put their papers aside and said hello. "He plays baseball and wants to see the bat in my room." They nodded us on.

Once inside, she closed and locked the door. I was impressed! Jay Bob didn't have a lock on his door. I didn't even have a door, just a curtain. A lock was neat. It opened up all sorts of possibilities. "What do you mean, a baseball bat?"

"Over there. One of my cousins from back east left it last summer."

"Wow! A Ted Williams! That's a good bat."

"He doesn't come very often. You can borrow it if you want. Now kiss me, you fool."

It was less awkward with Sherry. We just kissed and kissed and never talked about it. With Alea we had to think about what we were doing and discuss it. We had to hug and not hug, sit and stand, smack and not smack. She ran her fingers through my hair, which Sherry didn't do. Alea said it probably would have worked better if I'd had Elvis's hair.

Alea decided she liked kissing, but agreed that it would get boring after a while. "So don't you think I'd better go?" I asked. "Your parents will wonder what we're doing in here."

"Yeah, you're right. Here, don't forget the bat."

I went to get the bat and looked around her room. She had a whole wall that was a bookcase. I had never seen so many books in a house. "You read a lot, don't you?"

"Yeah, I don't have much of a life."

It was dark when I left Alea's. I pedaled the two blocks back to my house. No lights were on. I knew that Mom had left for her date. I read comic books awhile, and then went outside to practice swinging Alea's bat. I daydreamed about getting a letter from Mr.

Connell, and then lay down on Mom's bed to read *The Knute Rockne Story* by the lamp on her nightstand. I was going to get up and go to bed in the fort, but I was so tired I just turned off the lamp and fell asleep.

I was awakened by voices arguing, male and female. It seemed that for the longest I couldn't figure out who they were or where they were or where I was. One voice said, "I'm not that kind of woman! Leave, please!" And then as I fought off my sleepy-headed fog, I recognized it as Mom's voice. She was saying, "Get off me! Stop it!"

I got out of Mom's bed and walked to the doorway. I looked in the living room. A man was lying on top of Mom on the couch. He had both her hands trapped above her head with his right hand, and was trying to pull off her blouse with his left. "Come on, Lurleen, don't be this way!" he said.

Mom asked him again to stop, but he wouldn't. I tried to figure out what I could do to help. Then I remembered the baseball bat! It was on Mom's bed. I got it and hustled in to the living room. By that time I was wide awake.

"Leave my mom alone!" I said, threatening Mr. Harold Parks with the bat. "Get off her!"

"Joe Don?" Mom gasped, her hands still pinned by Mr. Parks's hand. She was surprised that I was there.

"Kid, get back in bed before I take a belt to you! Get out to that fort where you sleep right now. Your ma and I are busy." The man glared at me hard and pointed at me with his left hand, keeping Mom's hands pinned.

What to do? I had asked him nicely. I had no choice but to hit him in the ribs as hard as I could, connecting directly with the backside of his left rib cage. He made an "umph" sound and fell on the living room floor.

Mom got up, buttoning her blouse. I could tell by the frightened look in her eyes that she was confused as to what to do next, but by the time she stood up and straightened her skirt she had decided. "I'll phone the police! You guard him! Knock him out if you have to, but don't let him get up and hurt us!"

Strange-sounding words, given my recent history with Mom, but a good idea. Mr. Harold Parks had turned so he was lying on his good side. His eyes would open and shut as he grimaced in pain. He sounded like he was having trouble breathing. I wasn't going to hit him in the ribs again. That might kill him. I'd hit him in the shin if he tried to get up. If a line drive could keep Vic down for such a long time, a bat to the shin would keep Mr. Harold Parks down too.

I didn't have to hit him again. He stayed on the floor until the police arrived, although he had started saying that he was going to teach me a lesson. The policemen asked Mom what happened. She made me go outside while she told them. When the police were ready to leave, she called me back in. The cops helped Mr. Harold Parks up and were going to take him to the hospital. Mom made sure that one of them drove his car so he wouldn't have to come back to get it.

My stomach hurt. I was in serious trouble, worse even than when I hit Adam. Still, the cops didn't arrest me, and Mom didn't seem mad at me. I was confused. After the police left, she made us a cup of cocoa. While she was stirring the chocolate on the stove, I sat at the table. I was a three-time loser, and that didn't even count the fistfights I'd been in. I had kicked out a chuke's front teeth. I had hit Adam Choate with a track shoe. And now I had hit a grown-up with a baseball bat.

I figured it didn't matter that he was bothering Mom. A man had been arrested a week earlier for hitting his neighbor in the neck with a baseball bat during an argument. I had read about it in the *Roswell Daily Record*. He was in jail, and the neighbor was in the hospital. I didn't understand why the cops hadn't arrested me and taken me in. I was going to Springer for sure.

Mom was shaking when she handed me a cup of cocoa. She returned to the stove, got hers, and sat down at her place. She didn't look at me, just studied her cup. She was thinking hard.

"Mom, will I have to go to Springer now?"

She looked surprised. She reached over and patted my arm. "No, Joe Don, thank God you were here."

"Why not? Wasn't what I did assault and battery?"

"No. It was self-defense. You were protecting me. If there's anyone who ought to go to prison, it's Harold Parks."

"So I don't need to worry?"

"No. Drink your cocoa and go to bed. I'm going to stay up awhile. I'm too wound up to sleep."

It didn't take me long to finish. I got up to go out to my fort, but before I went I gave Mom a hug. She held onto me real tight and for a long time.

· · · · · · ·

Mom was worried. She worried all day Sunday about what would become of Saturday night. She found out first thing Monday morning. She got fired.

Mom was low and wanted to be by herself, so Monday afternoon I went to Jay Bob's to see if we could camp out. Mrs. Jones answered the doorbell and asked me what was going on. I told her something rotten. Mom had lost her job. "Good Lord!" she said. She put Mr. Jones in charge of the supper she had planned, got in the car, and drove over to be with Mom.

Jay Bob and I set up cots under the pecan tree and sat down to talk. Curty wouldn't be there. He was helping his dad clean Jake's Grill until late that evening. "What happened?" Jay Bob asked.

I told him how Saturday night Mr. Howard Parks was on top of Mom, and how I hit him with Alea's bat.

"You hit a man in the ribs with a baseball bat! Wait till Curty hears this! He won't believe it!"

"But I had to. He was hurting Mom. And when the police got there, they didn't even lecture me. It was like I did something right."

"Is he going to try and get you like Adam Choate is?"

"I think he already did."

"What do you mean?" Jay Bob asked.

"He got Mom fired," I said.

"Man, that's no fair! What's your mom going to do for money?"

"I don't know. She's been crying ever since she came home."

"Was she mad at you for hitting him with the bat?"

"No, she was glad I was there. I kept her from getting hurt."

"I can't believe no one's mad at you except the guy you hit," Jay Bob said.

"I know. It's weird. I just hope we don't have to move back to the farm and live with my grandparents. But if Mom can't find another sales clerk job, then we can't afford to live here."

"You mean not live in Roswell? Man, no way can that happen!"

Jay Bob didn't like the thought of Mom and me having to move to Texas. He started thinking of other places in Roswell where she might get a job. Then he started thinking of ways I could make money in addition to working at Whitman's Auto—mowing yards, taking a paper route, shoveling snow off people's walks.

I told him about the Oldfields. He thought that was a good deal. But then I got sad thinking how I had passed up the chance to make money selling firecrackers July 4th. Why hadn't I loaded up with Black Cats in Muleshoe?

When Mom came home and told me she had been fired, I told her she could have all my money. She smiled and said no, we'd be all right. But it seemed to me that unless she found a job soon, we were going to get behind on our bills.

Jay Bob had an idea. How about we rob an armored car? We could pull it off for sure. Number one, he had a criminal mind. When he grew up he'd devote his mind to being a great detective, but right now he just might be able to keep Mom and me in Roswell. And number two, given that I had hit Mr. Harold Parks with a baseball bat, I had the experience needed to make his plan work.

We'd be there just as an armored car picked up the cash from some big store in Roswell and was about to pull away. Curty would crash a bike that we had stolen a few minutes earlier into the front of the armored car and pretend he was badly hurt. This would be in an alley, so there would be no people around.

The driver would get out and see about Curty's wounds, and as he did Jay Bob would reach in and swipe the keys so no one could drive the armored car away. But the keys wouldn't open the back door to where the money was kept. To get the guard inside the armored car to open up, Jay Bob would toss smoke balls into the ventilation duct on top of the car. The guard would have to open the back door and jump out to get a breath of air. When he did I would hit him in the stomach with a baseball bat, knocking the air out of him.

While he was on the ground and I was guarding him with the bat—another part of the job for which I was now qualified—Joe Don would put on the World War II gas mask that he had bought at the Army-Navy Surplus Store, enter the armored car, and throw out the sacks of money.

Curty would have thrown liquid cinnamon into the other

guard's eyes, and handcuffed his hands to the bicycle frame. That way he couldn't use his pistol or run after us. Curty's dad had a real pair of handcuffs. We would need them and three red wagons. We would wrap the sacks of money in tarps and pull them to the fort in my backyard in the wagons. We would hide the money under the floorboard.

It would be a long walk across town, but that was okay. A heist this size was worth the effort. People would pass us by and think we were just kids pulling stuff in wagons. We would wear masks during the robbery, except for Curty. He'd wear a fake moustache and a derby hat. That way the guards would think that they had been robbed by adults.

"Yeah, but how will we give the money to Mom?" I asked.

"Easy. We'll leave it on the front porch in a basket like they do babies. And we won't leave the exact amount as the robbery. We'll leave less. That way no one will know it came from the armored car. You can keep the rest of it in your second ammo box until your mom needs it later. And here's an idea! We'll dump the empty money sacks in Adam Choate's backyard and tip off the police. They'll think he did it!"

I liked the thought of sending Adam Choate to Springer, but didn't think Jay Bob's plan would work.

Gerald came out the back door and grinned at me. He was on his way to his summer job working nights at a warehouse. "Ah so, how's Track Shoe Boy? Drilled any pimple holes lately?"

I didn't know what to say, and so I didn't.

"I hate to tell you this, but Adam's looking for you."

"Just let him come!" said Jay Bob. "Joe Don has a mean little surprise waiting for him," referring to my switchblade.

"He'd better have a big surprise, Number Two Son. Adam is mean and mad."

"What did I do to his face?" I asked.

"Not much really. I hear he wore a couple of Band-Aids for a few days. Some people say he had stitches, others say he didn't. But I saw him the other night, and he was his same old pimply self. I think what you did sounds a lot worse than it really was.

"But it sounds impressive," he continued. "Given how many people can't stand Adam, you're the toast of Roswell High School. Guys want to shake your hand, and girls want to give you their loving."

"See, I told you!" said Jay Bob. "Girls with curves! What you did makes girls go wild! They're out to save you. You're going to have to beat them off with a . . . baseball bat!"

"That's a fact," said Gerald. "You guys have good evening. I'm off to work. Confucius say, 'How can you tell a happy motorcyclist?'"

He waited for us to answer. We didn't have any idea.

"By the bug stains on his teeth."

We laughed. For a teenager, that one was pretty good. I'd have to tell my Sunday school teacher. Mr. Haynes didn't have a windshield on his motorcycle.

We watched Gerald get in his old heap and drive away. After he had gone, Jay Bob said, "Guess who likes you now? Janet Mitchum."

"You lie like a rug! Who said?"

"She came by here the other day when Curty and I were riding scooters on the sidewalk. She asked where you were."

"That doesn't mean she likes me," I said.

"I know, but she heard about you hitting Adam. And what I heard is true! Terry hasn't been her boyfriend for weeks. She doesn't like him anymore."

"What did you tell her?"

"I told her you were at your grandparents' in Texas. She said to let her know when you got back."

"Why didn't you tell me before now?"

"I forgot."

"You forgot the most important thing to happen to me this whole year!"

"How was I to know it's important? All we talk about is you and Sherry. We don't talk that much about you and Janet."

"Why would she want to know I'm back?" I asked.

"She didn't say, but I think she wants some kissing lessons."

"Sure she does. I wish she wasn't moving. Hey, guess who likes you."

"Who?" Jay Bob asked.

"Alea Ritchy."

"Big deal, Lucille. She's weird."

"I don't think so. I think she's the coolest girl in school, and I think she's pretty. I bet if you dance with her and treat her nice at Barbara Darby's party she'll smooch with you."

"Naw! You think?"

"Bet you a dime."

"Make it a nickel. No way she'll make out with me."

"A nickel it is, but you gotta try. You can't just wait around hoping it'll happen."

"Suppertime!" Mrs. Jones hollered from the kitchen. She had just come back from visiting Mom in time for Mr. Jones to take supper out of the oven. I didn't realize it beforehand, but I had interrupted a special occasion at the Jones house. Mrs. Jones had finally given in and purchased four TV dinners at the grocery store. The family was going to eat them off TV trays that her sister had given her for a birthday present.

Gerald had heard rumors about TV dinners, and so when he saw his mom leave to go visit with my mom, he decided to leave early for his job. He'd stop and get a hamburger at Smiley's. That freed up his TV dinner for me—Salisbury steak, peas, and mashed pota-toes. It wasn't that great. Mrs. Jones didn't think so either. I could tell by the look on her face as she ate, and for sure by what she said afterwards. "Well, we tried it. If that's what convenience tastes like, we don't need it."

• • • • • • •

Mom applied for jobs all over town, but with no luck. No one was hiring. On the afternoon of the Fourth of July, we went to Uncle Charlie and Aunt Elvis's for a picnic that would last until late evening. But I had permission to leave at seven o'clock. Curty had won four passes to the new South Main Miniature Golf Course. He had invited Jay Bob and me, and also Raymond Spencer, who rarely got to go anywhere.

Curty's mom picked us up, and then dropped us off at the miniature golf course around seven thirty. She would be back after nine to pick us up. All of us except Raymond had played miniature golf before, either on the old course on the north side of town that had been closed, or on the easy course in Ruidoso. This new course was hard. It had stuff we'd never seen before—anthills, windmills, castles, and water hazards.

We only got one game and so were trying to stretch it out, which wasn't hard given the crowd. After every hole we had to wait for the families in front of us to finish up the next hole. They were terrible, but we weren't much better. We even lost balls, though through no fault of our own. We would hit them inside the wind-mill or the castle and wait for them to roll out the other side, but they would disappear. We'd have to go get another one from the guy who checked out clubs and balls.

While we were waiting to play the seventh hole, some kids saw a snake in the grass by the chain-link fence that surrounded the golf course. It had wandered in from the vacant land to the west. Kids were screaming and adults were saying to kill it with a golf club.

I walked over to get a better look. It was a small bull snake, maybe three feet long. Some kids were moving toward it like they were going to hit it with their clubs. "Leave it alone!" I yelled. "It's just a bull snake. Let it go back under the fence."

"What do you mean, leave it alone?" a man asked.

"Bull snakes kill rattlesnakes and eat rats. They don't bother people. Let me get shut of it." I moved to a position between it and the kids and then used my golf club to steer it back toward the fence. The snake wasn't too feisty. It took a while to get it turned around, but once it was headed the other direction, it quickly disappeared under the fence and into the vacant lot.

Jay Bob, Curty, and Raymond were impressed. "I can't believe you did that!" Curty said.

"Me either," added Jay Bob. "Where did you learn about snakes?"

"From Grandpa and Grandma Snider, who live on a farm. My relatives don't kill bull snakes because they're good neighbors. Didn't I tell you the story about what happened to my grandparents?"

"No."

I was sure I had, but while we waited to play the eighth hole, I told them how last summer my Grandpa Snider was sitting in his living room reading the newspaper when he heard a thumping on the screen door. Checking it out, he found a bull snake striking the wood frame, not with its fangs, but with its nose. He had heard about this sort of thing before, and so he let the snake in.

He and Grandma stood aside and watched it slither into the small back bedroom and attack a rattlesnake that was coiled under the bed I always slept on. The bull snake killed the rattler and then slithered back into the living room. Grandpa opened the front door, said, "Thank you, Mr. Bull Snake, have a good day!" and it went on its way.

The three laughed. "I bet they were glad it came inside," said Jay Bob. "Imagine a rattler in your house and you don't even know it!"

There was an anthill on the eighth hole. The four of us got close on the first putt, but we all wound up taking a six for the score. We'd either shoot too easy and the ball would roll back, or too hard and the ball would continue over the other side, sometimes jumping the concrete curb and winding up in the grass.

While we were waiting to play the tenth hole, Jay Bob brought up the Electrical Safety Poster Contest. Raymond Spencer had had the neatest poster by far, but he got in trouble. His poster showed a boy with the seat of his pants on fire. It said, "If You Sit On A Wire You Might Catch On Fire!"

The contest had been held back in the fall of our fifth grade year. Jay Bob had been excited because he was good at art. His poster showed an electrical socket with a plug in it that had five cords running off the edges of his poster. All around the edges were flames like the decals on his model hot rods. It said, "You Will Be A Gloomy Gus If You Use An Octopus."

Jay Bob had come in third. Raymond had to go to the principal's office. "What did Miss Sherelle do to you?" Jay Bob asked.

"She didn't do anything. She's always been nice to me. She just said not to do it again. I was 'to refrain from calling attention to a person's bottom.'"

"Raymond, whose homeroom are you in next year?" I asked.

"Mr. Davidson for homeroom."

"Us too!" said Jay Bob. "And we have pretty much the same

teachers we had this last year: Miss Tower, Mrs. Taylor, and Mrs. Pfleugger."

"Aren't they going to replace Mrs. Pfleugger?" I asked. "She's just a substitute."

"No, Alea says they've hired her permanent."

"I wish my cousin Freddy lived here," Curty said. "He's a year younger than we are. He'd probably be in her homeroom class. We could really have some fun if Freddy was here."

"What do you mean?"

"Freddy learned how to be a ventriloquist a couple of years ago, and he's good. He does shows for the Kiwanis Club and Rotary in Dallas, where he lives. But the neatest thing he can do is throw his voice."

"How does he do that? I'd love to be able to do that," said Raymond.

"I don't know, but he can. It is so neat. He does it when our family gets together. And last year he did it at his school. He threw his voice out in the hall. He said, 'Mrs. Simpson, would you please come out here?'"

Raymond was beside himself to find out what happened next. "Did she?"

"Two times. After the second time the kids were giggling so hard she knew something was going on. But Freddy didn't get in any trouble. The teacher was so impressed that she helped arrange a school assembly so he could do his ventriloquism."

"Man!" said Jay Bob. "If no one else but us knew about Freddy, he could sit in Mrs. Pfluegger's class and call her out in the hall all day long. That'd be neat to see!"

"Right!" We laughed and laughed.

The fifteenth hole consisted of two "pup tents," as we called them, on the long straightaway to the hole. We knew we would have to hit the ball hard to keep it from going up the sides of the "tents" and rolling back down. But none of us hit it hard enough to get it over the second tent except Raymond. Raymond was the last one to putt, and he hit a drive fifty yards in the air over the fence that surrounded the golf course. It was beautiful, just like Sam Snead!

We laughed and laughed as Raymond ran to get another ball. But as we watched him, we saw Adam Choate in the concession area! And he saw us. He was with three friends, and they all made slit-your-throat gestures toward us. They shouted, "Come on in, guys! Let's get together when you're finished!"

What to do? It didn't look like Adam and his friends were going to play miniature golf. They were just hanging around the concession area playing pinball machines. Jay Bob said that we should just sit on the bench at the fifteenth hole and let everyone behind us play through until Curty's mom got there.

Curty disagreed. He said that we should go ahead and finish, that Adam wouldn't hurt me in front of that many people.

There were far more kids than adults around. I wasn't sure that Adam would leave me alone. I didn't have my switchblade with me, and I wasn't going to turn in my club until I could run and jump in Curty's car. We decided to just sit on the bench at the fifteenth hole and let people play through.

Curty's mom was always late. If she said nine, she might not get there until ten. Curty decided to go call her on the pay phone in the concession area. While he was on the phone, Adam Choate told him how he was going to mess me up. Curty's mom and dad came fifteen minutes later. When Adam saw Curty's dad walking in, he and his friends took off.

We replayed the fifteenth hole, then the next three holes, and turned in our clubs. Mr. McDonald treated us to cokes. I got a grape

Nehi and was standing in the concession area drinking it when a high school guy came up to me. He said, "Are you the kid who hit Adam Choate with the track shoe?"

I didn't know what to say. He had just checked out a golf club and ball. What if he was one of Adam's friends and was going to hit me? Then a pretty teenage girl came up and asked him, "Is he?"

"He hasn't told me yet. Look, we're no friends of Adam Choate. He's a jerk. Did you?"

"Yeah."

"Then let me shake your hand," he said. And the girl kissed me on the forehead! She winked at me as she took his hand and walked toward the first hole.

"What'd I tell ya!" whispered Jay Bob. "Girls are going to be all over you! You're going to have to beat them off with a golf club!"

We went back to Curty's house. We shot off some fountains and glow worms and ate watermelon. Curty had thought of something that puzzled him, and so we had to talk about it. Why didn't Tarzan have a beard? He wasn't an Indian, and he didn't have a razor.

We talked about Tarzan until Jay Bob brought up another question. Why didn't Jane have hairy legs? She didn't have a razor either. We wondered what hairy legs would look like on a woman. And did Jane ever fall in the toilet when Cheetah left the lid up? We laughed and laughed about Cheetah until it was time for Raymond and me to walk our separate ways home.

· · · · · · ·

Mom and I lived where Roswell stopped on the west. There was a cornfield to the south, a cotton field to the west and north, and houses to the east. The cornfield and the cotton field belonged to a farmer named Newt Tomlinson. Developers were waiting for him to agree to sell either or both fields so a new housing development could be built. They knew what a mean miser he was.

A couple named Atkinson, who didn't have any kids, used to live in our house and farm the land to the east of it. They sold the land and bought another farm in East Grand Plains a long time ago. As soon as they did, all the houses where Jay Bob and Curty lived were built. Our house was a tiny old shack of a farmhouse that was out of place among the newer, bigger houses. The curb, the pavement, the sidewalks, and the alley all stopped before they got to our house, but not the plumbing. The Atkinsons had kept our house as a rental. Every month Mom made out her checks to Orville Atkinson. She said he was a nice man.

One Friday afternoon the three of us rode bikes to my house from Jay Bob's. We had been shooting at tin cans in his backyard, and so we were packing BB guns. Curty and Jay Bob had their own air rifles. Jay Bob let me use Gerald's because I didn't own one.

Mom was at Uncle Charlie and Aunt Elvis's house, so we were alone. It was three o'clock and we were sitting in the shade of the elm by the fort. We had three hours to play before supper time.

"How can you tell when you outgrow toys?" I asked, thinking about toy cars and trucks and Tinkertoys. I sometimes liked playing with them, but at other times thought they were for little kids.

"I don't know," Jay Bob answered. "Dad says Gerald has outgrown comic books, but he keeps on reading them. I don't think you ever outgrow yo-yos. Adults have championship yo-yo contests. Maybe you do tops. What I'd like to do is go to one of those Mayan ruins in Mexico, one that has a thousand steps leading up to the top, and send a Slinky down the steps! That'd be neat!"

"Or how can you tell when you grow into stuff?" asked Curty. "My brother Darrell used to hate spinach when he was my age. Now he loves it, developed a taste for it."

"That's scary," Jay Bob said. "I hope I never like spinach. But I would like a mustache and a jockey strap. Hey, I know something we've grown into! A BB-gun war!"

Last summer Jay Bob had proposed a BB-gun war in Newt Tomlinson's cornfield. I had refused to go along because Mom had told me a jillion times never to point a gun at another human being, even a BB gun. Curty and Jay Bob didn't think it would be any fun just the two of them, and so it was called off. But this year I was game.

The rules were that we had to wear goggles to keep from accidentally shooting an eye out, else we might get in big trouble. Curty and Jay Bob had pilot goggles from the Army-Navy Surplus Store, and so they went home to get them. I had an old pair of my Grandpa Snider's that he used for plowing on his tractor when it was windy and dusty. They came from World War I.

Once Curty and Jay Bob got back, it was every man for himself. We would enter the cornfield to the south of my house from three different points. We would try to remain hidden while at the same time locating each other and taking shots. We had to aim for the legs. Nothing above the waist, and certainly nothing in the vicinity of the family jewels. The war was on!

I entered the field from the point furthest west. Most of the cornstalks were higher than my head. I was going to run straight south as fast as I could. My strategy was to get deeper into the cornfield than Jay Bob and Curty. Then I'd work my way back, sneaking up on them from the south. Almost immediately I took off my goggles. I couldn't see anything wearing them. After I ran a long ways down a row, I turned east. Like a fullback I barreled through row after row of corn, until I worried that I was making so much noise that I could be heard. I got down on my stomach and inched along until my elbows hurt, but I learned one thing on the ground. At times I could see better from down low than I could standing up. It was a scraggly cornfield in places.

I bent low and walked a zigzag route going northeast. I couldn't see Curty or Jay Bob, but I could hear them. Jay Bob had shot Curty, and it stung more than Curty thought it would. He was mad and was chasing after Jay Bob, shooting his BB gun as fast as he could cock it.

It sounded like they were coming my way, so I lay down flat and waited. Soon enough Jay Bob came into a clearing. I could see him from his waist down. He turned around with rifle raised to see where Curty was. I had a clear shot, squeezed off a BB, and got him right in the butt! He let out a yelp and turned around to look for me. Curty saw him and got off one that Jay Bob must have felt whiz by him. He ran south as fast as he could.

Curty arrived in the same clearing. I hadn't moved from my position, and so I shot and missed his legs. Suddenly he ran in the same direction as Jay Bob. But he didn't run for long until he ran straight into Newt Tomlinson, who had been inspecting his field!

Mr. Tomlinson was hauling Jay Bob by the arm. He grabbed Curty with his other hand, and said, "You juvenile delinquents are coming with me! You're trespassing in my field!" He turned them around and walked south. "We're going to my house and call the police." Jay Bob and Curty didn't say a word. They walked alongside Mr. Tomlinson as though they were captives. Apparently they couldn't break away from his strong grip.

The reason I had had such a clear shot at both Jay Bob and Curty, which I didn't know at the time, was that they had been standing in a pathway through the corn where some rows had not been planted. This was the same pathway they were now walking with Mr. Tomlinson. I stepped into it from the corn and watched as the three walked away. I didn't know what to do other than follow them. I moved over a couple of rows so I couldn't be seen, but soon made too much noise. Mr. Tomlinson stopped and turned around. "Who's there? You'd better come out too!"

I dropped down into a prone position so he couldn't see me, and once again I had a great view. I could see him from his stomach down. His fat belly stretched his khaki sweat-stained work shirt. I had a perfect shot and hit him right by his belly button. "Oww!" he cried. Both hands moved to touch the tender spot, and when he turned loose of Jay Bob and Curty they ran north toward my house. He took a step after them, but then thought better of it. He was too fat and stove up to catch them. He turned around and walked toward his house. I figured he was going to get his pickup and drive around the field in an effort to catch us.

I got up and ran toward my house too. Curty and Jay Bob, goggles around their necks, were waiting for me in the front yard so that the house was between them and Mr. Tomlinson's line of vision. As soon as they saw that I was all right, they jumped on their bikes and headed home, Jay Bob taking Gerald's BB gun with him. I went inside the house to read a library book. Since Mr. Tomlinson hadn't seen me, I wasn't too worried. If he showed up in his old green GMC pickup, I'd just play dumb. But he never came around.

The next Monday afternoon the three of us went swimming at Cahoon Park. I had a new decent bathing suit, and so I wasn't embarrassed like the year before. We had decided before we went that we were going to become better divers. We dove off the low dive for a long time, and then moved to the high dive. Jay Bob was the only one brave enough to dive off, although Curty and I jumped several times. It was fun. I had never jumped off the high dive before, and it reminded me of one of Uncle Caleb's stories.

Uncle Caleb had been in the navy. During training he and a bunch of sailors were supposed to jump off a high dive into a swimming pool. One guy got to the end of the board, but then wouldn't jump. The instructor screamed and screamed at him, with no success. Finally the instructor said, "What if you were on a sinking ship? What would you do?"

The sailor said, "I'd let it sink ten more feet." I loved the way Uncle Caleb laughed and slapped his knee when he told that story.

We got out of the water and lay down on our towels to get some sun. Curty said, "I can't believe you shot that farmer in the stomach. What did it feel like?"

"I guess no different from when you shot at Jay Bob."

"No, it couldn't feel the same. Jay Bob's a kid. We were playing a game. That farmer's an adult. You weren't playing. It was different."

"Why? How did you feel when you shot at Jay Bob?"

"Mad, because he shot me first and it hurt."

"How did you feel when you shot Curty," I asked Jay Bob.

"Weird, even though it was the rules. How did you feel?"

"It was weird shooting you and shooting at Curty. I didn't like it. I didn't like shooting Mr. Tomlinson either, but I had to save you juvenile delinquents."

"Here's an idea," said Jay Bob. "How about we not have anymore BB-gun wars?"

"Fine with me!" said Curty. "Where did you get the idea in the first place?"

"I don't remember. What do you think, Joe Don? You want to do it again?"

"Once was enough. Let's talk about something else, like how you two hightailed it out of there. It reminded me of that joke about the two buzzards. Have you heard it?"

"No."

"Two buzzards are sitting on a cactus when they see a fighter jet streak by with flames shooting out the back. One says to the other, 'Man, that bird sure can fly fast.'

"The other buzzard says, 'You'd fly fast too if your tail was on fire.'"

We laughed and giggled and Curty jumped into the pool to cool his tail off. He did his Hamm's bear walk in the pool, got back out, and asked, "What do you think about the All-Stars?"

The Sunday paper had been full of the Carlsbad Little League Baseball Tournament. Our Lions Hondo had won all three games, which advanced them to the state tournament in Los Alamos. Curty had worked at his dad's restaurant that morning, and some of the men who came in for coffee had been there. He had stuff to tell us, mostly about how well Tommy Jordan had played.

the SOAP BOX DERBY

IT WAS TIME FOR THE ROSWELL SOAP BOX DERBY, which was held on North Hill on Main Street. Curty and I went with Jay Bob so we could root him on. The race was on a Saturday, and so I took off work.

The night before, Jay Bob finally let us see *Hardesty*. It was amazing! I had seen soap box racers before, but none that looked as sleek and fast. *Hardesty* looked like it could go a hundred miles an hour. Jay Bob was a genius!

It was painted orange with black polka dots, although Jay Bob said the orange was tawny, the same color as a cheetah. "Hardesty" was printed in black using a stencil on both sides where car doors would have been. The black matched up with Jay Bob's interest in planning daring robberies. Jay Bob was "going to come like a thief out of the night and faster than a cheetah!"

The wheels and axles he had gotten as the standard package from the B.F. Goodrich Company, but the rest he put together himself, over two hundred pounds worth. I didn't understand all that Jay Bob said about ballast and the importance of it being wider than it was tall, but it was the coolest-looking soap box racer I had ever seen. Jay Bob let Curty and me sit in it and pretend that we were in the race.

We thought about having a campout Friday night, but decided against it because Jay Bob wanted to get a good night's sleep. He slept well, but I didn't. It took me a long time to get to sleep because of how things had turned out. Jay Bob had never been that interested in being a champion. I had. I didn't make the All-Stars, but Jay Bob had a great chance of becoming the Soap Box Derby champion of Roswell, maybe even winning the All-American Soap Box Derby in Akron.

As I tossed and turned, I was tempted to hope that he would lose. That way we'd both be losers, and I wouldn't feel so bad about not being a champion. But I didn't give in to the temptation. After I thought about it awhile, I wanted him to win. It was the right thing to wish. I wanted him to win not only in Roswell, but also in Akron. Just because I wasn't a champion was no good reason to wish anything less than the best for Jay Bob. Besides, it would be fun to talk about my friend, "the winner of the 1956 All-American Soap Box Derby!"

The next morning there was a crowd gathered along North Hill. Curty and I rode in the car with Jay Bob, Gerald, and his parents. Behind us we hauled *Hardesty* on a utility trailer. Curty was more excited than anyone. He had a notepad and pencil.

Curty had never made the honor roll, but was determined to do so as a sixth grader. In less than a month and a half we would be sixth graders. One of the first assignments would be to write a theme about something that happened during summer vacation. He wanted to get an A writing about Jay Bob and the Roswell Soap Box Derby. He was taking notes like crazy.

Curty figured it would be best for us to switch positions between Jay Bob's heats. I'd be at the starting line for one heat, while Curty was at the finish line, and then vice versa. That would give him a writer's well-rounded point of view. Three soap box racers ran at a time, with the winner going on to race again. Curty felt just like I did. Jay Bob had this thing won!

He won the first heat by two lengths. I was at the starting line, and moseyed down the hill to meet Curty. We had time on our hands before Jay Bob raced again.

Almost to the bottom of the hill was a vacant lot on the east side of Main Street. Curty was talking to an Indian lady and eating something. Several other people were eating the same thing. "Joe Don, come have some of this! It's just a nickel!"

There was a large handwritten sign leaning against the tailgate of a pickup, "Navajo Fry Bread 5 Cents." The lady was frying flat round pieces of bread in a big pot of grease over a campfire. I gave her a nickel and she handed me one that was cooling on a tea towel on the tailgate. I got some honey out of a pot, spread it on the fry bread, and bit in. It was about the best thing I had ever tasted!

"They're from near Gallup," Curty said. "Here, have some more honey . . . They're related to people south of town. Her son is entered in the race. They camped out here last night."

I wanted to ask the question I always asked about people who liked to camp out. Where did they go to the bathroom? I preferred something better than early-American plumbing whenever I went camping. But I didn't ask. Outside of Jay Bob's backyard, which had access to indoor plumbing, the only place I wanted to go camping was in one of the new Holiday Inns popping up across America, one of which was being built in Roswell.

Curty bought another piece of fry bread. I walked back to the race while Curty stayed behind to talk to the lady.

Heat after heat went by. After a while, Curty came and stood by me. We couldn't go talk to Jay Bob. We'd be in the way of other racers. Finally, we saw *Hardesty* at the starting line, and I ran down to catch the finish. Jay Bob won again! The closest car was about a length behind him, with the second car a foot behind it.

Mr. Jones came walking by. He was pacing back and forth like he was expecting Mrs. Jones to have a baby. He said for us to be ready for Jay Bob's third heat. It wouldn't take as long between the second and third heats as it had between the first and second. If Jay Bob won the third heat, his fourth race would be for the championship.

Curty said, "Don't you think it's interesting that an Indian kid is in the soap box derby?" Curty looked at his notepad. "His name is Clay Begay. I thought Indians just liked to ride horses. I never thought about them being interested in soap box racers. But he must be pretty good. He won his first two races."

"You're getting to be like a reporter, Curty. Like Jimmy Olson for the *Daily Planet*. It's like you've been interviewing that Indian woman."

"No I haven't. I just think she's interesting. We never have any Navajos in Roswell, just Apaches. Everywhere her family goes they sell something. She's got turquoise jewelry and some loaves of Indian bread. Her husband helps her for a while, then watches the races. He's a really big guy. I didn't know Indians were that tall."

Jay Bob won his third race, but by just half a length. I was supposed to have been at the starting line, but that was no fun. The finish line was where the action was, and so Curty and I were both there and surprised at how little he won by. We had thought of *Hardesty* as being much faster than any of the other racers.

Before the championship heat, Mr. McDonald came walking up. He had left the cook in charge of the Grill in hopes of getting to see one of Jay Bob's races. He hadn't been able to get away earlier.

Curty dragged his dad away from the crowd and introduced him to Mrs. Begay. They chatted awhile, then both returned with a piece of fry bread, Curty's third! I was more than full after one. Where could he possibly put it!

The three finalists were Jay Bob, Leon Chapman, and Clay Begay. I walked as close to the starting line as I could get before the race so I could see what the two other racers looked like. Clay's racer looked like it should be junked. It wasn't painted. It wasn't streamlined. It looked like something the Little Rascals would use to go down a hill. Leon Chapman's racer surprised me. It looked every bit as fast as *Hardesty*.

Leon Chapman was going to be in the eighth grade come September. He was two years ahead of me in school, and the one thing I knew about him was that he had been one of Mr. Connell's best art students. I had overheard Mr. Connell say so to Miss Tower. Mr. Connell said he was the most creative kid he'd ever had in class.

It was time for the race. There were so many tall men around that Curty and I couldn't see the racers as they came down the hill. We could only see them at the finish line. Leon Chapman beat Jay Bob by a foot, and Jay Bob beat Clay Begay by an inch, or maybe they tied. It was close! Curty and I were dumbfounded. We couldn't believe Jay Bob had lost.

We ran to see Jay Bob. We figured he'd be sad, mad, and disgusted, but he wasn't. He said that *Hardesty* ran well. He had no complaints about how his racer performed. Leon Chapman's just ran better.

Jay Bob had made friends with Clay as they spent time talking between heats. I had thought Clay's racer was junky, but Jay Bob said it was a really good one. It was like the saying, "Don't judge a book by the cover." He had looked it over. Clay Begay was nobody's fool. He knew what he was doing.

Curty's dad invited us back to Jake's Grill for lunch—his treat if we ordered the special—including the Begays, with whom he wanted to talk business. I was glad to be able to eat at Jake's, but not as happy as Jay Bob was to have the chance to talk more with Clay. The two of them were like long-lost friends. Neither did much more than pick at their food. They were too busy talking about how to improve their racers for next year.

Curty's dad wanted the Begays to come back to town during the fall and have a "Fry Bread Day" at Jake's. They agreed. Mr. McDonald said that he'd hire us three boys—actually four, counting Clay—to hand out flyers. Fry Bread Day would coincide with the beginning of the Eastern New Mexico State Fair.

Early that evening Jay Bob and I rode bikes around the neighborhood. I was still surprised at how gracious he was in defeat. He had come so close to going to Akron. I asked him why he wasn't upset. "It's like a jewel heist," he said.

"What do you mean a jewel heist?"

"I was thinking about it one time. Thieves can plan the most complicated jewel theft ever, but two things can trip them up. They can make the smallest mistake during the robbery, like dropping a tool and setting off the alarm. Or they can be up against a detective who is smarter than they are. So they get caught.

"Nothing went wrong for me today. *Hardesty* ran great. I was just up against Leon Chapman. He's two years older and so good that Craft Store displays stuff he makes. Losing to him is no disgrace."

"But did you beat Clay Begay?" I asked.

"We tied, and I was lucky to do that. I had all the tools and materials and books I needed to build *Hardesty*. I read books that you don't even know about. Clay didn't have my advantages. Given what little he had to work with, he's probably better at building a racer than Leon."

"So, you're not disappointed?"

"No. I did great!"

• • • • • • •

Sunday afternoon I went over to Jay Bob's to help him try out his new store-bought slingshot. He got it at the Army-Navy Surplus Store, and it came with ball bearings. They were more powerful than rocks. We set up some old mason jars on a sawhorse in front of his archery target. We shot at them until we lost all the ball bearings.

We were thirsty and got a drink out of the backyard hose. "The best water in the world comes out of a hose," Jay Bob said. "Lots better than out of the tap in the kitchen or in the bathroom."

I agreed. Hose water was the best.

Curty showed up just then and told us about the All-Stars. The Sunday paper was a morning paper, and the results had come in too late to make it to print. But people had phoned and told his dad all about it. Roswell had won the state tournament at Los Alamos, the last game being against Hobbs! Tommy Jordan had now hit home runs in five straight games. The district tournament was coming up the next week in Lubbock.

We celebrated by having a water fight. Jay Bob and Curty weren't strong enough to wrestle the hose away from me, and so I had a much better celebration than they did.

19

OWNING UP

FOUR WEEKS AFTER I SENT THE LETTER TO MR. CONNELL, I got a letter in return. I was sitting at the kitchen table when I read it. It was early afternoon, just after the mailman came. Mom was at the grocery store. It said,

> *Dear Joe Don,*
>
> *Thanks for your letter. You are kind to remember me.*
>
> *Of all my students you were the most interested in being a champion. Indeed, you have made a good beginning. Pursue excellence of mind and body, and one of these days you will know that you are a champion.*
>
> *Here is something we never talked about that may be helpful. When you fall down, pick yourself up and try again. Learning how to be a champion is like learning how to ride a bike. None of us get it right the first time, most not even the second.*
>
> *It is best that you do not write me again.*
>
> *Best Wishes,*
> *Mr. Pete Connell.*

My stomach started hurting. "Indeed, you have made a good beginning," he said. He was wrong. I'd made a lousy beginning.

I was crying about letting Mr. Connell down and didn't hear Mom come in until she was standing in the kitchen. She put down the sack of groceries and said, "Joe Don, what on earth is the matter?"

I wiped my eyes and said, "Nothing."

"What's that on the table?"

"It's a letter from Mr. Connell."

"Can I read it?"

"Yes ma'am."

She took the letter off the table, sat down in her chair and read it. "Why Joe Don, this is a nice letter. This is a wonderful letter! Why are you crying?"

"Because I'm a loser, not a champion."

"You're not a loser. Listen to the rest of the letter. 'When you fall down, pick yourself up and try again. Learning how to be a champion is like learning how to ride a bike. None of us get it right the first time . . . '"

"But he doesn't know how bad I've fallen down! There's no way I can pick myself up and try again."

Mom said, "Come sit down with me on the couch."

We sat down and Mom put her arm around me. "Joe Don, look, we all of us have bad days. Sometimes we have a whole bunch in a row. Sometimes they're of our own making, and sometimes not. You've just been going through a bad spell. I'm going through a bad spell. But things are going to get better. We're going to pick ourselves up and get on with the life God has given us."

"How do you know?"

"I just trust that things are going to work out, one way or another. You can still be a champion if you want to. Just get your dauber out of the dirt and try again."

"But I'm also sad because I like Mr. Connell."

"What do you mean?" Mom asked.

"I mean that if I agree that he's guilty, do I have to hate him?"

"No, you don't have to hate him."

"But everybody else does. You do."

Mom was quiet for a moment. "Joe Don, how I feel about Mr. Connell is hard to explain. I appreciate all he did for you, but I'm mad at him for what he did to those sixth grade boys. How about us agreeing that he did wrong, but we're not going to hate him?"

"I'd like that. I don't want to ever hate him."

All week long I thought about what Mom said about trying again to be a champion. In church the word "repent" was like what Mom was talking about. When you repented, you stopped backsliding and got back on the straight and narrow. But I didn't think I could repent. Adam Choate was too big a problem. He was still looking to catch me. He would hurt me bad, maybe even kill me, if I didn't do something to stop him.

The next morning I told Mom I was going to the school. She had applied for a job everywhere she could think of, but with no luck. To have some money coming in, she had taken a part-time job cleaning office buildings, and stayed at home until late afternoon when she went to work.

"What are you going to school for?" she asked.

"I've got to talk to Miss Sherelle."

"Walk by way of Curty and Jay Bob's house. Be careful. Watch out for Adam, and if you see him, you run straight in the closest house. Just open the front door and go in."

"Okay."

I had to walk because I had a flat on my bike. The school secretary wasn't there, so I walked through her office into Miss Sherelle's.

"Hello, Joe Don. Are you having a good summer?" Miss Sherelle was sitting at her desk going over school records.

"Yes ma'am."

"That's good. What can I do for you today?"

"I need to make a statement."

"A statement? A statement about what?" She stopped what she was doing and gave me her undivided attention.

"I was the one who, uh . . . urinated in Tommy's boot."

Whew! I had gotten it out. All I had to do now was take my punishment. I eyed the locked closet where kids said she kept the electric paddle, although I didn't think it really existed. I hoped it didn't. When she gave me five licks earlier, it was with a regular paddle. That hurt plenty.

"And does your mother know about this?"

"No ma'am."

"You just decided to come here after all these weeks and confess?" She acted surprised.

"Yes ma'am."

"Why?"

"Because it's the right thing to do."

"What else?"

"Because I felt bad." I could feel tears welling up.

"You felt bad? And why was that?"

"Because I told a lie." I was on the verge of crying, but pulled up short.

"Yes you did. You lied to me right out there in the hall. I remember it well . . . So, what do you think your punishment should be?"

"I don't know." I wiped my eyes.

She didn't need my help figuring it out. I had to work three hours a day until school started helping Mr. Richard Gallegos, the janitor, get the school cleaned up for the new year. And I had to go directly home and tell Mom about our conversation. I was to start helping Mr. Gallegos the next morning.

"How is your mother?"

"She's looking for a job."

"That's what I hear. Tell her to keep her chin up."

"Oh, I forgot. One other thing."

"What's that?" she asked.

"I don't want to be the newspaper editor."

Miss Sherelle looked puzzled. "You don't want to be the editor? You accepted when, last February? You spent months learning how. Miss Tower and I can't get another editor. It's too late."

"How about Curty McDonald? He'd be great! His father runs Jake's Grill, where all the reporters and politicians hang out. No one's more interested in news than he is."

"Why don't you want to be the editor?"

"I just don't. I should have never accepted."

"But you did. We have to live up to our commitments."

"But it would be good training for Curty. He doesn't have any other activities this year. He could go on and be the editor of the South Junior High newspaper, and then *The Howler* at Roswell High School. Who knows, one of these days he might win the Pulitzer Prize for being the editor of the *Roswell Daily Record!*"

She looked at me like I was full of prunes. "If Curty did become the editor, would you help him learn his job?"

I was right! Miss Sherelle was a sucker for the word "training." Her job was to prepare us for the future, and she was going to live up to her commitments. "Sure. I've got to be here three hours a day until school starts. He could come here every day and I'll show him how."

"I'll think about it. Scoot. Go on home."

I felt good walking home. It was like I hadn't been punished at all. I liked Richard Gallegos, the janitor. He was a kind man, and even Granddaddy Miller would be impressed by how hard Richard worked. It would be like working with Earl. But I didn't know how Mom was going to punish me. I figured it best to get it over right away, and so I told her what happened with Miss Sherelle as soon as

I got home. She was standing at the stove boiling eggs for tuna salad, and I was sitting at the kitchen table.

After I told her, all she did was look at me and say, "You did the right thing. I'm proud of you. Let me fix our sandwiches. Then I have something important to explain to you over lunch." She didn't mention any punishment. She was distracted.

As we ate she told me that she was out of money and could use whatever I had. People we owed were still okay with partial payment, like Mr. Orville Atkinson about the rent, but she was having trouble buying groceries. She didn't make nearly enough cleaning office buildings to pay our bills, and she could only accept so much help from Uncle Charlie. School started in Texas the same time it did in Roswell, the day after Labor Day. If she didn't have a job by Monday, August 27, Cousins Jasper and Stanley were going to come with their pickups and move us to the farm. That way I'd be there in time to start school at Bula.

I had known that we were in danger of having to move back to the farm. I just tried to pay it no mind. Mom setting a deadline made it real. I got up from the table and went to fetch my ammo box.

the PARTY

BARBARA DARBY'S PARTY WAS SATURDAY. Mom and I had a light supper—baloney sandwiches—because we assumed I'd eat a lot at the party.

Mom made sure I was scrubbed and polished and dressed in my Sunday-go-to-meeting best. I griped about wearing my sports coat and tie, but I knew all the boys would be wearing them. Mom said to take the jacket off when I got there. It was too hot to wear jackets at the party. If the other boys took off their ties after a while, I could take mine off too.

Mrs. Jones came by with Jay Bob and Curty and drove us to the Darbys' house. The place was packed. Cars were dropping off kids in front of the house, and the living room was filled with rising sixth graders from both homerooms. A sliding glass door opened to the patio and backyard from the living room. Kids were outside in the back too.

Mr. Darby met us at the front door and told us it was too hot to wear a coat. He took ours and said he would put them on the bed in the master bedroom. I liked the way that sounded, "master bedroom." When I grew up I was going to have one of those.

Mrs. Darby had the kitchen table set up with soft drinks, cupcakes, and cookies. We could help ourselves whenever we wanted, plus there were little cups of Pierce's Ice Cream in the freezing compartment of the icebox. Barbara Darby was busy collecting records from kids as they walked in and telling us to dance to the songs she was playing. I didn't know that we were supposed to bring records, and neither did Jay Bob or Curty.

This was the first time that many of us had seen each other since school let out at the end of May. Kids just stood around for the longest time, but then a few brave ones started dancing. From then on kids danced and ate and chatted. For a while I was the center of attention. Everyone knew I had hit Adam Choate with the track shoe. Guys wanted to be my buddy, and girls acted friendlier than usual, especially Jan Browning.

Roger Jamison was there. The last time I had seen him was when I belted him at Gizelle's for calling me a name. While I was having my second orange coke, he came up to me and apologized. He said again that he didn't know what the word meant. I accepted his apology and said I was sorry I hit him because we had always gotten along okay. We shook and were friends again.

Then Janet Mitchum arrived! From the time I saw her it was like she was in the spotlight and the rest of the party was around the edges in the dark. She apologized at the door to Mr. and Mrs. Darby for being late. This was her last evening in town. She had been packing with her mom and sisters and lost track of time. Then she turned from the Darbys and walked into the living room where the dancing was. She was beautiful as she said hello to this person and then to that one, finally turning to me.

"Joe Don, I like this song. Let's dance."

I couldn't believe it! She wanted to dance with me! Even though I had to go to the bathroom really bad, I held it for fear she might disappear if I walked away. I thought back to my night with Sherry at the Women's Club and assumed the position. It was a slow dance.

Janet put her right hand in my left hand, and her left arm around my shoulder. I put my right hand on her back. The song was "Wanted" by Perry Como. It wasn't one of Perry Como's best songs, but it was fitting. Being with Janet was what I wanted.

Janet was wearing a light blue dress. She had a darker blue barrette in her light brown hair, and she smelled of nice perfume "Have you enjoyed the summer?" she asked.

"Yeah."

"I was worried about you. I heard that some teenage boy was trying to hurt you."

"I think maybe he's given up."

"And then I heard how you kept that man from forcing himself on your mother."

Was that what he was trying to do? I had heard about men forcing themselves on women. "Yeah, we may have to move too. Her boss fired her."

"I hope you don't if you want to stay here. You were very brave."

Janet Mitchum thought that I was brave! I couldn't believe it! We danced two slow dances, and then she wanted something to drink. We went to the table in the kitchen, where I told her I'd be right back. I couldn't wait any longer. I had to find the bathroom.

I was afraid she wouldn't be there when I returned, that I would wake up from the best dream in my life, but she was. She had even poured me a Seven-Up. We walked out onto the patio and stayed together for the rest of the party. We talked and danced and walked around as Janet told people good-bye. And then the party was over way too soon.

Janet's mom was the first adult to come inside to pick up a kid. She told the Darbys that they were leaving early in the morning and she needed to get Janet to bed. We had no chance to say good-bye, other than Janet whispering in my ear, "I have your address. I'll write you." Then as quickly as Cinderella had left the Prince, she was gone. I stood there for a moment hoping Mom and I could stay in Roswell, if for no other reason than receiving her letter.

I got my jacket, thanked all three of the Darbys for the party, and went out in the front yard to wait with Curty and Jay Bob. Jay Bob was so excited that he was about to pop! He had made out with Alea in the backyard. And Curty was excited because he had kissed Charlene Bradley! I hadn't even thought about kissing Janet. Just being with her had been more than enough. I had been so swept away by her mere presence that I was surprised to find out I still had my tie on. The rest of the boys had taken theirs off.

"Here, I owe you this!" Jay Bob said. He handed me a folding dollar.

"I don't have change. We only bet a nickel."

"I know, but you telling me about Alea was worth a buck."

"But I can't take a whole dollar."

"Yes you can. Give it to your mom for groceries. Man, am I hungry! I spent so much time with Alea that I didn't get anything to eat except when the party started."

"Me either," said Curty. "I forgot all about food."

"Me either." All of a sudden I was starved.

Jay Bob's mom came to pick us up. At home I went to fix myself a peanut butter and jelly sandwich, only to find out that we didn't have any bread or peanut butter. I didn't say anything to Mom, who was folding clothes in her bedroom. I'd give her the dollar in the morning. I'd tell her I found it beneath the floorboard in the fort, that it must have fallen out of my ammo box.

I lay down in my fort and was really sad. My dreams had finally come true, only to disappear overnight. At seven o'clock the next morning Janet was moving to Alabama. It wasn't fair. And it wasn't fair that Mom and I should have to move to the farm. She had twenty-nine days to find a job. I said my prayers and fell asleep.

The next morning at church I found out that Roswell had won the District Little League Tournament in Lubbock by beating Albany, Texas, a team that hadn't been scored on in thirty-five innings. Roswell was on the way to regionals in San Antonio!

21

SHOWDOWN

MOM WAS STILL HAVING NO LUCK FINDING A JOB. There was nothing new in the classifieds, and none of the places where she had applied phoned back. By four o'clock Friday afternoon she had left me supper in the oven and was on her way out the door to clean office buildings. "And don't you leave the house. Hear me?"

"Yes, ma'am." Mom had worried about Adam Choate even more since he showed up at the miniature golf course. She didn't want me to leave the neighborhood during the day, and I couldn't go very far at night unless there was an adult present. Officer Brothers was still keeping an eye on our house. He doubted that Adam would try to break in at night when I was there and Mom wasn't. But if he did, I should call the police. And if there wasn't time, I should climb up in the attic.

I had never been in the attic until Uncle Charlie loaned us his stepladder. The entrance was a square piece of plywood that lifted up in the ceiling just outside Mom's room. It wasn't very roomy. If Adam broke in the house, he'd know I was in the attic because I couldn't pull the stepladder up behind me. But he couldn't get in the attic because I would sit or stand on the plywood so he couldn't lift it up. Or so we hoped. We hoped he'd get frustrated and leave for fear of being caught, but I put a supply of rocks in the attic just in case. Mom made me practice climbing up as quickly as I could. We kept the stepladder in the corner by her door.

Curty had gone fishing with his dad for the weekend, and Jay Bob and his family were on vacation. I listened to a couple of records—"Sixteen Tons" by Tennessee Ernie Ford, and a really silly song called "Santa Baby" by Eartha Kitt, who had a really neat voice. I had borrowed them from Curty.

I went outside to get the newspaper and studied the movies showing at the Chamisa. I already knew what was showing. I just wanted to check start times. Mom hadn't needed all my money. She left me a half-dollar, and it was burning a hole in my pocket. It would cost me a quarter for admission and a dime for a coke. That would still leave me fifteen cents for later. The theater owner had stopped admitting honor roll students for free in mid-July, six weeks after the end-of-May report cards.

The Chamisa was showing a double feature—*High Noon* with Gary Cooper, who I always got confused with Cary Grant, and *To Hell and Back* with Audie Murphy, my hero. These were movies I had to see! If I ate supper early and rode my bike, I could make most of the five o'clock movie and all of the seven o'clock movie. Mom got off work at nine thirty and was home within ten minutes. If I hustled, I could get home and be in bed before she arrived.

Audie Murphy was a poor farm boy from Texas who received more military awards during World War II than anyone else, thirty-three, including the Medal of Honor. He had killed about two hundred fifty German soldiers, while being wounded three times himself. He was a true hero, and was playing himself in the movie. I had never been to a movie by myself, but I had to see it. Jay Bob had helped me fix my old J.C. Higgins. It was riding better than ever.

I bought my ticket at the box office, and then handed it to the manager who was standing by the door to the theater.

"You need an adult ticket, kid," he said. "No way you're under twelve."

"I'll be twelve later this month, but I'm still eleven now."

I could tell that the manager didn't believe me and was going to give me grief, but an adult voice chimed in from behind, "He's telling you the truth. He's big for his age."

It was my Little League coach, Mr. Gilbert! He was with his wife and eight-year-old daughter, Hope. The manager let me in.

"We're going to get some pop," Mr. Gilbert said. "Let me buy you one too. What kind do you want?"

"An orange drink."

He went to the concession stand and got four drinks—two oranges and two Dr. Peppers. "Have you been following the All-Stars?" he asked, handing me my drink.

"Yes sir, I have."

"They're doing well. I still think you should have been on the team, but next year for sure. And we have a great chance next year to win the league! I'm looking forward to it."

I hadn't thought about Cathey-Jacobs coming in first, but baseball season was a long ways off. It was something to daydream about later. I didn't want to miss any more of *High Noon* than I already had, so I thanked him for the orange drink and pretended that I was meeting some kids in the balcony. He would think that I was weird if he knew I was by myself.

There weren't many people in the balcony, so I could hardly miss it when Sherry Watson came in a few minutes later with a guy in junior high, older than her by a year or maybe two. She didn't see me. She didn't see much of anything. They sat in a corner and made out the entire time. The one time she and I had come to the movies she got mad because I wouldn't kiss her all the times she wanted me to. I had wanted to watch the movie. She was a distraction.

I drank the orange drink during the first show, and then used my own money to buy a grape drink during *To Hell and Back*. By the time the double feature was over, I had to go really bad. I went to the men's room, thinking how great the second movie had been. I hadn't liked *High Noon*. It was too slow, no action until the end. But *To Hell and Back* was great! Lots of action!

As I walked out the restroom I saw Adam Choate standing at the concession stand. He was by himself, talking to the kid who had sold me the grape drink.

I slowly walked toward the outer door, hoping I could get outside without him seeing me. But the teenager working the concession stand said, "There he is!"

The concession kid must have phoned Adam and told him I was there. I ran out the door and didn't even think about getting my bike from the bike rack. There was no time. I ran south down the sidewalk, past Allensworth's, and turned right on West Second. After a block I cut catty-cornered across the parking lot, which was filled with cars. I ducked down behind them so that Adam couldn't see me. I made my way to the north edge of the parking lot. If I ran west on First Street, I could probably outrun him easy, but without my bike I'd never make it home before Mom. I decided to crouch down and cross the access road between the parking lot and Whitman's Auto. I'd hide behind the trash bin until Adam got tired of looking for me.

I hoped that the streetlights along Second Street weren't helping Adam see me as I ran toward the trash bin. It was a moonless night, and once I got there it was so dark that I could hardly see my own hand. I went around to the far north side, between the bin and the chain-link fence, and knelt down. A couple of minutes later I heard Adam's voice. He was out of shape and breathing hard. "Little moron, I know you're back there. Come on out and I'll go easy on you."

I said nothing. I hoped he was just fishing.

"Little moron, if I have to come back there I'm going to hurt you bad."

I heard him walking toward me. His footsteps sounded cautious. Maybe he couldn't see any better than I could. He was coming around the west side of the bin. I quietly moved toward the east side, hoping to sneak around the bin and escape when he was on the north side. But there was something in the way! Something that felt like a big display counter blocked my way. It filled the entire space between the bin and the outer fence. I couldn't get around it. I was trapped!

His steps came closer. I crouched down low and reached in my pants pocket. I couldn't see him, but I knew he was close. What was I going to do? Adam intended to hurt me bad, and I couldn't run away. I had a right to defend myself, but how? My mind was racing when I heard Adam let out an "uhh" and crumple to the ground beside me.

"Miller, it's me," a voice whispered. "Come on out."

"Earl?"

"Yeah."

"I can't see anything. Where are you?" A beam from his little flashlight hit the rabbit's foot in my hand and then traveled a bit to where it rested on Adam's unconscious face.

"What happened to him?"

"I just gave him a love tap. He's okay. Let's get out of here before he comes to." Earl had his '52 Buick parked on the west side of the building. We got in and drove north on Richardson Street.

Earl had been called back in to work that night to go help set up a bed frame that he had delivered earlier in the day. A family said they knew how to set it up, but when they tried they couldn't. He returned from their house to the store just before nine, expecting Mr. Rodman to still be there. But he had gone home. After Earl had hung up his clipboard inside the store, he locked up and was headed toward his car when he saw me running toward the trash bin, followed soon after by a larger, older kid.

"I take it that was Track Shoe Face?"

"Yeah, that was him. Thanks Earl. My bike is in front of the Chamisa Theater and I need to get on home."

"You can get it in a minute, but we gotta talk first." He drove real slow. "I know that you want to be a champion, but there's different kinds of champions, Miller. There's Greek heroes and there's Negra heroes, which I know about. Negra heroes like to win ball games too, but we don't always get the chance. And sometimes that's okay because there's more important things than ball games, like taking care of other people.

"I took care of you tonight, and you can't never tell no one, not even your close friends. If the law thought that a Negra man like me hit a white boy, I'd go to prison."

"I won't tell anyone, Earl. Honest."

"Good, but my point is you gotta be a champion in your heart, and not just your mind and body."

"What do you mean?"

"You gotta love people and help take care of 'em, like your mama. She lost her job. Ya'll are in a jam. If you can help her out, you got to do it. Wasn't that one of your New Year's resolutions?"

"Yeah, but I don't know what I can do to help. I'm just a kid."

"Well think about it. You're smart. I have high hopes for you, Miller. You made a good move when you came to see me the other day."

"I did?"

"Yeah, when you traded me your switchblade for my lucky rabbit's foot. That was a good move. What if you had had that switchblade in your pocket tonight instead of the rabbit's foot?

What if you'd stabbed that boy to death?"

"But what if you hadn't been there?"

"But I was. The good Lord called me in tonight to help you out. You did right, Miller. You left it to the Lord. The Bible tells us to wait for the Lord."

"I don't think I waited for the Lord, Earl. I just didn't know what else to do. I've been really worried."

"I know you've been worried, but don't say you didn't know what to do. You knew that you didn't want to stab Track Shoe Face, which the Lord took as you asking him to take care of you, which he did.

"One last thing and I gotta go. Times are changing. More and more stores are beginning to hire women salesmen. Your mama would make a dandy salesman. She was the best thing there was about Allensworth's. Everyone loved her. Tell her to apply to some of these stores to be a salesman. She'll make a lot more money too."

Earl let me off on Main Street several blocks north of the theater, far enough down the street that no one would see us together and figure out that he decked Adam Choate. The way Earl explained it, Adam would wake up and think I had knocked him out. Maybe he'd never bother me again.

I got my bike from the rack and beat Mom home by a couple of minutes, thanks to her running way late.

Sunday morning the paper was late being delivered. They had held the presses until they got the All-Stars results from San Antonio. The headline read "Roswell Wins!" Roswell won both games, against Beaumont and Houston. They were going to the World Series! I couldn't believe it. Our All-Stars, a team from the league with the worst field in America, was going to Williamsport!

22

CHAMPIONSHIP PLAY

MOST OF THE BOYS ON THE 1956 Lions Hondo Little League All-Stars had never been out of New Mexico, save to Lubbock and San Antonio, Texas. But now they were in Williamsport, Pennsylvania, with seven other teams. These were the best teams in America, including Delaware Township, New Jersey. It had been the runner-up in the World Series in 1955. Colton, California was also there. It had been the runner-up in 1954.

"ROSWELL, WHERE?" was the headline in one Pennsylvania newspaper. The people back east made fun of us, maybe because they didn't know their geography and thought New Mexico was a foreign country. Roswell was definitely a long shot. They figured we were no good.

But Roswell beat Upper Darby, Pennsylvania, in the first round. Tommy Jordan struck out thirteen batters and hit a home run. In the semifinals, Roswell put away Winchester, Massachusetts. Jordan smacked another homer. Going into the finals Roswell had won eleven playoff games in a row.

I figured that we'd listen to the championship game in Jay Bob's room, but Curty invited us to Jake's. There would be refreshments and two radios playing so we could hear better. There was a "CLOSED" sign on the door, and the shades were pulled since it was after Jake's business hours. But all Roswell businesses were closed in effect, no matter how late they stayed open. Main Street during the game was like a ghost town. Everyone was huddled around a radio.

What we kids didn't know, and what the adults didn't tell us if they knew, was that KGFL, Roswell's radio station, wasn't doing a live broadcast. KGFL couldn't afford to send anyone to Williamsport. Instead it relied on Western Union telegraph messages to recreate the game, including "bat noises" made by tapping a pencil against the microphone.

Roswell was playing Delaware Township, New Jersey, and after three innings trailed 1–0. In the fourth inning Sherrod and Storey walked. Tommy Jordan then unloaded his last home run as a Little Leaguer to put Roswell ahead, 3–1.

The last two innings we were on pins and needles hoping that Roswell could hold on. Every once in a while, some man would say something like, "Come on guys! Make us proud!"

Time passed slowly. There wasn't much action. Then the announcer said, "It's a grounder to shortstop. Jimmy Valdez picks it up and throws to first base. Out number three, and Roswell, New Mexico, is the Champion of the World!"

We cheered! People poured out of houses and businesses and filled the streets. We hugged each other and jumped up and down. I had never seen such carrying on, and it lasted into the night. We were the champions! I had played with the best!

I couldn't imagine how big a deal it was to be a champion of the world. I was proud to be from Roswell, even if my time was drawing short. Mom's August 27 deadline was less than three weeks away, and no one had even called her back for an interview.

• • • • • • •

Sunday I was sitting in the front row of the balcony during worship. If Mom didn't get a job that week, the next Sunday would be our last service at First Baptist Church. There was a difference between balcony seats and seats in the sanctuary. The main floor had pews, but the balcony had built-in chairs with wooden seats and backs. They were like the chairs at the movie theater, only the seats at the Chamisa had cushions. I liked sitting in the front row of the balcony. It made me feel like a daredevil, given that all there was between me and going over was the eight-inch retaining wall and brass rail. I liked to lean on the rail during prayers and hope it wouldn't give way, causing me to fall to my death on the floor below. It was an act of faith.

Jonathan Wilkins was sitting to my right. There were three vacant seats to my left, and then sat Tank Lowery, the giant starting tackle for the Coyote football team. He was also the state shot put champion, and dwarfed guys like Gerald, Darrell, and Adam Choate. To the other side of him was his grandmother, who always made sure he was in church. I didn't know anything about his parents. I had never seen them.

We stood to sing a hymn. Then as Rev. Harper began the prayer that followed, I heard a strange noise to my left. I opened my eyes and saw that Tank was hanging over the brass rail from his waist, the heel of the shoe closest to me was hung up on the armrest of his seat, but not that stuck. It was slipping off, and along with his legs about to follow the rest of him over the railing! His grandmother looked terrified. She was making an attempt to hold on to the leg closest to her as it went upward, but she wasn't strong enough to be of any use.

Tank had fainted, although I didn't know it at the time. All I knew was that I had to keep his legs from going over the rail. I darted the length of the empty chairs and jumped upward to catch his ankles. I grabbed both just as they were about to go over the railing, and then I swung from them like Tarzan from a vine in the jungle. Somehow in the process I went under the rail and over the side of the balcony, all the while holding on for dear life.

There we were: Tank's upper body draped over the topside of the brass railing, and me holding onto his ankles on the underside of the brass rail outside the balcony. I looked into his face. There was no one home. I hoped his pants weren't going to slip off, taking me with them to the floor below. They had started to move.

There was a loud gasp as people on the sanctuary floor looked upward. Rev. Harper, oblivious to what was happening, continued to pray. But Del Beene saw what was happening. He was the head usher that day, and with another usher charged up the stairway to the balcony. They made their way to the front row where they found Coach Johnson already on the scene. He had been sitting a couple of rows behind Tank and got to Tank right after I did. He had grabbed him by the belt just after I went over the side. He braced his legs against the retaining wall and was leaning back so as to be sitting on top of Tank's chair. Coach Johnson wasn't sure whether the brass railing would hold or buckle, or whether my weight would start pulling Tank under the railing. He was trying to be prepared for whatever moved next.

My weight didn't seem to be pulling Tank under, although his pants continued to slip. So when Del Been got there, Coach Johnson told him and the other usher to each get on one side of Tank. They were to reach down and grab his sports coat, which was bunched up around his shoulders. If they would pull from each side, he would pull from the back of his belt, and maybe the three of them could pull him back in. But first they needed some men below to catch me. They couldn't pull both of us back into the balcony. So when the men on the floor were ready, I needed to let go and drop. Del Beene signaled men below.

Rev. Harper continued to pray fervently as several men stepped up and stood on the pew beneath me. They could almost reach my legs. Coach Johnson said, "Drop!" I did, and didn't fall far until they caught me. As I was handed down to the floor, I noticed a familiar face. It was John Hall's dad. The Halls were back!

His eyes caught mine and he whispered, "It was you, wasn't it?"

I didn't answer, but turned and headed back to my seat in the balcony just as Rev. Harper said, "Amen." The congregation was sitting down, and I was reaching the first step of the stairway when Mom grabbed me from behind. She looked mortified, disgusted, and displeased. She ushered me out the front door of the sanctuary, where outside on the lawn she began giving me grief for acting up in church. "Joe Don, what am I going to do with you? What on earth were you doing up there in the balcony!"

I tried to explain what had happened, but it made no difference. Whatever I was selling, she wasn't buying. All she could tell from where she was sitting was that I was disrupting the worship service by hanging from a boy's legs from the balcony. And what was his problem? A boy that old should know better than to clown around like that in church! I was going to get it when we got home!

Thankfully, Coach Johnson had also come outside to see how I was, and he intervened. He explained to Mom that Tank had twice before passed out after he had taken medicine with codeine in it. Tank believed that he had outgrown his problem, and so he thought nothing about it when just before church he had taken a dose of cough medicine with codeine. Tank's grandmom had told Coach Johnson that part of the story. Coach Johnson then told Mom that if I hadn't kept Tank's legs from going over the rail, he could have been killed crashing headfirst into the floor below. And who knew what would have happened had he fallen on some elderly person— maybe two dead people. I was a hero.

When Mom seemed satisfied that I wasn't being disruptive, the coach got a big grin on his face. He said, "Joe Don, that was a quick move you made in there! If you can move like that when you get to high school, there's a place for you on the Coyotes. I'll turn you loose against the Carlsbad Cavemen, and we'll teach 'em what's what."

Coach Johnson made me feel really good. He knew who I was! After he turned and headed back into the sanctuary, I asked Mom if we were going back in too.

"No, let's go on home. You did good, Joe Don. I'm sorry I doubted you."

On the way home in the car I said, "Guess what, Mom? We don't have to worry about Adam Choate anymore."

"We don't! Why?"

"Cousin Greg had a talk with him, and Adam agreed to leave me alone."

And that was basically what had happened. I didn't give Mom the details, but it had turned out that Greg was tougher than I thought.

After Adam regained consciousness behind the trash bin, he wandered down First Street to the Eight Ball Billiard Parlor. He cleaned up in the restroom, and was in a real bad mood. He got a coke and sat down on a stool watching guys play snooker and pool. Greg was playing Eight Ball, and Adam started ragging on him. He said that Roswell would be a great place to live if it weren't for jerks like us Millers. Greg calmly walked over to where he was sitting and hit him across the chest with the thick end of his pool cue. Broke his collarbone. Adam fell off the stool and onto the floor. As he lay there in pain, Greg poked him with his cue, this time in the ribs, but not too hard. He told Adam that if he ever bothered us Millers again, especially a kid like me, he would hang him from the rafters and beat him like a piñata. "*Comprende?*"

Mom was glad to hear that Greg had intervened, although she was going to talk to him personally.

While Mom and I were eating peanut butter and jelly sandwiches for lunch, Mr. Del Beene phoned. Mom answered, and looked puzzled as she handed me the phone. He told me that as head usher he owed me a debt of gratitude for saving Tank Lowery from falling. Would I like to come to his store tomorrow, Monday afternoon, and pick out some baseball equipment, free of charge, for the next season? He had heard that I was pretty good.

Would I! I excused myself from the conversation and asked Mom if she could take me. I'd work at Missouri Avenue in the morning and ride my bike home. We could go right after lunch. She said she could, and so I told Mr. Beene I'd see him tomorrow.

Monday Mom wasn't dressed for going inside a store, and so she sat outside in the car. The same guy was behind the counter as was there the day I kicked out the chuke's teeth. He didn't seem to recognize me. I told him that I was supposed to see Mr. Beene, and he showed me to his office. Mr. Beene welcomed me and took me to the sporting goods section. He said I could choose any mitt, any bat, and to get me a ball. I couldn't believe he would give me so much, but I had decided to ask for more.

"Mr. Beene, could you give me something else instead?"

"Something else? What?"

"I'd rather you give my mom a job as a salesman."

I took him by surprise. His jaw dropped and he looked at me awestruck. He ushered me back to his office, closed the door, and asked me why I would ask such a thing. Who told me that he had been thinking about hiring a woman? It was supposed to be a secret.

I told him no one. All I knew was that Mom had to find a better job than cleaning office buildings, otherwise we were going to have to move back to Texas by next Monday. I told him that Mom was a good worker. Anyone who shopped at Allensworth's could tell him that. It was just that Mr. Franks' friend, Mr. Howard Park, was trying to force himself on Mom, and I had to hit him with Alea's baseball bat. That caused Mr. Franks to fire Mom. Since then she had looked all over town for a job as a clerk, but there weren't any jobs available. But that was all right because she would make a better salesman.

"Why do you think she'd make me a good saleswoman?"

"Because she knows all about refrigerators and washers and furniture. She used to come over here every Saturday when you'd get a new model in to check it out, even though she couldn't afford it. She can tell you what's good about it and what's not from the housewife's point of view. And she's a fast learner. I can teach her all she needs to know about sporting goods, and I have a friend who can teach her about tires and automotive."

"You're not a bad salesman yourself," he said. "And your mom is highly thought of in this town. Tell you what, I'm going to have to think about it. I've never had a saleswoman, only men. It's a big step. I'll let you know." He stuck his hand across the desk. We shook.

I got up to leave and had just walked out his office when he called to me, "Joe Don, I don't need to think about it any further. Your mom needs a job now, not later, and she has it. Is she at home?"

"She's waiting in the car. I'll go get her!" I flew across the store and out the door. I ran halfway down the block and went around to her side of the car. "Mom! Mr. Beene wants to see you in his office."

"What on earth for?"

"I can't tell you, but it's real important! Hurry!"

"Joe Don, I can't go in. I'm not dressed for it. I just jumped in the car to give you a ride down here."

"That's all right," a man's voice said. "I'll talk to you right here."

It was Mr. Beene kneeling down on the sidewalk and talking through the shotgun side window. "Mrs. Miller, I think you would make a great saleswoman for my store. Could I talk you into going to work for me?"

Mom was dumbfounded. "Are you kidding? What's this about?"

"Not kidding. I've been thinking about hiring a saleswoman, and Joe Don tells me that you know as much about appliances and furniture as anyone. You have a solid reputation in this town, and I think you'd be a good one. You want to think it over?"

"No sir, I don't need to think about it. I gladly accept. When do I start?"

"Why don't you be down here by eight in the morning? That okay?"

"More than okay. I'll see you then."

Mr. Del Beene headed back in to his store. I got in the car, and we drove home. Mom was so excited she almost got us in two wrecks on Main Street alone.

"Joe Don, what did you say to Mr. Beene? And where is your baseball equipment?"

"He offered me some, but I told him I'd rather him give you a job."

"You said that to Mr. Del Beene! What's gotten into you? You can't just reject a gracious offer like that and ask for something else!"

"Why not? It worked."

Mom thought about it for a moment, and then grinned and laughed. "It sure did. Thank you, Joe Don! Thank you for what you did for me."

"For us, and you're welcome."

"Here's a word for you to look up, Joe Don, 'gumption.' You've got a lot of it."

"I already looked up that word, Mom, remember? You need to get with the times."

"You're right, I guess I do."

• • • • • • •

Friday afternoon the team arrived back in Roswell. They had ridden the train home from Williamsport, just as they had ridden it to Williamsport. Coming home, each player took his turn sitting by the three-foot-high, gold-inlaid trophy. It had been donated by the U.S. Rubber Company and had forty ounces of solid gold in it. It was worth hundreds of dollars. The team was supposed to have visited the White House so they could meet President Eisenhower, but for some reason that didn't happen.

A parade met the team at the Santa Fe railway station and led them to the Chaves County Courthouse where the largest crowd ever gathered in Roswell cheered. Some people estimated the crowd at three thousand people. Others said it was more like ten thousand. Curty, Jay Bob, and I were there, and we had never seen so many people. There were some speeches, but we couldn't see or hear the speakers. All we heard was the applause. We figured the team was getting the key to the city.

When the crowd dispersed, we got on our bikes to ride home. As we rode along, Curty said, "Thanks, Joe Don, for helping me learn the newspaper. Miss Sherelle said you don't need to help me anymore. I've learned all I need to know."

"Good."

"And you're right, I do like the news. I love what I heard this morning at the Grill."

"What?" asked Jay Bob.

"Some people from Williamsport came to Roswell a couple of days ago, beat the team back. They heard what a terrible field we have and came to see for themselves. The word is that they're going to buy us a new ballpark!"

"Really!" I said. "With real dugouts and a real fence?"

"That's the news."

We were caught up in the joy of winning the World Series and getting a new ballpark as we bicycled home. We couldn't imagine that anyone in Roswell wasn't deliriously happy or might wish anyone harm. But we soon found out different. Someone yelled, "That's them!" We looked to our left and saw a gang of chukes sitting on their bikes in a vacant lot. One of them smiled. He didn't have any front teeth!

We pedaled for all we were worth. Curty and Jay Bob got away once again, but the chukes caught me. One of them hit me in the back with a bicycle chain as he rode alongside me. Another kicked my bike from the side so that I lost control and crashed. I hurt all over, but I got up and tried to run away down the sidewalk. I couldn't escape. There were chukes in front of me and behind. We were still in the business district. Stores had closed and most adults had gone home. My back was up against a storefront, and the guy whose teeth I had kicked out was coming toward me from the street.

I put my fists up to fight him, but he didn't want to duke it out. He pulled a switchblade. But just as he popped the blade, police cars pulled up with sirens blaring. The chukes started to run, but the police easily captured them.

I was picking up my bike when Officer Brothers walked up to me. "Joe Don, you don't look too good. How about I give you and your bike a ride home?"

"Is my back bleeding?"

"Yep, what'd they do? Hit you with a chain?"

"Yeah. Thanks anyway, but I'll ride on home with Curty and Jay Bob."

"Sure?"

"Yeah. It would only upset Mom if I came home in a police car."

Officer Brothers grinned. "At least you'll be safe. I have a feeling these guys are on their way to Springer. We want to question them about some robberies. I also hear that Adam Choate isn't going to bother you anymore. You don't know anything about that do you? "

"I think my cousin had a talk with him."

"Your cousin Greg? I heard it was Tank Lowery! Whoever it was, he took the starch out of Adam. Adam's a changed person . . . Well, take care, Joe Don. Tell your mom hello."

The three of us rode to Jay Bob's. Curty went home to get me a shirt, while Jay Bob sneaked some Mercurochrome out of the medicine chest and put it on my back. He talked his mom into a campout, and I slept on my stomach. My wound hurt, but no parent found out about it.

• • • • • • •

Monday morning, August 27, Mom left for her job at Del Beene's, and I reported for work at Missouri Avenue. But Miss Sherelle sent me home. She said to take the week off. It was the last week before school started, and I needed to be rested for a new school year. She gave me a five dollar bill and said I had done a good job helping Mr. Gallegos. I couldn't wait to tell Mom!

Mom got home about five thirty. I gave her the money. She said, "I'll pay you back later, but this will come in handy now. You need some new school clothes, and it's been a long time since we've had a hamburger from Smiley's."

It was strange driving to Smiley's on a Monday night, but even stranger when we got there. Mom didn't go to the walk-up window like usual. She just sat there and didn't move. I said, "Do you want me to go to the window? Two burgers and two fries?"

"No. Let's go into the dining room."

"Are you sure, Mom?" This was bigger than Williamsport!

"I'm sure." We got out of the car, and I held the door to Smiley's open for her.

A waitress showed us to a booth. The seats were red and white and looked like the seat covers of a hot rod. There was all sorts of neat food on the menu, and we studied it for a long time. Finally, we ordered our usual burger and fries, but also got chocolate malts.

"Joe Don," she said, "Today's our deadline, August 27. And I have some news!"

"What?"

"I think I can do this! I think I can be a good saleswoman."

"Way to go, Mom!"

"I sold washers and refrigerators and easy chairs this past week. I even sold a couch to Mrs. Pfleugger and her husband!"

"Do you think they can both fit on it?"

"What do you mean?"

"Nothing, Mom. Just kidding. Go on."

"Joe Don, it's the most fun I've ever had! I'm doing good, and even Mr. Del Been doesn't think it's beginner's luck. He thinks that more and more women will seek me out and buy from me over time. Women like to talk to me. They value my opinion."

"Do you make more money than at Allensworth's?"

"I did last week, and I only worked four days. Yes, I'm sure I can make more money."

"This means that we don't have to move to Texas, right?"

"Right. We're still behind on our bills, but I think I can make it up in a few months."

Suddenly a man and a lady were standing by us. It was John Hall's mom and dad.

"Mrs. Miller, I think I have something to tell you about your boy."

Mr. Hall wasn't much of a smiler. He looked serious, and that made Mom wary. "Hello, Mr. Hall, Mrs. Hall. It's good to see you back."

"Thank you. What pained me most about the thought of coming back was facing the burned-out utility room and my yard. I dreaded it. But some men from the church had gone over and torn the shed down. They did that just a few days before we returned. Fixed things up, painted the carport, made it quite nice. They were going to mow my yard, but it was already taken care of. It had been mowed and watered all summer. Do you know who did that?"

"No sir, I don't know anything about your lawn," Mom said.

"From what I can piece together from my neighbors, I think your son did it."

"Joe Don? How? We don't have a lawn mower."

"Son, whoever mowed my lawn was most kind. Was it you?"

I was embarrassed. I hadn't figured on being found out. "Yes sir."

Mrs. Hall said, "Thank you so much, Joe Don! It looked nice when we returned."

Every week I had borrowed Jay Bob's lawn mower. I told his mom why I needed it. Told her that John was my best church friend, and that the men outside at the funeral had wondered how Mr. Hall could ever face his yard again. She thought it was a good idea. I asked her if it could be our secret, and she said yes. She even provided the gas.

It was a long way from Jay Bob's to John's. I had to push the lawn mower five blocks along sidewalks, and then along the ditch bank for a quarter mile until I entered his backyard. No one ever came up to me while I mowed or watered. I mowed in the morning when Mom worked at Allensworth's, and in the evening after she started cleaning buildings. It was a lot of work, but it made me feel good.

"Do you have my bill?" Mr. Hall said. "How much do I owe you?"

"Nothing," I answered.

"Nothing! What do you mean? You put in a lot of work."

"I mean it was John's chore. He was my friend. I did it for him."

Tears streamed down Mrs. Hall's cheeks, and down Mom's too.

Mr. Hall thought for a moment, and then said, "We're moving to another house across town. As soon as we do, I'll need some help with that yard. It's bigger than the other one, and I'm going to pay whoever works in it what it's worth. Would you be interested?"

"Yes sir!"

"Okay. I'll call you."

"Do you really have a ceiling in your other house that has Rocky Marciano's scuff mark on it?" I asked.

"We sold that house. But I had that ceiling torn out and it's being installed in the house we're moving to here. And, yes, I do have Rocky Marciano's scuff mark, and those of a lot of other champions. I'd be happy to show them to you when you come over."

"It was nice seeing you," Mrs. Hall said, and the two of them turned to leave.

"What sort of a ceiling were you two talking about?" Mom asked. She had wiped away her tears and was smiling.

"I'll tell you after I see it. I'm not sure."

"Like you told me you were mowing their yard? Joe Don, when are you going to start talking to me about the things going on in your life?"

"I do, Mom. We talk a lot now."

"You talk more than you did there for a long while, I'll agree to that. Still, you haven't told me about the scar on your back. I hope it's not infected, and what did you do with that shirt?"

Oh man, how did she know about the chukes?

"Officer Brothers came in the store today. He was so pleased that I had found a job. He genuinely cares about me, I think, and cares about you too. I invited him to your birthday party tomorrow night."

"My birthday party?" This was the first I had heard about a birthday party!

"Yeah, the three of us are going to a movie tomorrow night, his treat, and then back to our house for ice cream and cake."

"What do you mean you invited him?"

"I mean that I have a date for your birthday party."

"Officer Brothers isn't married?"

"No. He once was, but she got killed in a car wreck about the same time your dad was killed in Korea."

"Mom, you just had a date the other night, and it didn't work out so hot. Remember?"

"That I do. But Mr. Connell, although wrong in what he did, is right in what he wrote, 'If at first you don't succeed, try again.' Both you and me! I think Officer Brothers is cute, don't you? Actually, his name is Bill. He's kinda shy. He was so flummoxed when I asked him to your party that he forgot I wasn't supposed to know about your back. He asked how it was. So, how is it?"

"It hurts a little, but it's not infected."

"Good. I'll check it when we get home. Probably needs some rubbing alcohol. I've told you about my day. Now you tell me about yours."

"I did. Miss Sherelle gave me a five dollar bill. I didn't have to work today, and so I went to Jay Bob's."

"Okay then, tell me what's on your mind. What have you been thinking about lately?"

"I've been thinking that you like to talk a lot, but Officer Brothers doesn't talk much. Have you noticed that? He's a man of few words, fewer than even me."

"You don't say? Unlike the letter delivered to our house today?"

"What letter?"

"I had to run home today at lunch. I met the mailman as I was leaving. And rather than take the mail back inside, I dropped it in my purse and carried it with me. There wasn't much, but there was a thick letter, lots of words evidently, a letter that smells of perfume. It's addressed to you. Who do you know in Alabama?"

"Where is it? Still in your purse?"

"Joe Don, I forget. I may have left it at work. Maybe I can remember by the time we get home. It depends. Now, what were you saying about Bill Brothers?"

"That I think he's a fine man." And I guessed that was what I really did think. If Mom was going to take a chance, it might as well be with Officer Brothers. "Mom, if it's my birthday party tomorrow night, do you get one of those things called an employee discount?"

"I do. But I haven't looked into it yet because I'm busy trying to learn my job."

"That means you can buy stuff cheaper than other people?"

"That it does."

"Then do you really want to know what I'm thinking?"

"I really do."

"How about a TV for my birthday? Think how cheap you can buy it!"

Mom smiled and pointed a French fry at me. "You're incorrigible, Joe Don. Look it up when we get home. 'Incorrigible,' but I'm going to keep trying anyway."